About t

Jo Johnson is a clinical psych[...] urological disorders and mind health. S[...] of nine health-related publications and writes [...]ral neurology charities. She worked within the NHS for sixteen years, and now trains individuals and groups on how to prevent stress and burnout, regularly giving talks and workshops on these subjects. *Surviving Me* is her first novel, and explores themes that, as a practising clinician, she can write about with conviction and authenticity.

I hope you enjoy
my novel.
Love Jo Johnson.

Surviving Me

Jo Johnson

This edition first published in 2019

Unbound
6th Floor Mutual House, 70 Conduit Street, London W1S 2GF
www.unbound.com

ISBN (eBook): 978-1-78965-062-4
ISBN (Paperback): 978-1-78965-061-7

Cover design by Mecob

Printed and bound in Great Britain by Clays Ltd, Elcograf S.p.A.

Dedicated to my four offspring – Joshua, Isaac, Oscar and Leah – in case they ever read my novel, and in loving memory of Nurse Lisa Black, a selfless and faithful friend, kindness personified. Wish you were here.

Super Patrons

Heidi Adshead
Stephanie Banfield
Petula Bladen
Noelle Blake
Veronica Bradley
Sarah Burns
Jean Bushell
Hazel Child
Jo Clark-Wilson
Carole Curtis
Caroline D'Arcy
Mrs Carla Daley-Howe
Katherine Dantanus
Gill Davies
DD
Christine De Bie
Loz Densham
Tim Downs
Sue Duncan
Matthew Duncan
Annaliese Edgington
Tara Elizabeth
Sue Elliott
Lit Eziefula
Edward Fardell
Julie Fisher
Jacqueline Forni
Noreen Frost
Lucy Funnell
Marie Funnell
Sue Gatland
Jed Goossens
Nick Gray
Paula Green
Judith Greengrass
Graham Hardy
Jackie Hardy
Elizabeth Hassan
Tineke Hauchecorne
Cheryl Hayward
Tracey Herald
Camilla Herbert
Mary Herbert
Peter Herbertson
Jean Herbertson
Kelly Hill
Jeannette Hilyard
Anthony, Sarah, Alexandra and Thomas Holland
Jaqui Hoole
Anna Hutson
Cathy Hutson
Charles Hutson
Rollo Hutson
Tallulah Hutson
Caroline Ingham
Paul Izzard Davey
Kerry Jeffs
Rachel Jeremiah
Misery Jeremiah

Naomi Jeremiah
Hope Jeremiah
Barnaby Jeremiah
Daniel Jewell
Lyndon Johnson
Maryrose Johnson
Leigh Johnson
Isaac Johnson
Oscar Johnson
Leah Johnson
Lewis Jones
Pat Kemp
Angela Kerr
Dan Kieran
Francis Lacy Scott
Ali Lutte-Elliott
Richard Maddicks
Richard Mansfield
Dorothy Marshall
Roy Matthewson
Sarah McCrimmon
Debbie Miller
John Mitchinson
Kieran Moon
Sarah Moon
Helen Moore
Delia Moorey
Patrick Morgan
Nadine Morley
Nick Moss
Hazel Nicholls
Elizabeth Noon
Ronald Noon
Maureen Noon
Sarah Noon
Sheila Nuttall
Joe Oliver
Beryl Ouseley
Jan Owen
Sally Palmer
Lisa Parsons
Jan Parsons
Liz Perry
Justin Pollard
Jane Pountney
Priyanka Pradhan
Tim Rice-Oxley
Justine Robson
Catherine Rowe
Sarah Rush
Susan Sale
Gráinne Saunders
Carl Sims
Hilary Smith
Annabel Solomons
Brian Solts
Alix Song
Jane South
Sandra Staples
Maureen Street
Wendy Syred
Pauline Szczerbicki
Helen Taylor
Sue Thatcher
Natalie Thompson
Emily Underwood
Emma Veitch
Suzie Venn
Maria Vermeulen
Stephanie Verry
Fiona Vincent
Tim Watson
Katja Weise-Lehmann
Robert Welbourn
Gillian Wieck
Phillipa Young-Raybold
Wayne Younger

Prologue

Siri

Marilyn is tapping on the glass, beckoning me to come out. My eyes meet hers through the transparent partition.

I shake my head and mouth, 'Not now.' She's not the brightest button in the box. She continues to gesture, beckoning and wobbling.

I shake my head. She continues to bend her finger at me like the witch from *Snow White*. I can't concentrate. 'So sorry…' I whisper to my guest. 'Let's play another tune. More from this inspirational lady in a few minutes. Here's the new single from Keane for a winter morning: "The Way I Feel". Enjoy.'

I rip off my earphones and march out to demand an explanation.

'What?'

Marilyn is unusually evasive. 'There are two policemen to see you downstairs, and they won't wait, or tell me anything,' she says through pinched lips, her arms folded tightly over her generous chest.

Police? What have I done?

I walk tentatively down the first few stairs. Marilyn follows me. Did I drive back stupidly fast last night? I was desperate not to be late for Tom… I pause before descending the second half of the staircase.

Two policemen in uniform are sitting on the settee in reception. They stand to greet me. One of them, slightly shorter than the other, says gently, 'Mrs Selmeston Cleary? I apologise for interrupting you at work, but I wonder if you'd mind coming with us.'

How do they know I'm the one they're waiting for? I see the outdated airbrushed photograph of me on the wall opposite. 'So sorry, I'm on air. If you'll explain what's going on, I'll come to the station at four-thirty, just after I finish—'

Marilyn interrupts. 'Danny's here, Siri. He can take over your show and then just carry on with his slot afterwards.' My head says, shut up, will you please, Marilyn? But she insists. 'It's fine – you need to go.'

'So, officer, tell me what's going on.'

'I'm Sergeant Chris O'Leary and this is PC Joshua Johnson. We're both from Sussex Police. Our car is by the side entrance. We can talk privately there.'

My feet drag my uncooperative body to follow them. What's all this about? I can see my colleagues watching me go. How embarrassing. Poor Helen, my guest, sitting by herself in a glass cubicle.

The police car is parked just a few metres from the office. DS O'Leary opens the back door. I expect him to push my head down like on the TV. He doesn't. He smiles, and instructs in a soft, kind voice, 'Just get in and make yourself comfortable. I'll come around the other side.'

I obey like a child. His colleague is taller than average: he clearly frequents the gym. His body looks too big for the space as he wriggles into the driver's seat. He doesn't fasten his seat belt or put his key in the ignition. I guess we're not going anywhere.

The police sergeant says again, 'I'm sorry to interrupt you at work, Mrs Cleary. We're looking for your husband.'

Chapter 1

Tom

At this point in time, I can accurately be described as unemployed, impotent, and a liar.

It still puzzles me that, just a few weeks after my first wedding anniversary, I am sitting alone in a café for misfits, miles from my home. I found this shambolic haven by chance. What does a man with a disintegrating life do by himself for hours at a time? If you hang about too much in the same street then other people get suspicious, and if you drive around aimlessly for too long then your own internal darkness is unbearable.

One day, just into November, I'd been driving for an hour, passing increasingly unfamiliar places, and felt confident I must be in a different county. I took the first turning off the main road, and after a few miles found an old-fashioned, largish village with instant appeal – quiet; no one was likely to know me here. The sign said 'Welcome to Middle Priory', and underneath another sentence asked me to 'Please drive carefully through our village'. I parked in a small car park – one of the few remaining where you could park for free. I spotted a woman in a heavy checked coat getting out of her car. Her hair was pinned into a neat doughnut on the back of her head; she looked old enough to be a local. I ran to catch her up as she was walking out of the car park. She spun around so fast, I expected to feel a thud from the umbrella she held in her fist.

'I'm so sorry, I didn't mean to frighten you. I'm desperate for a decent cup of coffee. I wondered if you knew the area.' Her mouth opened into a warm smile that reached her eyes and removed ten years from her face.

She pointed down the hill to the opposite side of the road. 'See that blue door? That's the Tea Cosy Café; it's usually quite busy but our Dawn will make sure you are well looked after. I recommend the jacket potatoes.'

The high street in Middle Priory was quiet. I walked past a gift shop, a butcher boasting organic meat and a fruit and veg shop. The fruit and veg shop had those old-fashioned scales with a silver bowl on the top, and was the sort of place where they choose your produce for you. I saw the shop assistant do that twirly thing to seal the top of a brown bag, and it brought back happy memories of shopping with my gran. I popped into the secondhand bookshop just to get a sniff of the smell of dusty books and the owner reminded me of the shopkeeper in the children's TV series *Mr Benn*. It was the one programme my father would tolerate and occasionally sit next to me and watch.

The café was warm and still smelled of breakfast. It was empty apart from an elderly couple sitting at a large rectangular table by the window. They looked like they were having an argument, but when the door closed behind me the sound of the half-hearted bell prompted them to stare.

I wondered if the décor was fruit of a brainstorm among drunken friends – vintage? bistro? fast food? cosy? retro? The owner obviously felt worried about offending any of the contributors. The walls were crammed with 'unique' art. The prices were more than I paid for my first car but the pictures reminded me of toddlers' self-portraits. The dark-haired woman behind the counter caught my eye and raised her unkempt eyebrows. I noticed a smudge of something brown above her lip.

'Bad idea. A local artist thought we could help each other but I've sold nothing. I suspect some of them give the pensioners nightmares.'

She saw me searching for the toilet sign.

'Mm, sorry. Another work in progress. Be ready any time soon, the builders told me a month ago. I'll make you a cappuccino. Go back towards the car park and there are council loos you can use.'

I don't remember being given a choice of drink. I thought this was a trusting offer to make to a stranger. Perhaps she felt sorry for me. Was I already wearing my mind on my sleeve? Wiping her hands on her apron, she followed me out of the door and gestured in the direction I had just come from. Despite their concrete exterior, the toilets were pleasant-smelling and clean. But I felt depressed to think a good day amounted to finding a cheap café and a urinal without puddles.

I wandered back. The woman called Dawn (I saw her name badge this time) presented me with an expensive-looking cup and saucer, a heart shape of chocolate dust floating on the coffee. Romantic love, I thought. A thing of the past.

'Follow me. Let me take that.' She snatched my rucksack from my arm so I could balance the drink. Did she think I was incompetent? 'Not many people know about this room. It's quieter, though I'm afraid the wi-fi is a bit temperamental.'

She set the cup and saucer next to the *Daily Mail* on a small round table with a wonky leg. I folded one of my business cards and stuck it under the base to stop it wobbling. The plastic tablecloth was covered in pictures of old-fashioned clocks… ironic, given I had all the time in the world. And as if I didn't already know how slowly time passes, there was also a disproportionately large clock dominating the wall. Next to it there was a small window looking onto the main road.

That first day, I stayed for the rest of the morning and most of the afternoon. People came and went, and I drank as slowly as I could. Dawn didn't seem to mind me out-staying the usual sitting time for two coffees and a pot of tea. She kept fluttering near me, but I left my eyes firmly on the newspaper print. I'd managed to fold it back on itself hoping other customers might presume it was a copy of *The Guardian.*

'I haven't seen you before,' Dawn had said. 'Are you new to the area?'

'No,' I answered, without looking up.

'You travelling for business?'

'Something like that.'

'Where are you based?'

'Sussex,' slipped out before I remembered the long journey I'd made to gain anonymity.

'Where in Sussex? I have several friends on the south coast. Beautiful scenery… I like walking the South Downs and we often visit Devil's Dyke in the summer. My son loves the chips at the pub on the top.'

I wondered if she'd ever pause for breath. I assumed she enjoyed the chips more than the walking. She had an attractive face and a warm smile. On closer inspection, I guessed she wasn't much older than me. Were the grey streaks a fashion statement or evidence of a lack of vanity? I wondered if she'd been one of the 'in crowd' at school who'd somehow lost her way. She eventually gave up the chatting and went to sit in the other room with the older couple taking a pot of tea and joined their heated discussion about whether the Co-op should be given permission to expand their car park. Being so unfriendly doesn't come naturally to me, but I had to be the grey man with a physical presence so unstimulating that he's invisible, forgettable.

It was on that first day I noticed the gleaming white house across the road. It had a small brass plaque to the right of the black front door, but would otherwise have gone unnoticed in a row of similar houses. The thing that struck me about it was the people going in and out of the door; it seemed a lot for such a small building in a quiet village in the middle of the day. Meanwhile, I carried out my usual online routine: paid bills, checked Twitter; I read the sports and finance pages. But now and then I found my eyes drifting back to that serious black door and a house that seemed somehow out of place in its environs.

I finished my tea, paid up and snuck out before Dawn could recommence her interrogation. Rather than go straight back to retrieve my car, I allowed a two-minute diversion to look at the gold plaque. The door seemed larger close up and more intimidating. It had an old-fashioned knocker that looked like it was polished more regularly than the similar one on my parents' front entrance (in our tree-lined lane, everyone had had an entrance). The plaque was unremarkable, mounted on a slightly bigger piece of wood, and simply stated in dark letters: 'Dr Pike. Admission by appointment only'.

I couldn't work out why I felt irritated at not knowing what lay behind that heavy door. The whole world seemed determined to frustrate my plans. I slouched back to the car, suddenly overwhelmed by a sense of failure. Spit it out, my mother used to say when I walked through the door hunched in defeat... And the thought of my mother caught me unawares. By the time I got into the car, I was wiping away tears.

Once upon a time, my mother hadn't been the person she'd

now become. I remembered the mum with bright eyes and a laugh that made me giggle too.

My best friend Harry's mum, Carla, was so kind. She'd say, oh, look at Tom's smile. He'll be the one all the girls will want to marry, or, Tom is so kind and brave. Look how he helps his sister when she's hurt or upset. I adored Carla. Because in my small boy head, I was silently screaming, look at me, Mum. I'm kind, happy and clever. But my mother's facial expression over the years became more and more inscrutable, removed, as if she wasn't participating in real life at all.

By the time my sister, Gemma, was nine, her school was saying she would benefit from a psychological assessment: other children were targeting her; she was socially awkward and very withdrawn. The ensuing discussion between my parents became my first traumatic memory. I heard my father's roar from the hall. So I sat on the bottom of the stairs and watched them through a gap in the door. His face was red and shiny and my mother had tears running down her cheeks.

'It's you!' His yellow-tipped finger was almost in her eye. 'You make her weird. You don't go out, and you have no friends, not a single one.'

In a tiny, high-pitched voice, my mother replied, 'Gemma isn't weird. She's kind and sensitive. They both are.'

'Don't get me started on the wimp. He's not much better, might as well be another girl. I wanted children to be proud of and you've raised cretins.'

Then he stepped back. Put his hands behind him on the base of his spine and let out a loud belly laugh intended to humiliate – I can still see and hear him, even today. Then he got a beer from the fridge, and turned around to look down at my mother who was sitting perched on a kitchen stool. He had the bottle in one hand as he slowly bent forward. I thought that, for the first time, I might see them kiss.

Instead, he swung back his right hand and slapped her hard across the face.

He stabbed a dirty fingernail towards her nose. 'You, lady, are a boring old loner. That's why our daughter is a mental laughing stock.' He spoke as if he was explaining how to work the oven. I crept silently back to my room.

All these years later, I still replay the incident as if it's happening right now. I can remember the orange kitchen curtains and how they clashed with my mother's deeper orange and pink dress. I can see her face, and her tears, and I can see my father, standing and watching. I have never told anyone about what happened that day, but my eyes sting whenever I remember the sound of my father's hand colliding with my mother's cheek. She didn't look scared or flinch when she felt his hand. It was as if she knew what was coming. As if it wasn't the first time.

I still beat myself up about not doing anything. I was too weak to protect my own mother: pathetic, over-sensitive, girly Tom, who'd never amount to anything.

Chapter 2

It was never part of my plan to be a double-glazing salesman, but then, let's face it, who would have that as a life plan?

I flirted briefly with the idea of going to college. Helpfully, my sister pointed out that the three local educational options would not be excited by applicants with fewer than five GCSEs even if they could do great impressions of their tutors. During my last week of school, I became, in Harry's words, 'increasingly not myself'.

One evening not long after I'd left school, my father was asleep in his chair and there was no sign of anyone else, which wasn't unusual in our house. There was no noticeable difference when the house was full or empty. It was always dark, cold and musty. Even when I was in the living room with my family, I felt alone.

The door-knocker woke me out of my teenage stupor. Such a strong slam of the lion's head could suggest only one person – my friend Harry. I heard my father swear under his breath as he shuffled along the hall to the front door, complaining about the late hour. No one visited my family after 8pm. Come to think of it, no one visited.

As my father opened the door, Harry greeted him with

a perfunctory 'Hello,' then rushed past him towards me and planted his hands on my shoulders. 'It's going to… be… okay… mate,' he gasped. Sweat was pouring down his face and his T-shirt had a large wet patch like a bib.

'What's going to be okay?'

'The rest of your life! You have to stop moping about up here; all that dark thinking is no good for you. You know that glass shop in Stane Street?'

'Can't say I do, Harry.'

'The one with the knight on horseback. You know, the blue ones – they're everywhere in town.' He was half pushing me upstairs as he explained.

'Oh yeah,' I said, having no clue what he was on about.

'I heard they want people like you, Tom, who can chat to people, work at different times. It's perfect for you. They just need a CV by the end of the week.' Harry was still breathing heavily as he sat back on my bed and leaned against the wall. His T-shirt had ridden up to expose his growing belly. I wondered when might be a good time to suggest he worked on his fitness.

From our first meeting ten years earlier, Master Edgington had taken it upon himself to rescue me. Initially it was from school bullies but, as I got older, Harry's heroics were more usually deployed when I was being my own worst enemy. I could see he was pleased that he'd found a solution to lift my mood. His smile started to fade as he waited for my response.

'Sorry, mate, I don't have a CV.' I couldn't tell him that working for a window company was not what I had in mind for my next step.

'No worries – Pa says he'll help you do one tomorrow evening. He's going to get an application form for you on his way to work.'

'Cool, thanks.' I plastered on the smile used only for school photos. It always convinced my mother.

I started an apprenticeship at Stane Street Glass the following week. The bloke who interviewed me, Mike, made it clear he thought I was too young.

'Window salesmen,' he carefully explained, 'are not welcome or invited guests, so you need plenty of confidence to be pushy and cope well with rejection.' I turned on my schoolboy charm, which wasn't hard: I'd been a schoolboy the week before the interview.

'I have the gift of the gob.'

'I think you mean the gab.'

'What?'

'The saying is the gift of the gab.'

'Well, I have that too – all my teachers said so.'

Mike relented in the face of my enthusiasm and made me do some role play: he was the uninterested housewife and I was the telephone salesman. We went on to complete three different scenarios with imaginary customers.

'Well, son, you certainly have admirable audacity for your age. I'll give you twelve weeks to prove you can replicate that in real life. If not, you're out.' And despite Mike's initial reservations, I was a sales genius, the first employee to win the national seller of the year award for an entire decade. I *was* a success, not the weak link my father predicted.

That was until Mike had a heart attack, and Leo Smales arrived as area sales director. He'd been in the year below me at school, a notorious bully. He took an instant dislike to me. I could see it in his eyes at the first team meeting.

'Good morning, comrades,' he said to a room of cynical middle-aged men, all older than him. I sat up straight and locked eyes with him, keen to make an impression. 'I think you will soon see big changes with me at the helm of this sinking ship. I can teach you every trick in the book to make the customer feel listened to.' He tapped his finger on the side of his nose. His lone guffaws were high pitched and sounded like an animal on heat.

'The best way to make the customer feel listened to, in my experience, is to listen to the customer,' I muttered quietly.

Ben, the new apprentice, sniggered, but I hadn't intended to make a joke.

My first formal run-in with Leo was at my annual appraisal. He invited me to sit down in my own office and offered me a cup of my own coffee. I suppose the writing was on the wall that day. I left with a performance score of three out of a potential five for the first time in my career. Old feelings of failure crept up my stiff white collar.

Six months later came a second appraisal, unannounced.

'Tom! Great to see you.' (I recognised this as Techniques Two and Four: *Start with a positive comment* and *Use the person's name frequently*.)

He leaned forward at this point. (Technique Three: *Lean towards the customer to make him feel secure*. It made me want to lean back to distance myself from his kebab breath.)

'Sales figures dropping, I see.'

I'd started to doubt myself. When I tried to take notes of customer requests, my mind wandered. The brain that held hundreds of relevant figures became my enemy. It would remind me of past mistakes, Leo's criticisms and the customers I'd lost. Work gradually lost its appeal, but 9am on 31 October still came as a horrible shock. The main office was decorated with Halloween balloons.

'Ten minutes late,' Ben smirked, pointing to his watch. A mocking pumpkin face stared down at me with a lopsided smile.

Leo was lolling against my filing cabinet, hands deep in his pockets, cosmetically enhanced teeth grinning at me like I'd won the prize. I am still angry that I knocked on my own office door.

'The company are making cuts…' I waited for him to say, Tom, buck up your ideas. But instead he opened his thin lips and calmly said, 'I'm letting you go.'

My personal effects were in a pile on top of a box file in front of me. The photo of my wife Siri was face down, balanced on my hole punch. I felt an indescribable physical pain from my belt to my scalp. I recognised it as my old friend, shame. I got to the entrance, clutching all my possessions under one arm, trying not to look back at the colleagues watching Leo throw me out. Leo had somehow got there first. He grasped my shoulder with his left hand and stuck his right hand out towards the door. I desperately wanted to run back, smash his display windows and punch his smarmy face. Instead, I crept towards my car like a pathetic mouse.

I was deep under water. Only some sounds were audible, the rest blurred. The thought of Siri's face when I told her I no longer had a salary made me want to be sick. I had to steady myself against a fence in the car park, my working life reduced to a pile of rubbish in a carrier bag.

A year ago, it wouldn't have mattered. Siri and I were both working full-time, the baby story had not formally started and she still smiled when I walked into a room. A year ago, I would have called her as soon as I stepped out of the building and told her what had happened. She would have said, Tom, that's awful, so unfair. You're too good for them. Stay put. I'm on my way to join you. We would've gone for dinner, laughed together, drunk too much wine. We'd have abandoned both our cars and stumbled home doing impressions of the way Leo said my name. The next day Siri would have phoned in sick, made me breakfast and helped me see there would be other jobs, that this didn't matter much in the grand scheme of things.

What a difference a few months can make. The fantasy, non-existent baby was now part of a ten-year plan that included two more siblings, a four-bedroomed house and an expensive school where our three perfect offspring were outperforming all their peers despite their father's lack of A levels.

I got into the car and drove. I thought about how to make this sound like good news. *You're right – it's the stress that's stopping us conceiving.* Or *I've decided to resign. It's time to move on, do something more truthful.* Or *I can tell your colleagues think you've married beneath you. I will go back to college, study, retrain as a teacher*. But however many scenarios I dreamed up, Siri's virtual response was the same: it involved words like stupid, irresponsible and lazy, phrases like default on mortgage, can't afford fertility treatment, and other, much less polite ones…

I spent the day driving around, out into the countryside, and back again, unaware of time, and I was over an hour late when I finally got home. The door opened before I could find my key. Siri had red eyes and blotchy cheeks. 'Oh, Tom.' She ran into my arms quicker than on our second date. I smiled back, puzzling over what she knew and the contrast with the images I'd been conjuring up. 'You're so late. I tried to ring but it kept going to voicemail. I thought you were dead, lying in an alley with a bashed-in head or in the back of an ambulance. I love you *so* much.'

'And I love you *so* much too, you daft lady.' I planted a kiss on her head and put down my briefcase. Her tender reaction to my lateness, and her ignorance of the real reason, meant I could almost imagine I had dreamed the last few hours. I opened my mouth to say I'd been made redundant. 'Really sorry, babe. I got a last-minute call from an old couple who want a whole new set of downstairs windows, and I didn't want them to wait until tomorrow for a response.'

Chapter 3

Harry Edgington has been my best friend for over three decades – for ten of those, my only friend. He rescued me in primary school.

'Good morning,' he said, angling a stiff right arm towards me.

I was sitting on the buddy bench studying trousers too short for my recent growth spurt, a bumpy scab positioned just above the cuff of my droopy sock to remind me of the kick I'd received the day before.

'My name is Harry Edgington. I'm six. I'm new here. I'm from London. Who are you?' His robot hand stayed horizontal in front of me until I lifted mine, uncertain about what he wanted. He grabbed my hand and completed what I later discovered was a firm and assertive handshake of a person with confidence.

From that day on, we were inseparable. His parents allowed me to fill the space of the second child they'd been unable to have. His house became my second home, or perhaps I should say my only home – my own was just a house. Unlike me, Harry has done predictably well. Every year in June, he throws an extravagant social for a large host of his peers, all of whom are either rich or successful, mostly both. For years, he'd used this annual event to find me a partner more stable than whoever had been my most recent choice. Things usually started on a positive note with a short line of suitable women willing to give me a first glance.

'Hi, Tom. I hear you are one of Harry's oldest friends. What's your specialism?'

'I'm not a doctor.'

'What are you then? Oh –' and the excitement is obvious – 'let me guess, a barrister? An investment banker? An accountant? Okay, I give up, tell me, tell me…'

'A salesman of windows…'

Cue woman making excuses: needs the powder room, to fix her hair, more food, to catch an old friend before she goes, to check on Grandma, etc.

Over the years I'd tried many ways to disclose my job without saying double-glazing salesman; I had tried 'home improvements manager' or 'glass advisor'. I'd tried really stretching the truth, but I wasn't a good liar. My more extreme falsehoods quickly tripped me up. As a urologist, I didn't know how her elderly father should manage his leaking equipment. As a legal executive, I didn't know the difference between a barrister and a solicitor.

The year I met Siri, I was already standing on my own with my father's voice of authority growling in my ears. *Stand up straight, boy, get your hands out of your pockets. Look at the room, not your feet.* I stood to attention at his command and realised an attractive young woman was staring. I checked over my shoulder, wondering where she was searching. When I looked back, she was heading over, marching as if on a mission.

'Hi.' I do get frustrated by my lack of imagination.

'Hi,' she said. 'You look slightly more interesting than most of the dullards I've spoken to so far. What's your name?' I admired her ability to be so blunt.

'Tom.'

'I like a simple name.'

I wasn't sure if that was supposed to be a put-down. 'What's yours?' I asked.

She launched into an explanation as to why she was at the party when she wanted to be in a bar with her friends. 'I've been dragged here by my boss. She interviewed the posh doctor bloke last week about the lack of rehab funding in the NHS. She was supposed to be bringing her bloke as her plus one but she dumped him this afternoon. I'm at the bottom of the pile so pulled the short straw and won this dull party as a prize.' But she wouldn't tell me her name. I wondered whether to make my excuses, but there were not many others queueing to chat to me. Then she told me her name began with 'S'. I guessed the obvious ones like Susie and Sophie but got nowhere. I teased her about reliving the story of Rumpelstiltskin. She clearly didn't know what I was talking about but didn't let on, which made me smile.

When I first saw her, I thought she was way too young. She had very short black hair in a severe cut most women couldn't have carried off. But, with her angular bone structure, it suited her perfectly. I plucked up the courage to obey one of Harry's persistent instructions and attempt a compliment. 'Your eyes are an amazing colour, similar to my first cat's.'

She laughed but her eyes didn't. 'It's been a while since a man compared me to a pet.'

'It was a much-loved pet… It's just your eyes are different, striking, like luminous peas. Are they lenses?'

'You're lucky I am deeply attracted to older men with receding hairlines. No wonder you're on your own.' Her tone was unclear. I wasn't sure whether this was flirtatious banter or the brush-off.

'Maybe my successful partner is visiting the bathroom.'

'Nah, my boss pointed out all the single blokes when we arrived and you were the only half-decent one. I've been waiting for the queue to go down.'

Her name turned out to be Selmeston but I didn't find that out for several hours. I couldn't pretend it wasn't a weird name, but I could tell her exactly where her namesake was on the map. I told her I would nickname her Siri after the know-it-all voice of an iPhone – giving direct and emotionless opinions in every situation. Later in our relationship, she confessed that by the time I spotted her, she'd included our wedding in her five-year plan. Siri works out her life in five-year chunks.

We were married five years, five months and twenty-four days later on a freezing cold day. Siri and the bridesmaids shivered in flimsy dresses she'd bought in the summer sale. To stick rigidly to her plan, we had to be married by 30 June, but the extravagant wedding venue had only two free dates: the end of November or the following summer. The manager at the hotel had joked that 'twenty-third of November man' had come to his senses just in time.

When we were planning the wedding, the one thing we instantly agreed on (and there wasn't much) was that Adam, Siri's older brother, should give her away. Siri's father had died suddenly when she was four and Adam, ten years older than her, had played substitute dad ever since. Siri says she barely remembers her father apart from his brown wool coat that smelled funny.

After the wedding, Siri's baby-making plan quickly sprang into action. She wasted no time bringing me up to speed: prepare for three months then move straight to the main menu: conception, pregnancy and birth. She'd described how our next five years would go before we'd ordered our first drink on the honeymoon flight. This included a house move, three pregnancies interspersed with two promotions for her and extended paternity leave for me. Phase one began one Sunday evening, thirteen months ago. We were talking about nothing in particular when she blurted out, 'I want to try for a baby.' It came as a complete surprise to me; we'd only been married a fortnight. She said that, with me being so much older, we were running out of time. My mother had warned me, do as you please, but mark my words – marry that toy girl and she'll be bored with a father figure before you reach forty. I'd convinced myself an eleven-year gap wasn't that much of a problem, and anyway having children was not something I'd thought much about before I met Siri. She'd joked about her plans, but we still hadn't talked about it seriously, in my view. Siri claimed we'd talked of nothing else for the previous eight months.

Siri plans her personal affairs with the same serious application as she plans her career. She's chosen songs for her funeral and how her body will be disposed of. I do feel the post-death plans are slightly obsessive. People say that opposites attract. Siri would have written the plan for her own birth whereas I stumble through life, jumping onto the next stone in my path without analysing how it fits with past, present or future. Siri plans the big things, but is useless with the small details like when or what we are going to eat, how we budget or pay the rent, or where we will put our many children in a two-bedroomed flat.

On that Sunday, Siri decided we were ready to enter baby-making stage one. It was never destined to be *let's just see what happens*. I knew her too well for that. We were entering the preparation phase when we get healthy, eat clean, sleep well, exercise regularly and give up everything nice.

'Don't panic, you've got it easy. Just take vitamin C, give up alcohol, avoid blue cheese and wear loose pants,' she'd pointed out to my fear-stricken face.

I nodded and smiled. I was prepared to step onto the next stone placed in front of me – and if it was going to be the baby stone, so be it.

Chapter 4

I'm so sorry, Siri. I didn't mean to end up like this. Please trust me on the big things.

All Hallows' Eve didn't end so badly. When I got home late on that last day at work, Siri was so relieved to see me alive that she allowed baby-making efforts when the calendar claimed it was pointless. It was going to be all right. We drank wine for the first time for what felt like months, ate a takeaway and life was good again. I decided it would be best to tell her at the weekend. Why ruin the great atmosphere when we hadn't had such a nice time in ages?

The weekend went surprisingly well. We ate together, we talked, we went out, we stayed in and we laughed. I can't remember the last time Siri laughed with me rather than at me. And I couldn't bear the thought of ruining the weekend either; we made plans to see Adam and Heather on Saturday evening and enjoy a pyjama day on Sunday. And I told her I was taking the first three days of the week off in lieu because of a conference I'd gone to earlier in the year...

Then Thursday came. 'Happy days are over, lazy boy. Wake up or you'll be on Leo's naughty step.' I got up, showered and made her a mug of tea which I put on the dressing table beside her. When the door closed a few minutes later and it all went very quiet, I looked at myself dressed in my suit, briefcase in hand, and realised I was unemployed.

Ten minutes later, the silence was shattered.

I'd taken off my jacket and tie and was about to switch the TV on – remote in one hand, screwed-up tie in the other – when I heard the flat door burst open. I threw my tie back round my neck but hadn't manage to knot it while I scrambled about in my brain for a plausible explanation.

'What do you think?' I stood like a dummy displayed in a shop window. 'I'm going for smart casual to invade the houses of the younger home owner.'

'Sure, good plan,' she said without looking. 'Watch it, Leo's ridiculous psychology is seeping into your sub-conscious.'

The silence quickly returned when she left and I felt a familiar sting in my eyes. A wave of nausea spread throughout my head and body. I had to lean on the door to steady myself; my heartbeat was so fast I could hear it; sweat was dripping off me. I thought I was going to end my working life just like Mike: a heart attack before forty.

As my body calmed, I felt cold. I guessed I'd had a panic attack. Anxiety was my only friend at secondary school. My first sensible thought was, what on earth can I do to fill a weekday afternoon? I still hadn't told anyone I'd lost my job, not Adam, not Harry, and, most importantly, not my wife. If anyone were around to go for an afternoon beer, they would question why I was free. I thought about going for a long walk, but what if I bumped into a friend who would then tell Siri? *Oh, I saw Tom yesterday – did he have a day off?* How would I explain that?

I decided it would be safest to go out in my car. I would be doing what's expected if anyone saw me – driving, smartly dressed, to sell windows. I would quickly find out that you can't just drive around all day: the fuel costs money and it's depressing and lonely driving without purpose, especially when the darkness starts to creep in as early as 3pm.

Then came the last day of my first unemployed week. Friday is the day the cleaner comes, which meant that I had eight hours of emptiness to fill. I needed to leave the house at the same time as Siri, so I decided to drive further away than yesterday and find somewhere I could settle for a few hours. That's how I found my café.

I'd been jobless for one whole week. 'Jobless' makes my predicament sound less threatening. My father berated the unemployed as useless benefit scroungers: no excuse to be without a job.

'Some people can't work,' I argued.

'Everyone can do something, boy.'

'Some people are disabled or ill.'

'They can sit down and work then, can't they?'

'They might be mentally ill.' I enjoyed winding him up: it was the best way to get attention. In fact, it was the only way.

'Don't be stupid, Tom. Mental problems are a modern invention. My grandparents got on with things. People used to ignore their problems, not snivel about them like children while I pay their rent.'

Gemma stayed quiet.

'Tom, can you please pass the salt?' My mother glared at me and changed the subject. Later, she reminded me, 'It's best not to provoke him, son. I know you chat to Harry's father like that but your father likes to feel his children respect him.'

I worry she may have suffered even more when I wound him up.

I'm still surprised by how easy it is to slip into a deceitful daily routine. I get up at the same time as Siri and we do our usual weekday thing: shower, make toast, chit-chat, say goodbyes, and then she leaves the house. I know she is disorganised but I hadn't realised how many days she comes back for something she has forgotten. So for the first fifteen minutes of every day I busy myself with things that can be easily changed to plausible 'just leaving' behaviours if Siri comes back. The only day I have to leave before nine is Friday. Mondays to Thursdays, at 8.30am I can take off my smart work attire and read the paper, feet on settee. Siri hates that. I am careful not to use food that will be noticed like cheese or ham, sticking with jars like jam and Marmite so Siri doesn't wonder why food is missing and blame the cleaner.

Six full weeks have disappeared and I haven't found an acceptable way to tell her I've been made redundant. Whenever I leave the house I make sure that the coast is clear – no nosy neighbours or late postmen hanging about. Sneaking about is disturbing. This isn't me, Tom Cleary, reliable and loyal, no side. I look in the mirror and still see that sincere and decent person but I don't recognise what he is doing. My mind interrupts with the truth: pathetic, weak, liar. You will never amount to anything, Tom. Give up now.

When I was working, I'd dream of this game: sitting at home relaxing, watching sport, reading or sleeping – but when you have no choice, it's not fun. The closest I have come to a similar experience is bunking school. I had no money or plan and, with every car that passed the park where I was hiding, my heart skipped a beat in case it was a teacher or my father. I didn't imagine I would be in the same situation as a grown man. What a ridiculous predicament: now I have all the unstructured time I've craved but what does a person do on their own for hours at a time?

I'd started at Stane Street less than a fortnight after leaving school. Show them you're really keen, Harry's parents said.

There'll be so many young people wanting a job this month. When I had secured the post, though, I realised, too late, that all my friends were enjoying weeks of unstructured time for the first time since reception class. I was dressed up in a suit pretending to be a grown-up while they were at the local park kicking a ball about or going swimming in the sea.

But then, as the years went by, I began to tell myself I was an optimist, a glass-half-full person. The dark days were gone; I was no longer that lonely kid in a cold house with uninterested parents. I was now a happily married man with a warm inclusive extended family and a nice flat, and my wife would soon conceive and turn us into a happy family.

And with that same learned optimism, I tell myself, I've been in window sales more than half my life – it will be easy to get a job once I've located some old contacts. I can say to Siri that I've been headhunted. She'll be protected from all unnecessary anxiety.

In the first fortnight I called or emailed fifty former colleagues and, of the few that bothered to return my approach, not one had anything to offer…

'Great to hear from you. Keep in touch.'

'I'll keep my ears open – something will come up.'

'They will be fighting over you, Tom, but nothing here, I'm afraid.'

My optimism continued until week four when after my third or fourth consecutive call, the tone changed.

'The market has dropped off.'

'Everyone is saving for Christmas.'

'Nothing doing at the moment, mate.'

'All gone quiet.'

'Just made redundancies ourselves.'

At the end of a particularly futile day of job hunting, I'd dreamed of Harry's dad. He was whispering his favourite saying in my ear: it's never too late to be what you might have been. If only that were true.

I can safely say the sudden death of Harry's parents in a car accident was the worst day of my life.

I'm so grateful that they made it to our wedding. As we were leaving the reception, Siri had dashed back to do more faffing rather than just stand and wait beside me for a few minutes for Adam and Harry to finish attaching cans to the car. Mr Edgington senior had pushed through the cheering crowd to come close to me, his back against the open driver's door. He'd taken my hands in his, just as Siri had done hours before, bending to my ear to overcome the noise. He'd whispered, I'm so proud of you, *my* boy. You'll make a fabulous husband. He hadn't looked away as my eyes moistened. Instead, he'd let go of my hands to envelop me in his arms just as he'd done so many times in my teens.

When they died, everything changed. For a while Harry was empty of content, as if someone had cut him open and scraped out his essence but left his exterior looking the same.

Chapter 5

I've realised pretending to have a job is more tiring than actually having one; remembering when you can be in the house and when you need to be absent is stressful. And I have to constantly make up details about my colleagues and my customers. That may sound easy enough, but it's not. If you keep saying mundane things it becomes dull, but equally you have to make sure your stories don't sound too dramatic or unlikely. The hardest thing is keeping track of what you *have* said, for example, don't tell a story about a couple who have broken up, and then blow it by mentioning their engagement lunch. I hadn't realised how hard it is to be a successful liar.

But it's the weekends that really kill me. I mostly have to share them with Siri's family, and that's when the stories I've told have the best chance of colliding with each other.

Our first wedding anniversary had fallen on a Saturday.

'Let's treat ourselves and go out to dinner,' I'd suggested, hoping to claw back some Brownie points, and thinking that maybe this was the one weekend that Siri and I could actually spend time alone together, and the stress of maintaining the fiction of my working life could be slightly reduced if I only had an audience of one.

When we'd first got together, I'd thought it ridiculous that Siri created so many anniversaries: the date we met, our first kiss, our first night alone and our first curry. Each had been noted and celebrated and for the significant ones Siri'd insisted on something new to wear, on a meal in a decent restaurant.

On a cosy night out for two.

So I silently fumed that, as it turned out, we would be spending our first *actual* anniversary with her family.

We walked in without knocking. Adam was looking as relaxed as always, spread out on the expensive leather settee, his arms stretched out either side as if illustrating the width of his world. Siri plonked herself next to him. They could easily be twins, raven-black short hair with matching eyes that seem more alert than everyone else's. He'd made no effort to dress up, but in comparison I still looked like a scruffy older brother.

Adam is a senior partner in a design company. To me he appears so successful, so attractive – and so fertile. I want to hate him but I like him an awful lot. I'm less keen on his wife, the immaculate Heather.

Distracted by the way she was filing her nails, I missed the beginning of a sentence emerging from her bright painted lips.

'I can't believe that Leo is taking the whole month of December off when he doesn't even have kids,' Heather said. 'Some people are so selfish – no wonder all the blokes with families were upset...'

I snapped out of my thought chain. I'd forgotten we'd had that conversation about leave issues at work and the stories I'd constructed around the extra demands that were being made on me.

'I thought it was a whole month at Easter next year that Leo was threatening to take as leave.' Siri was looking at me expectantly. '*Tom.*'

'What?'

'You weren't listening – again.'

Heather laughed in that fake way she does: small squeak, hand over mouth but not so close that it smudges the paint. 'What's happening to our men? It's like having two grumpy kids with ADHD.'

My heart was pounding so hard I thought they would hear it. I muttered something about Leo threatening to take both December and March while thinking how easy it would be for my life of deceit to be blown apart. The longer the lies went on, the worse it would be… Then, thankfully, right on cue, Adam knocked a saucepan full of hot water off the stove, creating a welcome distraction from my awkward body language.

All attention turned to clearing up the mess and rushing our godchild, Indya, to the tap as a few drops of hot water had splashed on her arm. I think she was more distressed by her mother's hysterical shrieks than any injuries.

'For goodness' sake, man,' Heather shouted, 'Not again!'

'Sorry,' Adam muttered in a tone that sounded like my current domestic self.

'How many times have I told you to turn in the saucepan handles? That could've gone all over her.'

'But it didn't,' Siri chipped in.

'No, but it's the third time he has spilled hot stuff in the last fortnight. Next time it might be life-changing injuries.' Heather sounded like she was going to cry.

Adam is one of my favourite people to be around. Working full time and being a great dad would be enough for most human beings but he also volunteers as a student liaison officer travelling all over the UK to help underfunded colleges get kids into work. When Adam talks, his body speeds up: he waves his arms around as he enthrals his audience with talk of his latest project. He says that being with the young keeps him optimistic.

At any social gatherings, he attracts plenty of female attention, which annoys Heather who says he is a flirt. This is patently untrue; it's just that he gives *everyone* his full attention, whether they are male or female, old or young. Talking to him makes you feel validated, as if you have something important to say.

Heather doesn't ever let up. I think it suits her to keep Adam firmly in the doghouse rather than letting the incident go with a 'no harm done'. I've never heard *him* complain about losing his dad when he was young or about the barely concealed fact that Siri is their mother's favoured child. They have three girls, Amelia, Indya and Rebecca – Meelie, Indy and Becca. Most of the time they are lovely but occasionally, when they're all screeching and competing, I find myself craving the peace of my as yet child-free abode.

When we decided to buy our own flat, Siri insisted we found somewhere rural with a community feel. She wanted a village school, country walks, a tea room and a decent pub. I wanted a convenience store where we could get milk, chocolate or beer after dark. We had decided to buy in Ditchling, and luckily a flat came on the market a few days after our engagement. It was cheaper than most in the area because it had no garden and the parking was limited. And the main reason this flat ticked all the boxes was because it was within walking distance of her big brother.

Now, much as I love Adam, I was beginning to wish they lived further away. We had fallen into the habit trap. When we first moved, we went to supper a couple of nights a month. Now we go to Adam and Heather's every Saturday evening unless we or they have something else on, which these days never seems to happen. Not even on our first wedding anniversary.

'Guess we need to get home, Heather,' Siri said when the

conversation turned yet again to how many activities the children were doing in comparison to everyone else.

'I need my bed,' yawned Adam. 'I've got an early start tomorrow.'

'My brother working at the weekend?' Siri exclaimed with mock surprise.

'Sadly, yes. I've got a college visit so I'll go in the morning and stay over till Monday.'

'Lucky old you,' she said as she gave him a high-five.

'Less of the old, baby sister – you're catching up fast, not far off thirty now!'

'Night, favourite bro.' She kissed him as he set her back on the ground from a bear hug.

It's hard not to be jealous of their closeness. Why did I have to get the family from the psychology case files and a sister who'd touch me only to break her fall over a crumbling cliff edge?

Recently, Siri tends to be in tears on the walk home. She is fine when we are with the girls but the contrasting quiet against their noisy chatter makes it painfully obvious what we lack. The endless failure to do something so seemingly simple as give her a child is so unbearably demoralising. The story of my life.

Well, people might say, okay, so Tom didn't amount to anything, but at least he didn't pass on his frail DNA.

Having stayed in the preparation phase for eight months longer than she was planning, Siri has made an appointment to see the GP next Friday after we both finish work.

Chapter 6

Only the regular customers know about this back room at the café so I deceive myself that it's my personal space. It has three tables: mine, which is a table for two, another small one by the window, and a larger rectangular one that seats three. The only person who regularly joins me is Philip, a middle-aged man with mental problems. He likes the window table but the room is large enough for me to feel sufficiently alone. We make a good pair.

If he catches my eye, he haemorrhages historical information, but if I avoid his gaze, he happily chats to himself, no need for a conversation partner. When people see him here, they instantly retreat so he gives me added protection. I find his chatter strangely comforting.

However, unusually, today Philip is absent and there are two strangers on the biggest table: it's impossible to relax and I deeply resent their intrusion.

I haven't seen them before: well-dressed ladies with accents to match are not Dawn's typical clientele. They could be mother and daughter. I am bizarrely drawn to the face of the older one. Her vein-laced eyes are directed at the picture behind me but the expression on her face betrays her thoughts. I can imagine what they are saying.

Why is a bloke his age on his own in a café in the week? It's not normal, is it?

Bet he's on benefits. There is a lot of that around here…

Happy to spend our taxes on coffee and cigarettes though, aren't they?

Two years ago, if I'd told Siri about them, she would've said, bet they fancied you, hun. But I know my looks don't invite a second glance. I don't think even she would say I'm classically attractive – especially these days when any natural desire she had seems to have disappeared. I have less hair than is optimal and a nose too generous for my face. Mind you, I don't think it would matter if I had two heads at the moment. It's my downstairs equipment that's important.

Siri has become obsessed with exorbitant fertility treatments, including one offered on Harley Street.

'Eleanor gave me the details of this amazing doctor – she's one of the leading experts.'

While Siri was at work, I looked up the fabulous Dr Camber. She sells Chinese potions for £200 a month. Her website boasts great success for thousands of childless couples. Siri and I had a blazing row.

'Listen to yourself, woman. You are losing your rational judgement.'

'Don't patronise me, you arrogant idiot.'

'Look for the evidence, Siri. You're not stupid. How can herbs and spices change anything? It makes no sense.'

'Dr Camber said there are lots of things we don't yet understand about fertility. I emailed her and she replied straightaway.'

'I bet she did. If what she does was supported by science, the NHS would offer it for free.'

'There are loads of valid treatments the NHS can't afford to offer. She has no reason to lie.'

'Don't be ridiculous. This treatment costs hundreds of pounds a month and the website says six months is recommended.'

'She said people have to make a long-term commitment, psychologically.'

'I saw her new BMW with personalised plate – 5PERM 1 – online. That just shows you how many couples have made a commitment.'

'Really?'

'No, of course not… but I doubt she lives in a poky flat or drives a Fiesta.'

She used to laugh at my jokes. That stopped weeks ago…

A crash interrupts my thoughts. An elderly gentleman is struggling to gather pieces of a floral tea cup.

'Sorry, I am so sorry.' He sounds like he's going to cry. There is blood on his hand but he continues to seek out the china fragments in the carpet as the dark stain spreads outwards.

Dawn rushes in, puts someone else's green soup on my table and bends to join him.

'Isaac, leave that.' She dabs his hand with a tea towel and gently pulls him back to standing.

'You sit down.' She guides him to Philip's table and helps him to sit. Her skirt stretches as she bends. I wonder if the material will hold as the zip widens.

'I'm so sorry, I get distracted.' A loud out-breath escapes him as his body finds the red velvet chair and he notices me watching him. No doubt he too is wondering why a middle-aged sloth is lazing about here on a weekday morning.

The man has flaky skin and the marks of old age on his face.

I try not to stare but his posture matches mine, slumped and hopeless.

'Here you go, my friend.' Dawn unloads a solid mug onto the plastic tablecloth.

'Thank you, dear. Do charge me for breakages.'

'Don't you be silly. I have far too many cups. I've got a friend who volunteers in Oxfam and she's always bringing me bits and bobs.'

'You're too good to me. I don't know what I'd do without this place.'

'You're very welcome, my friend. Coffee cake is on its way. We're a bit behind this morning,' and she nods towards the other room. 'I think Jess had a late night.'

'Shall I take these?' Without waiting for a response Dawn grabs a tray and piles up my debris – the cup from my first espresso, a teapot and a latte glass.

I was hoping my props would allow me a further hour. I must be due to get another drink but I'm not sure how much money I have left in my wallet. Dawn's is half the price of the coffee chains, but I am on a tight budget.

'Thanks, but this soup isn't mine,' I point out.

'It was a wrong order and I thought you looked hungry. I've told Jess to turn up the radiators. I can't believe how cold it is today.'

Does she think I am homeless or just a sad old bachelor? Can't she see how busy I am? That my wedding ring is obviously platinum?

I turn sharply to retrieve my phone from my briefcase as if it's ringing. Dawn disappears back to the serving area. Fortunately, the glass is misted over with condensation, so only vague human shapes can be seen from outside. Isaac has nodded off, and thankfully the old bats have gone.

'Can I have another latte, please?' I'm not sure I can stomach more caffeine but I feel obliged to order at least one drink an hour.

'Jess, give him a free one,' Dawn shouts over her shoulder. She takes her arms out of the soapy water and peels off her yellow gloves to wipe her forehead with the back of her hand.

'No, it's fine – my articles have been well received this month. Save the charity for next quarter.'

'Sorry, didn't mean to offend. All my regulars get freebies, part of the service.'

I don't want to be having this conversation. I produce an exaggerated open-mouthed grin but I catch a glimpse of my reflection in the window. I look like I'm having a stroke. Being believable and invisible is hard.

'You okay, love?' she says in my grandma's tone.

I paste on the smile that sells windows. 'Great, thanks. Finishing off a few bits before I get back on the road.'

'Tight schedule?'

'Indeed. Sometimes too tight.' It's hard to maintain eye contact. I've never been a liar.

Endless coffee makes me feel as bad as beer does, but I can't afford to keep buying food. I am supposed to be using my daytime hours to job hunt, search the employment sites and send out my CV. Instead, I sit down in preparation for all that, and before I know it Dawn is mopping the floor and I should be driving home from 'work'.

I realise I'm great at expressing my emotions in my head. I can spend hours staring into space listening to my own mind. I've opened a trunk I haven't looked in for years. Now its contents are out, I can't resist digging deeper into long-forgotten aspects of my history – and I'm not sure this is a good thing.

My gran used to pay me to unravel the contents of her knitting bag. There you go, she would say as she plonked a tangled mass into my lap. That should keep you out of my hair for ten minutes. I can remember staring at the mess: I knew the solution was to choose a strand and pull gently and patiently until the chosen snake wove its way out. With each colour gone, the 'mother' ball would shrink and change shade until the tangle was replaced with neat piles of single colours. For some reason, I found it entrancing. Right now, my life is that mud-coloured muddle of confusion. If I could find the end of even one strand, maybe I could disentangle the tight ball of brown despair. The problem is I can't see where to start.

Siri has started to hint that's why she's not conceiving. Buttoned up like his father, was how she described me to her irritating friend Eleanor. I came back early from work one evening last week; I could hear them chatting in the kitchen.

'We've tried the scientific approach and even the crazy stuff like him wearing the right pants, eating goji berries and not washing for three days, blah blah blah...' The conversation became hushed and I found myself being drawn closer to the kitchen door. 'You just never know with Tom, you never know what's going on inside his head. The mystery of Tom's head,' she said, and they laughed.

She might as well have said it outright: Tom is so uptight even his sperm are held in.

I could help Siri solve the mystery of what's in my head. It goes something like this. What's wrong with me? Why can't I get my wife pregnant? Why can't I keep a job? Or reassure myself I am not losing the plot? My feelings are increasingly dark, dismal and terrifying. I think about death, illness, grief and funerals more than I think about laughter, sunshine or happy-ever-afters. I feel a failure, rejected, pointless, but mostly, just dark. That's what's in Tom's head. Perhaps they're right. Maybe my head is the reason my sperm can't fulfil their sole purpose. That night we went to bed in silence.

Chapter 7

'Tom. Dad's dead.'

My father would have approved of his final departure. It was New Year's Eve going into the millennium, and I was out in Brighton drinking with some old schoolfriends. The millennium provided an excuse for a big celebration. The plan was to meet early and then go into central Brighton, working our way from bar to bar, starting at one end of the main road with a view to reaching the clocktower by midnight to join the crowds for a drunken rendition of 'Auld Lang Syne'. Sadly, I didn't get beyond two drinks.

The phone's vibration in my pocket took me by surprise. It was an even greater surprise when it displayed my sister's name, Gemma Cleary. (That's how close we are: in my contacts, she is listed not as sis, Gem or even Gemma.) She had never phoned me before and we've not spoken on the phone since.

'Oh hi, Gemma… it's very noisy. I think I misheard you… what did you say?'

'Dad's dead.'

There was a long pause. I couldn't think what to say. 'How…?'

'They think it was his heart but…'

'But what?'

'Nothing. Mum didn't seem to have all the facts. But I think it was… straightforward. Anyway, he's dead, so it doesn't matter. Let me know if you have any ideas about the funeral. Mum wants the full religious piece.'

The line went silent. At first, I thought the signal had gone. Then I realised that she'd ended the call.

I had absolutely no idea what to do. I couldn't hear myself think for drunken shouting. Should I call her back, invite her to mine, go to her? Isn't that what families do? Weep together, huddle together in their shared sorrow? I was twenty, my dad was dead, and I felt nothing. I had no desire to seek solace with my sister or mother. I realised we were related but not in any way connected.

I went home with Harry, the street noise ringing in my ears. I didn't get angry or upset. Harry reassured me it was shock, and that grief would hit me later. But it didn't. Gemma made all the funeral arrangements without asking me again if I wanted to contribute. I presume she consulted my mother but I can't be sure.

I received a voicemail a week after the death call to inform me when and where the funeral would take place. The service was formal. There were three hymns, even though my family only go to church for weddings, christenings – and funerals. It was one of those occasions where no one knows the hymns apart from the church-goer with the most tuneless voice.

I didn't know anyone there apart from Gemma, my mother and her only friend, Freda. The pews were full of clones in dark suits, crisp white shirts and black ties. One after another they sought me out.

'Such a shock. No age to go…'

'So sorry, so hard for you to have it happen like that.'

'You must get on with your life. No shame on you.'

I didn't care sufficiently to ask what they meant. That day, I made a commitment to be the best father to my own kids. They would know me, love me and weep at my funeral. Adam is that kind of dad.

My mother didn't appear upset.

'How are you feeling about Dad?' I asked my sister.

'Not everyone feels the need to talk about their every emotion, Tom.'

My wife says I'm buttoned up, and my sister thinks I am emotionally incontinent. No wonder they don't spend any time together.

I left in the middle of the wake.

When I describe my childhood, people look sympathetic. My father worked long hours as a company director and weeks went by without us seeing or speaking to him. This was no bad thing as when he was around there was tension I couldn't explain. He left the house before 6am and rarely returned before my mother was in bed. My parents didn't show each other any affection. They lived parallel lives, coming and going at different times, rarely sharing a conversation let alone a bed. I'd often get up for school and find my father asleep on the settee in a crumpled work suit, an overflowing ashtray on the floor.

I once overheard my mother complain to Freda. She was saying, I sometimes wonder what he is avoiding by staying at work all those hours. I blushed as I overheard Freda say, maybe he has a fancy woman, and my mum laughed, which was unusual. Who would have him? she'd said. He's as fat as a pig and snores like one too!

I loved it when Freda came. I didn't like *her* much but when she was with my mother, Mum changed. She drank wine and moved like a dancer; sometimes they sounded like screeching schoolgirls. Mum would tell her what she'd do if she won the lottery; she would share her fantasies about holidays and adventures that never included my father. Even as a child, I knew this was my real mum, the one who got excited and jiggled about as she chatted. As I grew up, this mum went away more and more often. My dad had consumed her completely by the time I left home. He spat out a flat, pale and spiteful person who looked a bit like my mum.

I am unaware of any friends she has other than Freda. They still meet every Tuesday for coffee and a toasted teacake, to talk about TV soaps and who in the neighbourhood has died.

My mother has never phoned me. I was impressed she and Gemma made it to my wedding. When every couple of months I summon the stamina to check she's still alive, the conversation follows a familiar pattern.

'Hello, son. Do you remember Basil?'

'Can't say I do, Mum.'

'Oh, you do. He was married to Marion; they had Karen. Funny girl she was.'

'Can't recall anyone like that, Mum.'

'They lived on Cranleigh Road. Brown dog. He was manager at the butchers.'

She makes no concession to the fact this is supposed to be a dialogue. 'We were in the flats then. Marion drove a van. Freda and I thought that was odd for a woman.'

'Really have no idea who you are talking about, Mum.'

'Oh, well. Basil died. Funeral is Thursday. I've booked a cab.'

Funerals seem to be the only events that motivate my mother out of the chair. She and Freda go together and have a pub lunch afterwards. Obviously, the corpse changes but the punchline's always the same: Oh, well. — died. Funeral is —. I've booked a cab.

As I got older, I spent more and more time at Harry's. With

him being an only child living with his parents and grandparents, I was always welcome. When we came in after school, Harry's mum hugged me as she did Harry. There was cake in the tin and the promise of a home-cooked meal before seven. I loved it there.

Chapter 8

'*Love, love, love... Love is all you need...*' Dawn is jigging about as she makes toast and sets out cups and saucers. The radio is on far too loud.

When she's cheerful, she sings, smiles and nothing is too much trouble. Today is going to be a good café day.

'Morning, Tom.' To be known by name wasn't the plan. 'Your usual?'

I'm desperate to defy Siri's most recent criticism. Last night I'd said we couldn't afford an all-inclusive holiday to relax our reproductive systems.

Boring and predictable is what you're becoming, she'd spat, balancing her dinner on her lap while watching some drama she preferred to talking to her husband at the table. I should've listened to my mother's alerts when I married someone over a decade my junior.

'I'll have toast but with strawberry jam, and green tea please Dawn.'

Dawn lifted her head so fast you'd have thought I'd insulted her. 'Well, there's a surprise. I opened a fresh tin of marmalade when I saw you come down the hill.'

'Oh well, I'll stick to my usual then, but with green tea.'

'Green tea?' Peter looks up from his conversation as if I've offended him, too.

'Good for testosterone levels,' leaks out of my mouth. I can't believe I've said that in public. I might as well wear a sticker on my head, declaring my status as faulty.

Peter and his wife, Cilla, have been here every day since my first visit, always at their table in the front room; I think they like listening to everyone's business. Cilla can't seem to sit still.

'We come every day, every day since it opened five years ago,' she'd said to me.

'How nice,' I'd said without turning towards her. I didn't know how to communicate any more effectively that I was here to work, not socialise.

'Dawn does a lovely jacket potato, lots of butter. Those modern cafés scrimp on everything, don't they, Peter?' Cilla didn't wait for Peter to confirm. 'We come for a hot lunch and have a sandwich and a cup of tea in front of *Pointless* at home later. Do you watch the tea-time quiz programmes?'

'No, I'm usually in the car.'

Peter then pushed to get a word in as his wife got up, wandered over to the door, looked out, came back, sat down again. 'How's your belly off for spots, lad?'

'I'm sorry?'

'Don't you worry about him,' said Dawn. 'He's from foreign parts up north. He's asking how you are.'

'Not from round here, though, either, are you?'

'No.'

'What do you do for work?'

'I've just started working on a country magazine, researching businesses that specialise in producing or selling organic foods,' I explained with a tone that sounded impressively authentic.

The voice in my head told me that I sounded like the worst

combination of Leo and my father. I had absolutely no idea where that career came from. I'd never bothered about organic food in my life until we started the baby preparation phase, although these days I am of course not allowed to eat anything exposed to chemicals or hormones. I was in a recurring nightmare: the old me had changed from a normal bloke to one with no control over what came out of his mouth. I thought, I need to see one of Harry's cronies to assess me, and they'll diagnose an unusual medical condition where people spontaneously tell untruths – although I guess those people are called liars.

This morning, as if she understands in her childlike way what's on my mind, Cilla says, 'We don't have any children. Do you have any?'

'No.'

'Such a shame, but it might not be too late for you.'

'Maybe not…'

'You need children. All your friends will die. Won't they, Peter?'

'They sure will, but don't depress the poor boy.'

'Sit down Tom, your table is empty,' says Dawn. I'll bring the green tea and toast over when I've finished Peter's porridge… Hello, Isaac. How are you?'

'Terrible. My knees hurt, the woman in the Post Office was sour, and the bus was late.'

'Never mind,' Dawn soothes. 'Take your coat off and I'll make a hot tea to cheer you up.'

'It will take more than that to cheer me up.'

'We know,' she mutters under her breath.

Isaac shuffles himself into his favourite chair and continues to rant about all that is wrong with what used to be a perfect village. 'There are no young people here. God's waiting room, this village.' No one responds. 'No one visits me. Why did I bother? Twenty years I slaved away in that supermarket to put bread on the table and pay for them to go to college. What thanks do I get? A card at Christmas if I'm lucky.'

I wonder whether his irritable ways pushed people away or his misery is down to rejection and loneliness. He reminds me of my father.

Carol is another regular. She says her chats with Dawn are all that stand between her and insanity. When Carol left the café on my first week, Dawn filled me in on all the details. 'Her second child died during birth, which was awful, and she got post-natal depression. Then, her good-for-nothing husband went off with the woman who worked at the supermarket on East Road, leaving Carol to bring up her other daughter, Alice, who has learning difficulties. The ex then emigrated, never to reappear. Carol had just got Alice settled into a home when her mother got diagnosed with dementia and had to move in with Carol because she can't live by herself.'

Dawn usually moves on from me to Cilla when she's telling her long stories and my eyes glaze over. I have no idea why all these people treat me as if I'm one of them, as if I'm one of their day centre colleagues. Peter has even started asking me to fix his computer problems. Why would a journalist know how to do that?

But yesterday, there was a new buzz in the café: for the first time in ages a new customer pitched up. Dawn looked like she wanted to rub her hands together at the thought of a new victim to interrogate. A novel guest is as dramatic as a fresh murder at the police station. Dawn likes us all to spot the clues so the suspect can be identified as soon as possible. We were all sitting at our allotted tables when the door opened and closed quicker than usual. As if part of a synchronised team, all eyes went to the newcomer, even mine. The good thing about my table in the back room is I can hide but also have a clear view to the front entrance. In shuffled a customer who was still in her teens, a rare sight in these parts. She had the blonde hair of a much younger child tied in a high pony tail that swished from side to side faster than she walked. Her eyes stayed firmly on her boots, perhaps because they were disproportionally large in comparison to the rest of her.

'Hi, good to have a customer under forty,' Dawn said before the girl had reached the counter.

The girl didn't look up; only her eyes lifted.

'What can I do you for, lovey?'

'Coffee, please,' she said in a whisper. All ears were straining to listen.

'What sort of coffee? Latte, cappuccino, flat white…?'

'Any is fine.'

'Latte?'

'Thanks.'

I have no idea why but she captured my full attention. I could see she was barely an adult but there was something about her to distract me. I confess I'd watched her walk from the bus stop half an hour earlier. She'd headed purposefully towards the black door opposite but at the last minute juddered to a stop and retreated. She stayed in the café an hour with her one drink. Dawn popped over with a chocolate brownie but she kept her head down. The treat remained untouched when she left.

Before she was even properly out of the door, Dawn muttered, 'That was an odd one. Pretty though, behind those red swollen eyes. Name's Lydia and that's all I got out of her…' Then, 'I wonder if she's at the college,' she said to no one in particular.

I thought she looked too young to be at college. Cilla sprang up before the door had clattered shut, grabbed the teenager's abandoned cake and devoured it before re-joining her husband.

Peter smirked, superiority plastered all over his face. 'I bet you didn't spot the bespoke badge on her bag.'

'Actually, I did,' Dawn quipped back.

I couldn't resist joining the competition. 'Black badge, "John three sixteen",' I shouted through the gap.

'Thought the cat had got your tongue today. Welcome back. I'm guessing John's the boyfriend and they met on the sixteenth of March,' said Dawn.

Cilla had her hand in the air and was shouting, 'Me, me, me,' like a primary school child desperate for her teacher's attention.

'Wait a minute, Cill – let the youngsters guess first,' Peter grinned, leaning back in his chair with his arms folded.

'It'll be a tour date for a teenage indie band,' was my best guess.

'I know, I know, pick me.' Cilla continued to thrust her raised hand. 'It's the Bible.'

'She's right,' said Peter, leaning towards his wife like a parent urging on a toddler to take her first steps. 'It's the most famous Bible verse – can you remember how it goes, love?'

Cilla stood up, straightened her body and said in the best Received Pronunciation: '*For God so loved the world, that he gave his one and only son, Jesus, so that whosoever believes in him, shall not die but have everlasting life.*'

'Indeed.' Peter sat back, proud of their winning team.

'How do you two know that? You're always here on a Sunday morning.'

'Sunday School. In the 1930s, it was the only place open on a Sunday.'

'It can't be that,' I pointed out. 'What teenager would have that on a badge?'

'Maybe she stole it,' Dawn surmised.

I think I can now be counted as a Dawn's café regular, someone who six weeks ago thought frequenting cafés was for women. I can now recite the difference between seven types of coffee. I know this lot better than the colleagues I worked with for years.

I've been officially unemployed for seven weeks. I have my 'real' life and this other life, a place where I spend many hours with people whom my wife, friends and family know nothing about. It is unlikely anyone who might recognise me would be in a village miles away from my home – but stranger things have happened: Siri once met her neighbour on a beach in Menorca. Siri works full time, my mother stays in her dining room, Harry is stuck in his clinics... But Leo travels. That would just about be the cherry on top of his cake, to see me snivelling into my laptop when he marched in for an espresso.

When I arrive, I lay out my newspaper, my phone, my laptop, my iPad and my journal, which I bought to jot down ideas for events in my working day and what I have told to whom: it is my diary of deceit. I am ashamed to admit that I also scribble what I am thinking and feeling, and it helps me make sense of my double life.

The idea of me writing expressions of emotion in a journal would make Siri smile. When was the last time I saw her smile? I convince myself I'm at home, that I'm not hiding from my real life because I am a testosterone-deficient specimen who can't tell his wife he has no job.

Chapter 9

I haven't felt this excited since I was, what – ten? Spending two weeks at home being myself, in my real life, without pressure, is exhilarating. It makes me recognise the utter madness of hiding the truth from everyone around me.

Usually, Christmas Day is spent with Siri's family. Margaret and Adam share the catering, and the lunch table is an overflow of seasonal dishes cooked to perfection. Heather takes charge of the aesthetics, ensuring the serviettes match the crackers; our only responsibility is to ensure there is sufficient alcohol to last a week. Since his parents died Harry has chosen to lunch alone but he joins us for ridiculous party games in the evening. My mother and sister are always invited but have rarely attended. Their plans have to be worked around the TV schedule, and, if my sister does turn up, she makes it clear she wants to leave by 4pm. Must get back for the neighbour's cat, is Gemma's excuse. I realise the last time I saw my only sibling was a good few years ago.

This year though Adam and Heather have gone to her parents, and Harry has decided to break with tradition and join his colleagues for a ski trip in France. I suspect he's sniffing around the new female consultant. Siri has offered to cook lunch at ours. My mother isn't inspirational in the kitchen and eats sandwiches for most of her meals. If you'd told me last year the festivities would be spent trying to fill the awkward silence separating my wife and my mother I would've openly wept, but I'm so relieved to be 'off work' I'm content to be anywhere. And Siri is relieved she doesn't have to cope with Adam's children while our pregnancy plans are still at first base.

In the days leading up to Christmas, I was horrified to realise that our relationship was becoming just like my parents': meals in silence, a chair each at different ends of the room. But on Christmas Day, Siri is surprisingly cheery and we exchange gifts and have a baby try without checking the calendar or her temperature. She apologises for her misery and we agree that next year will be different. But I resist the temptation to say, this is the year we will get pregnant, because I doubt my abilities.

The ordeal of Christmas lunch with my mother over, the rest of the holiday is unusually quiet. We get up late, watch films and eat loads of junk food; Siri switches off from her healthy mission and eats the anti-fertility foods she's been avoiding for months. She even appears to like me.

On New Year's Eve we stay in and watch *Love Actually*, one of her favourite romantic comedies, and I make an extra effort not to complain about the lack of action. We have a real baby try, and we invite in the New Year in bed watching the fireworks. I go to sleep promising myself that this is the end of 'fake work' and rehearse how to be honest with Siri without exposing myself as being a weak, deceitful pig. By the time I get up on 1 January, Siri has gone for a run.

She has now convinced herself that the reason for her failure to conceive (despite eating organic rabbit food for months) is that she hasn't done any cardio exercise. As soon as I wake up, my resolve starts to disappear, so I decide that a compromise is to tell my secret to Harry. I have to share it with someone.

I send a message saying 'BBN' to Harry – this means 'Beer, Bar, Now'. We used this code when we were living together if either of us had stuff to mull over without our flatmates overhearing. We would text that code and meet at the White Horse on Corn Street at 7pm. The White Horse has been converted into flats for older people but we still use the code if we want to demand attention from the other in a hurry.

My phone pings late into the evening. Siri and I are in bed. She is fast asleep but I am wide awake even before my phone announces Harry's text message. 'DTP?' This means 'Day, Time, Place?' and is another code, meaningless now as Harry has no choice over when he's on leave.

'You name time and place but make it soon,' I type.

'Can you leave early on Thursday and meet at 4? Am on call at 7. Pizza Express in Lewes?'

'Will be there.'

Siri stirs, moaning she can't sleep with the phone light flooding the room. She turns over and loudly sighs as she does when she has something to say but doesn't say it.

She was keen enough to be friends earlier in the evening when the calendar said her ovaries were wanting to party. It was not long ago that my wife's attention was something I desired above all things; now I dread the calendar calling for my services. It feels like a mechanical act bereft of emotion and, if that's not depressing enough, I then have the period joy to look forward to two weeks down the line. Every month, Siri's spirits lift as she allows herself to believe that this will be the end of phase one. I think her stress levels are so high her cycle is altered: her period is frequently late, which gives her a few days of euphoria and time for fantasising about our first son. This is followed by the inevitable subsequent devastation.

Last month I tried to have a rational dialogue about this. 'I know it's hard but try not to invest so much in the thought of a baby until it's a fact.'

'I can't believe you said that. You have no idea. You're stupidly insensitive.'

'I was trying to help, protect you from disappointment over and over again.'

'Maybe that's the problem: your attitude is sabotaging the process. If you aren't prepared to believe it will happen, it won't.'

Note to self: stay quiet next month, Tom. Perform when told. Keep your mouth shut.

I allow myself to fall asleep knowing I am seeing Harry on Thursday and the GP again on Saturday morning. I haven't been to the doctor in years. But since I consented to be a sperm machine, I've been in the medical centre more often than the pub.

The first doctor Siri and I consulted looked as if he should have retired many years ago. I stayed silent: Siri likes to lead.

'We've been trying for months without any progress.'

The GP leaned forward as if he might kiss her. 'What do you mean by trying, my dear?'

Pleased to make a contribution, I piped up. 'Having sex.'

'Ah, yes, I was thinking more of frequency and following cycle patterns.'

Siri shot me a look and carried on their conversation. 'We've tried everything it says on the website the nurse suggested. I'm doing it all to the letter – eating well, restricting alcohol, exercising… and Tom is trying his best.'

My hands were hard to keep still. Siri hates my fidgeting. I felt helpless, an idiot. Even the old man looked at me with withering concern. He pushed both hands on his desk to stand up and spoke like he was at the front of a university class. 'You might find it interesting to know studies report approximately thirty-five per cent of couples conceive within two years, while other studies of mostly young women report natural pregnancy rates of up to eighty per cent within three years.'

No, we didn't find that interesting; eight out of ten cats prefer Whiskas but that doesn't help the two who despise it.

'Conception is harder than it looks, young lady. It takes time and patience,' he said to my wife as he shook her hand. I imagined him thinking, give me a call: I could do much better than his best, even at my age. Then I imagined him talking later with Mrs Ancient over dinner. *You should have heard the naive couple I met today, trying for a baby for five minutes with no results and now they can't cope. Perhaps some inconvenience in their neat life plan might teach them a thing or two.*

'You're still very young, Mrs Cleary, no reason to panic,' were his parting words. This was clearly the end of the consultation. The smile and the pat on my back made me really want to knock him back into his plush revolving chair. 'Enjoy the process, Mr Cleary. Come back in six months if there's still no action.'

Harry is waiting when I get to the restaurant. Harry is never a minute late for anything: my pint is on the table waiting for me. Seeing Harry makes the tears well up. He gets up for a man hug and holds my gaze for longer than normal before we both sit down. I don't know where to start and for a moment we sit in silence.

'How's work?' I ask.

'Fine. Now, cut the small talk. What's up?'

'Don't know where to start.'

'At the beginning. How bad can it be?'

'As bad as it gets.'

'Please tell me you're not having an affair.'

'Harry!' If my oldest friend could think that of me, there's no hope.

'I thought not, just can't think of much else that matters.'

'I got the sack.'

'What? Why?' Harry's eyebrows are pulled down. I imagine this is his professional 'giving bad news' face.

'Being me. Not up to the job any more. Lost my edge.'

'You can't be sacked for that. Challenge it. It's unfair dismissal. I'll come with you.'

'I left at the end of October.'

'Tom! How come I don't know my best friend has changed jobs?'

'Your best friend is jobless. I thought I'd find something but I haven't been able to.'

'You will, mate. My nan always said you could sell duffel coats in Africa.'

'Once upon a time, maybe. Leo said I was past my prime, that all the juniors were doing much better on half my salary. We just didn't see eye to eye. He was shallow, insincere, thought nothing of swindling old people, pushing contracts with quick turnaround dates. It's not my way.'

'Nor should it be.'

'I got a payout but that is dwindling, even though I spend on nothing but coffee and toast.'

'So, you weren't sacked. You were made redundant.'

'Sacked sounds more courageous at least, like you did something exciting. Pathetic, isn't it?'

'Why are you so hard on yourself? You don't have to step in where your old man left off, you know.'

'Dad was right. He'd point out I couldn't keep a job, and couldn't father a child.'

'Stop. We are not going back there. You are kind, intelligent and a great husband. One idiot tells you rubbish and you're back in your bedroom being fifteen. You'll find work, you have a great marriage and you'll get pregnant when she stops stressing. How has the home master taken it? I bet she's on it. Surprised she hasn't phoned Buckingham Palace to see if they need new windows. Has she written your CV and given you a list of contacts or do you just have to clean the house in your free time? Surprised you're allowed time off for beer drinking...'

'Siri doesn't know.'

'Well, you don't have to tell her every time you meet your friends, do you?'

'She doesn't know I am not working.'

Harry stays quiet for a minute. I notice how different he looks now: no sign of his teenage self. In a flash suit and with a fresh haircut and neat beard, it's obvious he's a professional man.

'I don't understand. You said you left on Halloween.'

'I did. I went home to tell her but when I arrived, she'd been panicking because I was late and for once was affectionate. So I planned to tell her the next day.'

'And...?'

'She's obsessed with private fertility treatments, going on spa breaks to relax, looking to cut down her hours. I chickened out. I thought if I had time to call some contacts, I'd be in work before she knew.'

'But she'd understand. It wasn't your fault.'

'Not many grown men get bullied by a new graduate, do they?'

'Plenty do actually, and by consultant medics; it happens everywhere. It's the bullies who deserve the shame.'

'I keep thinking about what I should have done differently.

He threw me out in front of everyone. I was so humiliated. Old feelings are surfacing.'

'It'll be okay. You just need to get Siri back on side and the three of us can make a plan. Why does she think you're home?'

'I'm not. I drive miles every day to a café for a group of odd-balls and fit in very nicely. No one knows, only you.'

Harry is laughing as he swigs the dregs from his glass.

'What?'

'It's pretty cool you've managed for two months to live a secret life and not get caught, especially knowing Siri and her mother. There's undercover work waiting for you some-where.'

'It's not funny,' I say, but I realise I'm laughing too. It's been a while.

I tell him about the café, about Dawn who could definitely be employed as an undercover agent, Philip and his historical genius, Cilla's irritating ways, and Lydia, the newbie who's been on my mind.

'She just looks so young and vulnerable. She reminds me of Olivia Newton John in *Grease* before she fell in with Rizzo and the Pink Ladies. Do you remember how many times we watched that film in your parents' house?'

'You're not falling in love with someone who is not yet through adolescence?'

'No, nothing like that. Any feelings I have are strictly fatherly. I am working up the courage to ask her about why she's in the café so much.'

'Let's hope they don't ask you the same question.'

Chapter 10

I forgot it was Friday when I woke up this morning. I need to pay more attention.

I get dressed for Siri's sake but leave shaving, showering and eating until she goes. I did the same thing one morning when I was running late and worried she would notice, but she didn't. Now, I treat myself to a quiet shower and sometimes even a leisurely bath after she's left for work.

She moves towards the door, bag in one hand, toast unattractively hanging from her mouth. 'Don't forget clothes need picking up off bedroom floor.'

'Darling, it's me who clears the floor every day, as well as collecting your many tea cups from the previous evening.'

'I know but Friday's cleaning day.'

I have no idea why she can't have one tea cup she refills. There will be a cup in the bedroom, two in the sitting room and at least one in the bathroom. They will stay there until we run out of mugs. Then either I collect them for the dishwasher or it's the day the cleaner comes.

As I drive away, in my rear-view mirror I see the cleaner's blue car pull up outside the flat. I find my playlist and turn up the volume to silence the thoughts. On a good day it works, but often no sound can drown out my misery. On those days, the words in my head come fast.

Why am I alive?

I am a waste of space.

I am a burden.

If I can't get her pregnant, she'll hate me.

I've never been good enough.

Then, the childhood stuff comes back, the relentless bullying, the questions about my family: what was it about me that my own mother couldn't love? Why was my father so angry? Why me, why me?

Dawn's tone of panic jumpstarts me out of a horrible mood.

'I am so glad to see you,' she shouts from outside the café before I've crossed the road. She is carrying one of the metal chairs that go with the outside tables.

'My mum's ill again and Jess has gone on a hen weekend. She phoned in sick but she's forgotten she friended me on Facebook so I can see she's in Paris. They do my head in, these college students. No wonder they're all in debt.'

'Oh dear, can I help with the chairs?'

She pauses to mop her brow with her sleeve. 'Music to my ears! Yes, please, thanks so much. I haven't started the coffee machine, the bins need emptying and the jackets won't be out for lunch unless I get them in now.'

'I can get the furniture out front and empty the bins. You focus on the food and drink.'

'Deal. Free coffee all day for you, Tom… I don't even know your surname!'

'It's Cleary.' Was that a mistake? I wasn't quick enough to come up with a realistic false one. As I drop the square silver table into the centre of two matching chairs, I see my belly creeping out from my T-shirt. Mr Blobby feels like an accurate pseudonym.

I don't sit outside. I would hate to be on public display, even if I was a smoker and it was a reasonably mild day, and it is stupidly close to the main road. Trucks have knocked against the wall on more than a few occasions.

'Wow, you've done it already. It takes Jess most of the morning to get these all out.'

'I'm not sure the outside tables are safe. Cars come very close and the fumes are awful.'

'You think too much. It's fine. If people choose to smoke, they should be happy to breathe carbon monoxide and risk death.'

I don't sit down until eleven. My table has a reserved sign on it with my favourite girly tipple of a weak extra-hot latte and one of Dawn's divine chocolate brownies. Life is strange: just over two months ago, I thought I was successful, working at a fast pace on a reasonable salary. Then my world caved in. Now I have a reserved table in a café for oddballs that nevertheless feels as much like home as my own.

'Sorry, Tom.' Dawn interrupts my typing. 'I don't suppose you could pop to the supermarket and get some milk. I'm almost out. I can't believe no one I could ask has popped in, today of all days…' It's a while since I felt useful to a woman.

I don't manage to get out of the door before her next request comes flying.

'I feel awful, but when you return, you couldn't help with taking out the lunches, could you? No worries if you're too pushed today.'

'That's fine – milk, then my waiter's charm on my return.'

'You're an angel. Your wife must love you, Mr Helpful.'

I leave without comment. I haven't said I'm married. I know

she wants more detail. I've watched her with others. I'm happy to do favours for her café but my life will stay my own.

Serving the lunches gives me an excuse to move close enough to Lydia to take a sneaky peek at what she is up to with her pen. She comes in most days, arriving early and sometimes staying as long as me. Her notebook page is full of doodles. I pluck up the courage to say, 'That's exactly what my wife does when she can't solve a problem.' To my great embarrassment she starts to cry – not slow silent tears like I do, secretly, but big, gasping, breathless sobs.

Dawn rushes over, shoots me a look and wraps her arms around Lydia in a motherly gesture too intimate for a virtual stranger. Lydia doesn't seem to mind. I hover awkwardly; I don't know what to do. Should I go and leave the girls to chat or, as the instigator of the outburst, am I obliged to stay and sit it out? In the end the decision is made by Lydia. After five minutes of sobbing, she pushes Dawn away, says, 'I'm sorry,' and walks out. Dawn and I watch in silence as she crosses the road and disappears.

'What on earth did you do?'

'I have absolutely no idea.'

Dawn is unruffled though. And she is disproportionally grateful for my help. 'Thanks so much for today.'

'You've said that three times in an hour. It's fine. I have less to do on a Friday.'

After the morning rush, the café empties and she wanders through to the back room and sits at my table. Then, she's quiet. It's unusual for her to be so unforthcoming. Dawn is great to chat to when you can't be bothered to communicate properly – or don't want to – because, like my mother, she talks at you rather than to you. Her typical topics of conversation are the lives of her regulars, made-up lives she creates for the less regular, and her struggles as a single mum to three children.

She had her first baby, Ned, at sixteen. He is now twenty and she tells everyone he's been 'a challenge since he was born'. He is currently living with his father so Dawn only sees him at weekends. Her younger two, Daisy and Phoebe, are nine and eleven; I haven't heard anything about the man they came from. They get collected by their nan or a friend's mum each weekday but come to the café to do their homework or watch television in the office upstairs. They arrive not long before I leave but they chat happily to a boring middle-aged man like me and have lovely manners. I love my nieces, but they are less polite and generous by comparison with these two.

'Spit it out! I haven't got all day.' I presume she's going to have another go at extracting my life story so she can share it with Cilla.

'I know you have a job, but don't suppose you fancy helping me out for a couple of hours on a Friday morning on a regular basis? Jess is going to university in the autumn and wants to go travelling when her exams are finished. I could do with some muscles to do odd jobs…' I must look as shocked as I feel, because she gets up to go. 'So sorry, Tom. How insulting of me to imply a successful journalist would want to be a skivvy in a shabby café.'

I stop her in her tracks – which is a pretty impressive feat. 'Dawn, I would love to,' I say with too much enthusiasm. She gives me a hug then pulls away quickly and laughs while we both flush a shade of pink.

'Just need to work out terms and conditions then?' I say with a smile.

'Whatever is fine. I've enough money.'

'Dawn, I was joking, I don't want to take your profits. You can't be getting much with all that you give away.'

'I need to pay you! I can pay the bills even without selling flapjacks.' She doesn't offer an explanation. Is she some rich aristocrat disguised as a waitress, a secret millionaire?

I agree to do a couple of hours on a Friday morning and bits and bobs across the rest of the week, doing odd jobs, lifting and fixing. Dawn isn't bothered about the details and it's me who suggests keeping a record of my hours. So, that's how I've made the transition from window sales into a career in hospitality. It isn't what I could ever have imagined, but it's a few hours' money to top up my lump sum and it's stress-free, with people I like and who trust me... sort of.

If you ask Siri what her husband would be least likely to do, expressing his emotions and working in a café would both be near the top of her list.

Siri was out visiting her mum when I got back. A Post-it Note was attached to the microwave: 'Back by 8, wait to eat'; I read it again and assessed her mood as upbeat. I made a fish pie, her favourite meal, and cleaned the kitchen before she came home. I am not great in this department and only have a small repertoire, but what I cook, I cook well. I have Harry to thank for that.

'Hey, Tom Tom.'

It's a good sign when she repeats my name like that, a habit she developed in our early months together. If I'm the annoying voice of the iPhone, you must be the condescending instructor on the satnav, she'd said on one of many tension-filled journeys. No idea where you're going but good at directing everyone else...

I went over and kissed her. 'Hello, my wife. Dinner is in the oven. Good journey? Your mum okay?'

'Yes, though she's worried about Adam. Apparently, he is overloaded at work, calling her two or three times a week, which is never a good sign.'

I can't imagine a situation that would result in multiple calls to my mother. But Siri rarely misses a day without chatting to Margaret on the phone and they text constantly.

'He seemed okay at the weekend.'

'That's what I told her. I think he exaggerates his woes when he's with Mum, turns into mummy's little boy because she is so different from Heather who just tells him to man up. I need the loo, then we can eat. I'm starving.'

We didn't talk about the medical appointment booked for the next day.

Chapter 11

We arrive at the GP surgery fifteen minutes early. It is unpleasantly dark in the waiting room. A row of faces look up, their minds accusing the unemployed bloke of stealing a scarce Saturday morning slot.

'It's horribly gloomy in here,' I note, trying to fill the silence.

'Tom, it's not gloomy. It's you, not the room,' Siri snaps.

We sit in silence watching a black tubular screen. Every few minutes, it makes a demand for someone to move: *Will Mrs Kerry Milton please go to room four?*

After what seems much longer than fifteen minutes, the voice behind the red writing says, *Will Mr and Mrs Cleary please go to room seventeen?* I listen in case the voice adds, because they are unable to make a baby.

'Have a seat,' Dr Marsh says, staring at his screen.

Why are modern GPs either about to expire or still in college?

'Shall I call you Tom and Selmeston, or Mr and Mrs Cleary?'

Simultaneously, we answer.

'Mr and Mrs Cleary is fine,' I say.

'Tom and Selma,' says Siri, louder. It's odd to hear her use her proper name. I use it so infrequently I forget Siri isn't for real.

'We've been patient but I have been off the pill for nearly two years.'

She has the foresight to catch my eye. I thought it was only ten months.

'It's not unusual,' he says with a softer tone than Dr Ancient.

'I know, but I'm in my late twenties and my husband is much older.'

'Only eleven years.'

She ignores my presence. 'I have totally overhauled my diet. I haven't had any alcohol for months. I am doing everything right.'

She makes it sounds like a one-man, or I should say, a one-woman project.

'I am wearing loose pants and drinking less alcohol,' I offer in an attempt to be included.

The doctor hands Siri a tissue when she starts to sob uncontrollably. I take her hand and she accepts the gesture.

He is encouraging; I suppose he doesn't have enough life experience to be realistic. He notes we came in before Christmas and that Siri has been off the contraceptive pill for a long time.

'You will probably conceive naturally, as most people do, but perhaps it's sensible to get the ball rolling with some exploratory tests at a specialist service. Give me a moment to check waiting times and see which clinic would be best...'

'We have private health insurance,' she says. I was unaware. Apparently, she's had it since she was eighteen and most things include me now we are married.

'That'll speed up the process. I'll refer you to the polyclinic.'

'Is that for students?' I ask in an attempt to break my own sense of despair. No one laughs.

Siri is not picking up the GP's non-verbal clues that the consultation has come to an end. I stand up and hold out my hand to her; she obliges and lets me haul her off the chair.

Dr Marsh smiles and says to Siri, 'When you have both had the tests, come back and see me – the results will be sent here. You each need to make an appointment as we feed back the initial results separately. Not everyone wants to process the implications of the results with their partner present. We can then see you as a couple if further tests or treatment are needed. Stay positive. These things come right in the end.'

At this point my simmering desire for self-flagellation takes a dark turn into rage. 'What a patronising idiot,' I hiss at Siri as soon as we are back in the corridor. I expect her to empathise.

But she spits back. 'It's not his fault I'm not pregnant.'

The medical centre shares a car park with a large Tesco, which gives me the perfect opportunity to stomp off in a different direction.

'That's it, buy some beer. That'll help, after all,' she shouts after me. I ignore her but throw the car keys so she can wait in the car.

When I get in to join her I'm intending to make amends. I hand her chocolate. She is sticking to the dark stuff but I thought her favourite white chocolate might soothe the mood. She manages a smile and we drive to Adam and Heather's, pretending to listen to local radio. I can't believe we agreed to go to theirs after the GP.

It's a surprisingly mild day for January and the women and children are outside. I stand and chat to Adam who is cutting the vegetables in a professional, efficient manner. Despite a minor hiccup when his hand slips and blood tinges the potatoes with a subtle hint of red, he manages to produce a delicious lamb curry at top speed. He chops, stirs and blends and I keep him company with easy chat.

'More wine?' I top us both up, without waiting for his response.

'What's with you guys? My sister had a right face on her when she arrived.'

'Embarrassingly, we are having tests for infertility. We've been trying for nearly a year now with no joy.'

'Tough?'

'Mostly for Siri.'

'You too though?'

I shock myself by giving him a detailed description of our appointment with Dr Marsh. 'It makes me feel useless. I hate not being able to give Siri what she wants.'

'She's used to having things her way,' he says without malice. 'This is not your fault, mate.'

'I am not sure your sister feels that.'

'I'm sure she knows it's not your fault. You know what she's like – Mrs Life Plan. This will be the first time since she was six that plans haven't quite worked out yet.'

'It's not really her, Adam. It's me. Harry says I'm a self-bully. Can't help feeling I'm being punished somehow.'

'That's mad. You need to stop thinking like that. In my experience, it pulls you down.'

'I keep a journal, putting my dark thoughts on paper.' I hold my breath, expecting a chuckle.

'Good idea. When I saw a psychologist, she told me to write it down.'

'Psychologist? But you're always so cheerful and optimistic...'

'I used to be. When I was younger, I could suck up high levels of stress. But the last few years have been tough. Becca wasn't planned, money is tight, work is hard. I had a panic attack at work and one of the partners said I needed someone to talk to. So, he gave me the psychologist's name; his wife knew her. I expected it to be all beanbags and candles but it helped... I'd recommend it.'

'Are you still going?'

'No, my insurance policy only paid for six sessions. I could probably do with going back... Work's awful at the moment.'

'Are your colleagues supportive?'

'They try, but they're getting fed up. I haven't been myself recently and have made some major mistakes – forgetting important details about clients and the like... lost three accounts.'

'I'm sorry. I didn't realise.'

'Like you, I tend to keep it inside. It's not very manly saying you feel like crying most days, is it?'

'I guess not.'

'You should try talking therapy before it gets on top of you, Tom. I should've gone earlier. I ended up on heaps of medication which I still have to take.'

'Not for me. When Siri gets pregnant, everything will be fine. The GP said most people get there in the end and Siri is on the right side of thirty. Sounds like you need some help now, though?'

'I think I'll be okay. Heather says I'm not myself. I keep forgetting things and flying off the handle at the slightest provocation, but Becca is not a sleeper and that's hard. When I get some consistent kip, all will be well.'

'What does Heather think about what's going on at work?'

'She doesn't know. That would give her too much ammunition; work bullets as well as home ones – no way!' Adam laughs in a way that shows it's not funny.

Then, before I can probe further, the girls, all five of them, come in to eat. End of man chat.

On the way home, Siri asks what Adam and I were talking

about. 'Heather came in the back door and heard you talking in hushed tones…'

'What a ridiculous exaggeration – we didn't know she was there and were just talking at a normal level, not screeching at top volume like she does.'

'Don't take it out on me.'

'I'm not. I told Adam about seeing Dr Marsh.'

'You didn't tell him we can't conceive?'

'I did. I haven't told anyone else. It sometimes feels too much to keep in.'

'Great! That's what Heather will now be gossiping about at her baby yoga class.'

'He's your brother Siri! And he doesn't tell her much, so you shouldn't worry.'

We arrive home in silence.

Chapter 12

My drive home from the café has been particularly pleasurable. I've had a better day. Perhaps chatting to Adam did me good. I'd never have thought someone like him would get down or worried.

Unusually, Siri is home before me, sitting at the kitchen table with her arms tightly folded. She has on 'the face'.

'You okay?' I ask, not wanting to know.

'When you didn't call, I presumed you were in a meeting. That would be bad enough. But now I realise your lack of interest is total.'

'What have I forgotten?' I ask, though I want to say, give me a break, it's not easy holding two lives in your head.

'You really don't know, do you?'

The fear starts in the pit of my stomach, slowly moving up my body until it sticks like a lump in my throat, making it difficult to talk. She knows. Maybe she's been to the office, bumped into Leo or Ben in town…

'Put me out of my misery. I'm doing my best but Leo is constantly on my back. When I come home I am expected to perform at the drop of a hat. It's hard for me too,' I say with a confidence I don't feel.

'Today was my fertility tests.'

'Oh blast... Oh I'm so sorry... I saw it on the calendar yesterday, but yes, it flew out of my brain... Leo keeps on about my dropping sales...'

Her shoulders drop quicker than I'd anticipated.

'It's just I start worrying you don't want a baby.'

'I really do, but it's so much harder for you – it's you who have to go through so directly the raised and dashed hopes every month, and it's your body that will be nurturing a baby, not mine—'

The shoulders shoot back up to her ears.

'What's that supposed to mean? It's somehow my responsibility, just like the childcare will be? Should've remembered that from last month, silly me!'

'What...? That was just a theoretical conversation. I was just saying, what's the point of having kids, if you stick them in nursery all day?'

'No doubt it will be me who gives up work, and you'll get to continue up the ladder.'

I boil the kettle in silence and hand her a mug of camomile tea which she snatches without comment. Dawn told me camomile tea was a magic sedative.

'So, what did they say? Is it me?'

Wrong move. 'Did you not listen to anything the GP said? Even if you didn't listen, are you the only person on the planet who thinks you can have a hundred complex tests and then, on the same day, they tell you the answer?'

She goes off to sleep in the spare room.

The next thing I hear is her snoring, or what she calls sleep breathing. I lie awake until the early hours of the morning thinking of ways to make amends. I want to explain I got chatting with Dawn. That she wants me to work in the café. That she listens to me as if I am interesting.

I wake up with a start after a couple of hours' sleep: the clock says 6am. I've been dreaming Siri was giving birth and I had forgotten to set an alarm and missed the birth so the doctors told Siri she couldn't keep the baby.

When Siri surfaces, there is a full English breakfast on the table. She resists the temptation to criticise me for using organic sausages intended for the casserole and lets her pre-baby-trying grin slip out. She says goodbye with good cheer.

I load the dishwasher, enjoying a stress-free morning. For once I could chat truthfully about my plans for the day. Siri said it would do Harry and me good to have some chill time. I know her only concern is for the impact of stress on my testosterone levels. I'd been embarrassingly euphoric when a few nights ago my phone beeped.

'BBN.'

'WWW,' I replied before starting a sensible exchange.

'Unheard of, I know, but have space on Wednesday. Need a leave day. Fancy London?'

'Yes, please. Plan?' I typed as fast as a teenager.

'Eat, shop, sort out your life?'

We planned to meet at Victoria station.

The train pulls in as my phone beeps. 'Outside shop of offensive-smelling bath products, follow nose and look for handsome doctor.'

Once I've been pressed through the ticket barrier by a crowd of unruly schoolchildren, I see Harry. He is looking at his phone so I can only see his angular nose and full eyebrows. Each year his hair seems to thicken as mine falls out.

At work he wears expensive suits but his casual is more elegant than my dressed up. His beard makes him look older than his years; he says it makes him look more like a consultant so patients feel he is worthy of respect. I don't look a day over twenty-five. Well, that's what Siri tells me.

Harry smells of bath products for the first half of our day.

'You smell interesting,' I point out.

'I'm sure it's better than stale beer.'

I get the hint. My attempts to drown my sorrows have failed – they keep finding the life boat.

We negotiate the Tube and find ourselves in the freshest fresh air London can offer. It's midday and we head off to a restaurant we have frequented many times as students. Well, he was a student and I was a window salesman. From the outside, it doesn't look dissimilar to the newsagents in Middle Priory, old and unloved. The paintwork advertising delicious Chinese food is long faded – the only visible letters are C and A; the interior isn't appealing either with its plastic white chairs and red sticky tablecloths; it has a handful of locals and doesn't attract tourists. But it has the most consistently delicious food for miles.

My chair squeaks as I move. I can breathe, I am completely relaxed and present in my real life. There is no need to watch what I say or make up stories or remember what organic foods are on trend.

Harry has always loved food. His nan and mother cooked well. His mother baked every day – a range of amazing cakes and pies. As soon as Harry was old enough, he enjoyed making food for others. His legendary bacon sandwiches at school became the full English breakfast everyone wanted as we got older – all of us keen to pile back to his after a football game or a long drinking session.

Harry digs in his bag for his phone.

'Went out with this one for a few dates. What do you think?'

'Looks okay.'

'An accountant from Surrey. Bit boring though. Kept checking her appearance in the restaurant mirror, reapplied her make-up at least twice in the few hours we were out. Don't think she's my type.'

'But Helen who only cared about animals was too scruffy to be your type. What exactly is your type?'

'Mm, maybe I'm just not ready to settle.'

'We're middle-aged men!'

'You are. I'm young, free and single,' he grins.

'Anyway, who'd put up with a stressed medic who's always on call?'

'You seen Adam and Heather much?'

'Bit too much. I told Adam about our fertility issues.'

'Bet that got you in the kennel.'

'Certainly did. She can tell him what she likes but if I share, it's private.'

'That's women. Never happy or consistent.'

'Is Adam drinking?' Harry asks out of the blue. Harry has known Adam as long as I have and we frequently socialise together.

'Don't think so. Adam isn't a big drinker. You know what he's like: first to go home early complaining he will suffer the next day.'

'He called me a couple of days ago. He thought he was calling you.'

'He often does that, calls me instead of Heather or Siri.'

'He was slurring his words.'

'Maybe he'd been out.'

'It was ten in the morning.'

'Must have been the phone line. He would never drink and drive – he takes the girls to school.'

'I did think it was out of character, but his speech was slurred, no mistake. I wouldn't mention it if I wasn't sure.'

'I know Adam's under pressure at work, but he's the last person I'd expect to turn to the bottle for support.'

Harry backtracks. 'It was just a quick call. Might have been the line.'

We eat as much as we can manage of the food piled high on our plates.

'Buffets are for the young, old man.'

'The offer of as much as you can eat is irresistible.'

'It used to be four courses and run home. I'll be lucky to walk after this.'

The food and drink bill is less than you would pay for one course in the restaurants close by.

'Mr Chaeng, you are too cheap.'

'I know, Mr Harry. You like though?'

'Reprint your sign, wipe the tables and get student help – you could triple the price.'

Mr Chaeng smiles politely. 'Mr Harry, then I be too busy. You have to book table, you no like that.'

We stagger out, full of food. Now the previous plan of visiting more bars has lost its appeal, we take a brisk stroll along the river until our bellies feel manageable. It's a gloriously sunny day and I can delude myself I'm on holiday, a welcome break from my deceitful-husband role.

Harry and I can spend long periods without saying much. Eventually he describes his new job. 'It's exciting, Tom. I will actually get to know my patients and the staff.'

'Explain what's wrong with them?'

'Neurological disorders like MS, brain injury and stroke; they will come to us for a few weeks or months for rehab.'

'A care home?'

'Not at all; they will be under sixty-five, most younger. The brain injuries are often blokes in their twenties. They will be stable, so not dependent on nursing care, and stay Monday to Friday. I will get weekends off and more evenings.'

'I haven't heard you talk about work like this for a while, all fired up with medical-student passion.'

'I know. I was getting more and more disillusioned, which I didn't like. This will give me more control and I have the freedom to work as I see fit. I intend to stay for years so no more moving from pillar to post.'

'I am pleased for you, and for me if you'll be about more. Shame I appear to be infertile. You'd make a great uncle Harry to our non-existent kids.'

'When are you going to lose your old man's tone? It'll happen. If it doesn't, there are plenty of other options.'

'Can you imagine my wife settling for anything that's not the home-grown organic best?'

'She might have to grow up a bit and accept that we don't always get what we want or deserve, however meticulously we plan.'

'Bit harsh?'

'Maybe. I love Siri almost as much as you but Adam still indulges her like she's his first child.'

'She kind of was.'

'When she was a kid, fair enough, but you took over where he left off. She's nearly thirty for goodness' sake.'

'Thanks. That makes me feel so much better. You're saying she married me for the parenting? What kind of walking cliché does that make me?'

'Get over yourself, sugar dad. You suit each other. No question you two are a match made in heaven. But life happens.'

It isn't until we are back at the station that he broaches my job situation. I know full well the timing is deliberate. 'Tom, you told Siri about your job?'

'No.'

'You are going to have to, mate. You'll get caught.'

'I know, but I just don't know how.'

'It will be the deceit she won't like, so tell her soon and the job will come; don't risk your marriage over it… It's over two months, Tom. What are you doing all day?'

'I'm still at the café. But I'm doing hours for Dawn now.'

'Great, so you have a new job. Just tell her.'

'I will, when our tests are finished. If all is well, she'll forgive me anything.'

'I hope you're right.'

On the train journey home, I stare out of the window at nothing specific, caught in my head. I'm stuck in a sick board game that I don't get to choose. If the dice throws well, I get the ladder: it's happy ever after, stay-at-home dad to triplets. If the snake takes me to infertile, I am off the cliff, no way out. My head feels crowded by my double life, my fertility worries and a diminishing redundancy fund. The thought of the return to 'routine' tomorrow fills me with dread.

Chapter 13

Today, for the first time since I discovered this litter-strewn car park, I feel a little like the old Tom – worthy of respect, walking with his shoulders back and looking people in the eye. I am not sure why. Nothing much has changed. Maybe it's seeing Harry. And Dawn trusting me to help her. If the fertility tests are optimistic, Siri will conceive and the job issue will be obsolete.

'Morning.' Dawn finds it hard to talk quietly. I open my mouth to return her greeting, but she's there first. 'Don't suppose you saw a bald bloke in a jacket and cap, bit older than you?'

'No, but that could describe most of the locals.'

'Walked out without paying.'

'Deliberately?'

'Who knows? Probably. I have a feeling he's been before.'

'Doesn't that make your blood boil? People walking all over you like you don't matter?'

'I don't take it personally. Maybe he needs it more than me.'

'How do you make ends meet? Do you have a secret benefactor?'

'Sort of. My ex left me four months' pregnant. His guilt provides an income that's more than sufficient.'

'Lucky indeed. Why don't you put your feet up or lunch with other local women with no personality?'

'Thanks a lot,' she grins.

'Sorry – I didn't mean you're dull. But I'd love to be rich enough to retire. I wouldn't take on a stressful business.'

'That's what my mother says. But I'm not someone who can sit about. I get down. It gives me a buzz to provide this for people like Cilla, Isaac and Philip. What would they do without a place to come? The chains won't allow people to chat all day without buying stuff. We all need a reason to get out of bed, don't we?'

'Yes, we most definitely do… So what's wrong with Cilla?'

'Not sure, probably dementia. She wasn't like that a year ago. But Peter hasn't said anything.' She pauses and studies my face. I pretend a car has caught my attention.

'You look better today. Haircut?'

'Long overdue.'

'You look brighter though. Watched you walk down the hill with a bit more bounce.'

'Must be the Weetabix. I've been overdoing it at work… been tired, not sleeping so well. Going to slow down a bit.'

'Well, you look better already!'

My brow is damp. I wish a customer would break up our chat. I must keep up my guard. The grey man is gaining colour.

She pauses. 'It's odd you don't talk about your life outside of the café. We've all been guessing what you get up to when you're not here. Peter thinks you have two families, Mum named you The Morning Murderer and jokes you take a break from violence on a Friday morning.' Dawn responds to my face. 'We haven't talked about you that much, maybe once, perhaps twice.'

'Pleased to hear it,' I smile, unconvinced. 'Nothing to say, really. I have a dull life. I'm supposed to be writing up the visits that I make when I'm not here – either that or I'm out slaughtering the public.'

'I don't really know you at all; maybe you're not even called Tom.'

'My mother will reassure you that my birth certificate says Thomas. If I'm such a mystery, how come you trusted me enough to leave me with the till?'

'Flippin' heck... have just seen the time. I need to get the bins out today.'

'I can do that. Pass me the cupboard key and I'll go now.'

She runs her hand along the high shelf where the key for the bin storage space should be, but her hand finds only dust. She searches the deep pocket in the front of her apron, back pockets of her jeans and then buries her head in a big leather bag.

'It's not here. I must have left it at Carol's. Can you hold the fort? They have to go out today. They're overflowing and we'll get rats again.'

I catch my face in the window reflection. I'm in charge. Might only be for an hour in a village café but hey, everyone has to start somewhere. As my posture straightens, the voice on my other shoulder butts in. *Shut up! Ridiculous! You were a team leader. You're now putting out chairs at a shabby hole for misfits, working fewer hours than a Saturday boy. Get a grip, Tom.*

Typically, Dawn is longer than she promised. By the time she gets back, most tables are occupied and a queue is building up. Jess keeps me busy with demands for tables to be wiped, floors to be swept and cups to be washed. She only raises her eyebrows once, which is a dramatic improvement from my training session. I've always been clumsy but breaking seven things in two hours is pretty extreme.

Lydia is back at the café and looking sheepish; she always sits at the window table in the front of the shop. It's the only space in the café to fit eight people, but for some reason it doesn't attract many customers; perhaps people on their own don't want to risk uninvited chat and the women who come in pairs want to gossip in private. Dawn lets our only teenager sit for hours gazing out at the road unless a big group arrives, and then Lydia is ousted onto a table for two. Without asking her I make her an Earl Grey tea the way she likes it in pink china with the teabag left in. I don't know what it is with this girl but she makes me forget my inhibitions.

'Here you go.' The wobble of the cup in the saucer prompts her into the present and for a moment we eyeball each other in silence.

Remembering Harry's raised eyebrows, I puzzle over what to say. I must look odd standing with my hands buried in my front pockets like an awkward adolescent about to ask a girl on a date. I pull out a chair a couple of seats from her.

She gives me an instant mega-wattage smile. 'Sorry, it wasn't personal.'

'Didn't think it was. I'm used to girls crying when I speak. So what's up, kiddo?' I ask, with what I hope is a cheeky, not creepy grin. Lydia withdraws her eyes and turns her attention back to doodling in her drawing book. Her hand tenses around the pen and her black scribbling becomes purposeful and dense. I can't quite see what's she's working on.

'I have to sort it out on my own. There's nothing you can do,' she says to her illustrations.

'Maybe not, but I know from experience that a problem shared does make it feel lighter.'

'I've told Dawn.'

'Did that help?'

Lydia keeps her head down. Her pale skin is suddenly flushed. Am I being intrusive, unfair, bullying even?

'No, not really. Now I feel ashamed when I see her as well as when I look in the mirror—' and her words come in a rush. 'I wish I hadn't told her. Before I could pretend everything was okay when I was here – that I was a normal student, at college, using a coffee shop to do my coursework. Now she knows, it's ruined here as well.'

'I know what it feels like to pretend; it's harder than it looks and soon it makes life even harder, whatever your secret.'

She looks up. Now it's me feeling regret. What am I doing, hinting to young girls that I'm living a double life? How is that going to help her? I remember what Gemma said to Harry last time she visited. We were actually talking about how open his grandmother is with all her nursing home chums, but Gemma can twist any conversation around into a character assassination of me, and so she said, oh, he always puts his foot in it, our Tom; even as a child he told our private business to all and sundry. I can't remember exactly what Harry said. I know his response would've been in my defence, but even so, now would have been a good time to keep quiet.

Lydia is silent. My feet are restless, desperate to do what they do when situations get too intimate. I push my palms firmly into the tops of my thighs, wiping off the moisture at the same time as steadying my legs. Harry would say, come on Tom, say what you feel without second guessing others.

'You don't have to tell me anything, but I promise you there is nothing you can say that would make me think less of you.'

'I'm pregnant.'

My eyes flit unintentionally to her belly. I try to sound casual, as if I don't feel sick. 'I'm guessing not planned?' My voice sounds prepubescent. I'm desperate to sound kind and supportive rather than judgemental, but my thoughts are racing. Why does it have to be *that* secret? Anything but that would've been okay. I'd predicted she'd run away from home, fallen out with a friend, a boyfriend, was in debt, had been shoplifting… but pregnant? She's rake thin, for goodness' sake.

Her revelatory speech speeds into a cascade of words as the story floods out. 'Definitely not planned… I don't believe in sex before marriage, let alone pregnancy.' Her eyes fill with tears that perch on her eyelashes. I want to touch but when I try and pull my hand from my pocket, it goes deeper. 'My parents will be so sad.'

'What does your boyfriend want to do?'

'He isn't my boyfriend. It was a one-nighter.' The tears overflow and run down her cheeks.

'It was a pre-Christmas social at college. I was chatting to Charlie, my tutor. I get on better with people older than me.'

'Are there not rules about that?'

'It wasn't him. It was someone he knew, not a college employee. It was such a bizarre evening, great music and this good-looking bloke was openly flirting. We discovered we were both born on Christmas Day, twenty years apart. He said, I can be your Father Christmas. He was nice. We chatted for a bit as part of a bigger group… he was wearing some amazing shoes. I said, I love your shoes. Love *The Lion King* – and Converse, and he said, do you, my Christmas elf? A Christmas present. They're bespoke, sprayed especially for me in Camden market. It's my favourite film. So I said, mine too. I know it sounds ridiculous but I thought, wow, I don't know anyone else born that day. We both love *The Lion King*, this is meant to be. Looking back, he was just a middle-aged slime ball who knew the right things to say.'

'Did he push himself on you?'

'No, I have no defence, Tom, but thanks. I got drunk. He

was too – he could hardly walk. We went to my room and by the time I sobered up, he was doing up his trousers. He said sorry.'

'Why?'

'Because I was crying.'

'A bit late to be sensitive.'

'I think he did care, especially when I was sick on his beautiful shoes.' She manages a weak smile but keeps looking at her feet. 'He couldn't cope with vomit… he rushed out of the door backwards leaving his shoes behind.'

'That's very odd. So did he come back for them?'

'No, I was left with the most amazing pair of yellow and orange Converse, with shadow silhouettes of Timon and Pumbaa. The irony was the *Lion King* mantra was scrawled in black italics on each shoe: *Hakuna Matata*.'

'I don't know what that means.'

'It's Swahili for no worries. I haven't watched that DVD since… somehow it's one of the things that really angers me. It's like he robbed me of so much… and like he's ruined every memory I have – of all the times watching that film with my friends or my family… it's like… my childhood has totally gone. Sometimes I think I hate him.'

'Did you keep them?'

'They weren't my size… I gave them to a bloke in my halls. I washed them first though…' She gives me fleeting eye contact before her gaze is pulled back to the floor. 'I can't face my tutor. I think he knows. He wouldn't look at me in the canteen. I haven't been to any lectures since that…' and her voice wavers.

I try hard to keep up the sympathetic nodding. I don't want her to think I'm judging. I know she feels awful. How can this be? Siri and I desperately want a child. And this young woman – girl, who desperately doesn't, has a one-night stand and gets pregnant. I lose focus and my stomach is threatening to eject breakfast…

'Tom! Tom!'

I hear Dawn's voice from a long way off.

'We need to call an ambulance! He could have epilepsy… a heart condition…'

'Oh Tom, thank goodness, I thought you were dead… What happened?'

Dawn and Lydia help me to sit at my usual table as if I'm the unsteady pensioner. Lydia sits down beside me.

'Here you go.' Lydia hands me a glass of water.

'Stay next to him and I'll make a strong coffee,' Dawn commands.

'You okay? Shall I call a doctor?' Lydia looks very young. She is whispering. 'I'm sorry. Did I upset you with… my news?'

I try to think what she means. Then I remember. 'Oh no, please don't think that! It was honestly nothing to do with you… It must have taken a lot of courage to tell me… I know… what shame feels like. It's awful for you, but no, you mustn't think like that. You made a mistake.'

'Now I have to pay.'

'No, no. And there are other options. You need to talk to someone, get the right help.'

'I spoke to a nurse at the GP surgery. She sent me to a specialist clinic to talk. I already knew what my options were. It's not rocket science.'

'No, but hard to work it all out on your own.'

'The father offered to sort it.'

'How so?'

'For weeks after I found out, I didn't see or speak to anyone, lied to my mum every few days when she called on the land-line. When I switched on my mobile, there was a message. I recognised the voice straightaway, which was weird because I'd only spent a few hours with him. He said he'd got an inkling… oh no, I thought, I knew my tutor had worked it out… He'd heard he'd… left behind more than he'd intended.'

'What a disgusting thing to say.'

'Yeah. I was so sick after that, I thought it might solve the problem, but it didn't. He asked to meet in a pub. I didn't want to, but what else could I do?'

'Did you?'

'Yep. It was a pub out on the edge of town. I walked there on my own. It was miles from anywhere. I thought of my parents finding out I'd been murdered and was pregnant.'

Lydia starts crying as Dawn pushes a coffee at me. 'It's got lots of sugar.'

'Thanks.' I've been so distracted I've forgotten the drama I've created.

'Here Liddie. Hot chocolate solves all problems; do you want me to join you?'

She looks at me. 'It's okay, I told you, Dawn knows this stuff… Well, I saw him in the far corner with a pint in front of his face. When I sat down, he grinned like we were back on the dance floor. I remembered how he'd pulled me in with his hypnotic green eyes and cute smile, and for a minute I liked him again. As soon as I leaned back into the chair, he stood up, swigged the last of his drink and nodded towards a brown envelope. He mumbled, "I've got a family. That'll sort it out… so sorry," and walked out. The envelope was bursting at the seal, full of twenty-pound notes. When I got home, I counted them on my bed. It was five hundred pounds.'

I don't know what to say.

She picks up her drink and I pick up my coffee, and Dawn

does a great job in changing the subject. 'Carol was in a right state this morning. It was good I went, meant to be. Her mum had fallen. She was glad I came. What is it today? Drama following me everywhere. You okay, Tom?'

'I'm fine, just tired I think, maybe low in iron or something.'

'Gotta go.' Lydia retrieves her drawing book from her table and almost runs out of the door.

I shuffle a few pieces of paper out onto the table and bury my head in my bag. I need time to process Lydia's man, her pregnancy, Siri's unpregnancy.

'Tom, can we talk?'

'I'm fine. I'm a bit stressed at the moment. Lydia surprised me...'

'I mean, can we talk honestly... about you?'

'Sure, but you will be disappointed. There's no mystery.'

'Tom, you don't have a job, do you? I've watched you. You're looking on job sites, fiddling with CVs and most of the time staring out that window.'

'What are you suggesting? I'm freelance, like to check what's out there, not get stuck in a career rut.'

She stays silent.

'Anyway, what's it to do with you? I'm not a love-sick teenager. I can manage my own life, thank you.'

She continues to stay still and quiet: it's very unsettling. This lady doesn't do still or quiet.

'I'm a bit down on my luck at the moment, yes.'

'It might help to talk. I can tell you're struggling.' She looks straight at me.

It's suddenly a relief to tell her. 'I... got made redundant. I was good at what I did. I functioned well as a man, you know? Before you met me.' I try and make it sound like a joke.

Dawn doesn't laugh.

'I have always been appraised well by colleagues, won salesman of the year. My team liked me.'

'What happened?'

'New manager *didn't* like me. And that brought up old stuff. I've always been a soft touch. I thought I'd changed... until he came.'

'That's tough.' She has her hand on my knee like she's my teacher. I wish she'd move it before Cilla and Peter arrive and think something is going on. That's all I need – for Siri to be told I'm having an affair.

'Is your wife not supportive? Does she work?'

'She's a radio presenter. She's great. But I haven't told her I'm out of work. She's desperate for a baby and I'm not fulfilling my job description right now: I can't get her pregnant.'

'I knew all along there was something. Seen it before.'

'All along?'

'Since week two. No one your age sits in the same café for such long hours if he has work to do.'

I think of Jess, Cilla and Lydia and my cheeks flush with embarrassment.

'You've all been laughing behind my back but playing along, asking about food and features?'

'No one knows, not even my mother. Tom, I like to gossip about people I don't care for, but I'm not spiteful. I play along with them. We were guessing what you could be... Tom, the reason I told you is not to make you feel awkward. I want your services. I have an idea and I can't do it on my own. I may prove to be misguided but I trust you. From the moment you walked in, I liked you. You have an honest face.' When Dawn gets going, there is no point interrupting or asking questions until she breaks for air and that can be a while. 'You know who I mean by Carol?'

I nod, glad the topic has shifted from me and babies.

'She's desperate to lose weight, but doesn't like the idea of joining a fat club.'

'What's that got to do with me? I'm not going with her.'

'You won't need to,' Dawn says briskly. 'Just listen. I picked up some Slimming World cookbooks in the Cancer Research shop over the road. I've been cooking the recipes for Carol, and she's lost four pounds in three weeks.'

I think back to the last time I saw Carol: Dawn's efforts are not yet obvious.

'Got me thinking about a diet café. I can cook, slimmers can order meals on their diet plan. I can do them all: Weight Watchers, Slimming World, Rosemary what's her name. I'll prepare them for collection or people could eat their food here and not have to wash up.'

'Minor issue, you don't have an oven.'

'Well spotted. I'm going to prepare the food at Carol's: she'll be glad of the company and gets healthy food for free as payment for kitchen rental.'

'Mm, I can't deny it sounds reasonable. Every woman beyond puberty is on a diet.'

'Exactly.'

'Still not getting my part. I've many weaknesses, but think my BMI is still okay.'

'Wish I could say the same. I need reliable staff at the café and someone to create an order system. You're great at ideas.'

'How do you know?'

'You sorted the door. I've complained for years about customers bursting in after closing time demanding to be served. It made me furious.'

'I bought a closed sign.'

'No one else thought of it. You spend an awful lot of time fiddling with your computer... You can create a brochure with menus, take the orders and keep this place ticking over when I'm at Carol's.'

Dawn leans back in her chair and grins. 'So, what do you think, Billy-no-job?'

'You're on!' I indulge her in a small smile. 'Until I get a proper job.'

I can't make Siri's tea to an acceptable standard so how on earth will I cope with a latte, a cappuccino or a mocha? I have heard the way customers complain: too hot, too cold, not hot enough, too much froth, too strong, too weak, no chocolate sprinkles – and that's only the drinks.

I'm being asked to design a brochure and order form, take orders, communicate with Dawn who'll be cooking ten minutes up the road, and listen to Isaac and Cilla while fixing Peter's IT problems and handing tissues to a hormonal teen.

I can't help feeling excited.

'Can my new manager please lock up?' she shouts on her way out to a school meeting, as she pauses to turn the door sign to closed.

I arrive home without conscious memory of how I got here. I've been thinking about Lydia. I empathise with her terror that the people she loves will find out about her deception. I know she thinks it will be the deceit that breaks their hearts…

My chest is tight as I gasp for air – too much free cake. I no longer find it easy to run up my stairs two at a time… It's not Harry any more who has thighs that rub together; maybe my BMI needs checking after all or I need to start refusing Dawn's free samples. Or join in with the customers she now wants to cater for.

Vibrations in my back pocket jolt me back to the present.

It's Heather; her words are blurring like Dawn's when she has a juicy piece of gossip to impart whilst rushing about in the café.

'Oh Tom, I'm so glad to have got you.'

'What's the matter? Are the girls okay?'

'Shut up and listen,' she snaps in a recognisably Heather tone. 'It's Adam. He's in A and E in Brighton. I'm miles away. Margaret can't go – she has the children. Can you and Siri go? He needs picking up.'

'Siri isn't back, but I can go.'

'Thanks.' She rings off abruptly without further explanation.

I scribble a note to Siri – 'Gone to hospital, to collect Adam. Don't worry' – and rush out the door to my still-warm car. Thoughts of coffee, cafés and how to reveal a new job are pushed to the back of my mind. I've no idea why Adam is at the hospital. Maybe Siri should be worrying.

The hospital is a twenty-minute drive from our flat but it's rush hour so getting into Brighton is a nightmare. A smiling nurse welcomes me as I stumble through the automatic doors I've tried to force open. I suspect she's laughing at my clumsiness; it'll be a good story to tell her colleagues at tea break.

'Hey, Tommo. Thanks for coming. Sorry.'

Adam is lolling across three chairs with his dirty trainers resting on a fourth one. A lady reading a magazine gives him a sideways glance. His fringe that usually flops fashionably over his left eyebrow is interrupted by a blood-stained bandage covering his forehead down to his brow. His other eye is showing a bruise that is going to develop into a shiner before the night is over.

'What on earth happened to you?'

'I was popping out to the pub at lunchtime and didn't account for the step, tripped and caught my head on the side of the door. The admin staff panicked – there was lots of blood.

I was too dazed to protest. I said it was overkill but the paramedics insisted I be checked out – so here I am.'

'I didn't realise you've been here so long. Why didn't you call?'

'I called Heather but she didn't pick up.'

'Why didn't you try me or your mum?'

'Didn't really think about it. Finally got Heather, who of course shouted at me.' His lopsided smile doesn't reveal the negative emotions that would be raging inside of me.

'You okay, ready to leave?'

'Yep, all stitched up.' Adam's voice is overexcited, as if we're off on a camping trip.

'You need the toilet before we go, mate?'

'No, why?'

'You're jiggling about like Becca when she's bursting.'

He frowns at me and then looks down at his body as if he's Doctor Who, just after a regeneration, unsure of the body he's standing inside.

On the drive home, he still seems more exuberant than usual. Not long out of the hospital car park, he presses the button to open his window and shouts, 'Great legs!' at a pack of nurses. I put my foot down and use the central controls to close the window.

'Didn't think that was your thing,' is all I can think of to say. Adam's usually a bit of a feminist.

'Long day,' is his explanation as he moves on to cracking jokes about falling over and doing accurate impressions of what Heather will say on our return. 'Her welcome home question will be why on earth did you do that – I've had to bath the girls, Meelie is screaming in her room because she missed some stupid cartoon, and Rebecca won't settle. Sorry, I tripped, I'll say. I told them not to call 999. Not again! she'll yell at me.'

I leave before I say something I regret. Harry's question about Adam's drinking comes back to me.

Siri's gratitude for my picking up her brother has put steak and chips on the table, and a rare glass of wine while cooking has brightened her mood. I watch as she clears the dirty plates and loads the dishwasher; she does it with energy and a certain grace even though she's impatient and I have to resist the temptation to interfere with how she stacks things. I remember with a pang why I fell in love, something I am losing sight of with evenings ruined by baby and job thoughts elbowing their way into my mind.

I fall asleep planning how to reveal my change of status in a way that makes it sound in line with her plan.

Chapter 14

Dawn pokes her head out of the back-room fridge. 'Hey, it's Billy.'

Walking in here is like home used to be: tension goes, mind and body recognise the familiarity. I want to feel this way at home, in my own bed, in front of my own TV and looking in my own fridge.

The café is surprisingly quiet for mid-morning. Peter and Cilla are sitting in near silence. Dawn and Jess are in the serving area but not speaking. They've clearly had a spat. Lydia is in the corner drawing away; she looks up and raises her eyebrows – we are used to the way these two females relate.

I try not to get irritated at the name she has been calling me since guessing my employment status. I know she doesn't mean it unkindly but it makes me 'spike'. Siri nicknamed me 'hedgehog' the first year of our mating. She reckons I have three emotional positions: happy and smiley; curled in a ball / leave me be; spikey / don't touch; or it will definitely hurt. Annoyingly, she is right.

'You missed a friend.'

'What do you mean?'

'A bloke who knew you popped in.'

I can feel my chest heaving. Who knows I am here?

'Bloke came in. Posh suit, nice teeth. I couldn't resist an interrogation,' she cackles.

My mind scrambles about for someone to fit the profile. Leo comes first.

'What did you find out?' My voice refuses to comply with the disinterested tone I want to generate. I casually swipe the tea towel from Dawn's shoulder and start drying up some cups.

'That he's a very charming consultant on his way home from an assessment a few miles away.'

My relief must be visible. 'Harry?'

'Spot on. He said his oldest friend told him about my pad and he was close enough to pop in. Nine out of ten. Is he single?'

'Yes, but I think he likes it that way.'

'Shame.'

'Hey, Tom, what do you think about this?' A familiar tone immediately eases my tension. Lydia has on her usual uniform of black leggings, black hoodie and silver headphones. The headphones look massive on her and remind me of the ones I wore as a kid. 'Look,' she points outside. I notice she has bitten her nails down to the quick. 'What will it be? Dodge, chat, ignore?' She is pointing at an older woman we've nicknamed Nosy Nicola. She can't cover a hundred yards before stopping someone for a chat.

We think it's hilarious to watch how Nicola's chosen victims avoid eye contact as they see her coming in the opposite direction. The people walking towards her get trapped by her ample proportions blocking the narrow path; some risk death by swerving into the road to get past. Lydia and I amuse ourselves copying the facial expressions of irritation, fidgety polite and downright rude. Siri would say we are very immature.

'Tom.' Dawn says my name but without the usual warmth.

'Yep.'

'Could I have a word, please, before you get into some deep chat with madam?'

'Sure.'

'I was thinking about relaunching the café as a way of publicising the diet ideas.'

'Good idea.' I find my eyes watching out of the window to see whether Nosy Nicola has gone.

'Your attention might be nice.' I haven't heard this teacher tone in her before.

'You have it.'

'If we do a launch afternoon, can you source some blackboards so we could display all the various slimming meals on three boards? I also wondered about some helium balloons outside, and free cake.'

Before I can point out cake and a diet café are maybe incompatible, Cilla pipes up from their table in the front corner. 'Helium can kill you.'

I smile an acknowledgement. She is coming out with some off-the-wall comments lately.

'It can. I was reading in the *Argus* last week a man had taped up his car, opened a bottle of helium and off he went, happy as Larry. No pain.'

Peter leans over and taps his wife's arm. 'I don't think they want to hear about that, love, especially when planning a party.'

As Cilla turns her back on us again, Dawn manages a smile. 'A dead man, happy as Larry!'

'Just let me know when you want to do it and I will spend a few hours on Amazon,' I promise.

I turn back to Lydia, who is consumed with her drawing. I feel suddenly cold, and rub my hands together.

'Please don't!' She puts her hands over her face. 'That's such a dad thing to do!'

Lydia frequently pokes fun at my routine habits, labelling them as dad ways, dad jokes or simply 'so dad'. Here I am, impotent Tom with a pretty young thing showing me how easy it is to get pregnant, then mocking me for my stereotypical father-like behaviour.

'I was thinking about what you said the other day about not feeling good enough. I think everyone feels that. It's just what the Bible says about humans,' she says with her serious stare.

We've been chatting quite a bit. It strikes me as odd, spending this time with a teenager, but it's an unexpected fountain in the midst of all the current drains. We've talked politics, psychology and relationships, but our most frequent source of heated conversation is religion. When she told me she was pregnant, she admitted to growing up with parents who are evangelical Christians. In my head, religious types are all the same: three Hail Marys and you can keep sinning while judging everyone else.

'Do I feel more preaching on its way? Go on then, sock it to me.' I hold my hands up in resignation.

'Well, we don't feel good enough, because we're not. The Bible says so. All human have done wrong, and when people do wrong, they become disconnected from God.'

'Speak for yourself. Before this year, I was a decent human.'

'By your standards, maybe, but compared with a perfect God, you're not okay. The first commandment is to love God with all your heart, soul and mind, but we don't. We worship anything else but God – ourselves, stuff, qualifications, families.'

'I never said I was as holy as God, but surely no one is.'

'I agree. No one's perfect so God sent his son, Jesus, to take our badness and receive his goodness!'

'So, the bad people get to go free? If it's all about forgiveness and your parents believe this stuff, why don't you tell your parents about your sinful behaviour? Would they still stone you for getting pregnant?'

She snaps at me, which is unusual. 'You just don't get it, do you? My parents are good people, they love me unconditionally. Everyone messes up – you, me, the pastor, the Pope – so they won't judge me, I know that. They'd forgive me without a second thought... That's the problem.'

She looks at me with a very serious face, staring straight into my eyes, and says, 'Why don't you tell Siri you have no job?'

'Because it will devastate her and I love her too much.'

'Exactly.'

Dawn is frothing milk with her back to us but hears us laughing and gives me a look over her shoulder that's way too similar to the ones my mother would fire at me in 'letting down the family' moments. It takes me by surprise and makes me feel like I did when I was seven and had wet my pants in public; that feeling is a frequent visitor at the moment, but not usually in the café.

'Any chance of a hand, Tom?' There is only one person in the queue. Dawn is not usually bothered about people being kept waiting. I ignore her.

Lydia stuffs her drawing book, pen and phone into her bag. Without looking up, she says, 'I speak to my parents most days. I tell them I am thriving at college and studying hard for my second module; I keep them in the dark to protect *them*, not me.'

'So, what can I do about my deeply flawed and sinful self?'

Her chest heaves upwards and she lets out an impatient sigh. 'I know you don't care, Tom, but you should. This stuff's important. You can't do anything yourself – but you can ask Jesus to save you from your inside mess, and he will.'

She smiles, turns on her heel and walks out. I'm so lost right now, even this Jesus stuff sounds quite appealing.

Immediately, Dawn is standing in front of me. 'Can we talk?'

When women of a certain age use that tone to invite you for a 'chat', you know a lecture is coming. My brain searches for a plausible excuse. Too busy, I'm afraid: urgent email, need to check in with my boss, Siri will be worried... Since Dawn found me out, though, there is only one acceptable response. I nod silently. 'Love to.'

'You don't know, do you? The reason she came here, the reason she went to see Dr Pike over the road?'

My preoccupation with the goings-on behind the black door are long forgotten. I rarely look out of the window these days. I realise Dawn is waiting for a response.

'I am not sure what I don't know... No, I don't think I do.'

'The house over the road is an abortion clinic.' Dawn takes a long intake of breath: this is the warning sign you're not going to be free any time soon. 'The poor kid had discovered she was pregnant. She found the clinic online and arranged a private appointment – apparently it's perfectly legal after you're eighteen.'

It makes me sad to think of this young woman, who seems hardly older than Meelie, going through that alone. She'd come into the café two days running after failing each time to attend at the clinic.

'Can I be honest?' She is going to be, whatever I answer. 'You're getting too close to that kid. She's vulnerable. You need to watch yourself, especially given her predicament—'

'What? What are you implying, Dawn?' Wet eyes are becoming an embarrassing habit of mine.

'I'm worried about you.'

'Really?'

'Tom, I didn't mean to upset you.'

'What? By accusing me of abusing vulnerable teens? Not at all.'

'Come on, you can't think I meant that.'

'Creepy old Tom, unemployed, unhappy marriage, sniffing

around a teenager who is all alone. I know exactly what you've all been thinking. Sad I didn't realise earlier.'

'Absolutely not. You've got it all wrong.'

'Have I though? And I guess Carol and Cilla agree with you.' I can hear myself being irrational but have lost control of my tongue.

'Tom, you're getting this totally out of perspective.'

'I don't think so. I am many things Dawn, but not that.'

'I have no idea what you think I'm implying. I have trusted you since the first time you spoke. Sit down, let's talk.'

'There's nothing to say. Watch out. I might start on your girls next… I thought you were my friend.'

'I am, but I'm worried for you both. She's getting attached to you. I don't want you getting hurt when she swans off like teenagers do…'

'I have to go… I might take a few days' annual leave this week and next.'

'Tom, come back. Please don't…'

The closed sign crashes back on the glass as the door slams behind me.

The conversations with Dawn and Lydia had given me some brief relief from the gnawing sensation in the pit of my belly. By the time I get back to the car, the sense of being overwhelmed by my own misery hits me like a sledgehammer. I can't access what's going on. My head feels full: GP, Lydia, Siri, Dawn, others thinking I am on the prowl.

'Hello, you have reached the voicemail of Doctor Harry Edgington…'

I don't bother to leave a message.

Chapter 15

My stomach wakes me up. My eye sockets feel like sandpaper and February sunshine is streaming horizontally into the room through the big Velux window. It was one of the things that attracted me to this flat when we first viewed it: it makes the room feel airy and spacious. But the blind doesn't work properly. When I realised how much the genuine Velux ones cost I got the cheap imitation. It doesn't quite fit and frequently springs up at night, which is terrifying – and is something else that is held against me – and means that even in winter you are often dazzled awake.

I'm approaching today with the same degree of optimism as I did the day of my GCSE results. That day didn't end well. I hope Siri might forget it's my fertility results day so we can avoid an awkward conversation over breakfast; I would then be vindicated for forgetting *her* appointment. Stupid. As if Siri wouldn't have this date marked on her calendar, emblazoned on her diary and engraved on her brain.

As we were told, the GP wants to see me on my own for the verdict. I am on my own everywhere. The café was the only place I could hold on to the remnants of the real me, and now that's gone. If these tests results are bad news, there really is no place to go.

I thought I'd hit the shame jackpot when Leo escorted me out of the door, but any remaining fragments of self-respect were dispersed last week at the East Sussex Poly Clinic.

'Thank you for waiting, Mr Cleary.' I didn't know I had a choice to skip the queue of men in garments with matching triangular exposure gaps. I felt slightly less dim when the man undressing in the next cubicle knocked to ask which way round the gown had to be worn. If the aim was to make men feel weak and vulnerable, they achieved it.

'Have you got your sample?' I handed over my pocket contents in a sealed plastic pot.

'Thank you,' she said as she held it up to the light as if checking a diamond was genuine.

'Let's hope these little fellas are healthy and fast, shall we?'

She handed me a double-sided list of questions.

'Please complete this. I'm here if you get stuck.' Did she think I was illiterate as well as impotent?

I worked my way to question forty-six, watched carefully by the lady in a blue dress that matched the gowns, but without the revealing window at the back. She didn't look away. I wondered if she could tell my fertility status by my writing. What was she expecting? Is it possible to cheat?

'You doing okay?' She caught me looking at her looking at me.

I wanted to say, absolutely, nothing more stimulating than a multi-choice exam on your private life, is there? Instead I lifted my head and offered what my mother would describe as an adolescent grunt.

My private parts were squeezed and prodded as if I was being assessed for an organic market. I was unsure of the etiquette. My father must've left that out of his father to son instruction manual, although I guess he hadn't truly admitted to having a faulty son. I didn't know whether to laugh, cry, run away or simply snap her lubricated wand in half and chuck it out of the open metal window.

'Well, the good news is I can't see or feel any obvious abnormalities.'

I was expecting her to say, but just because abnormalities are not visible, it doesn't mean they are not there, but I think she muttered something about my little fellas being sent to the lab to check their shape and mobility. Let's hope they are better sportsmen than me.

I tried to stand up but she shoved me back into the chair and said, not so fast, sunshine. Siri says I must've imagined that part.

She ripped open a sealed packet, nodded towards the couch and took out a small lethal weapon...

'All done, brave boy.'

My eyes were watering. I've never been a violent man, but lately feelings of rage are coming fairly frequently.

'We'll send the biopsy with the samples to the lab. Good luck.'

I struggled from the horizontal position like a disorientated old man.

I was informed by the receptionist on my way out that the results would be on the medical centre system within the fortnight. I was told to request an individual appointment to receive the results, and that we would then be invited to a joint appointment back at the clinic to discuss the way forward if necessary.

So, here I am waiting for my name to flash in red lights. I wonder how many couples make it to the joint part.

'Ann Summers to room twelve to see Doctor Marco.'

I can't help sniggering as a round elderly lady responds to the tannoy's command.

'Tom Cleary to room fourteen to see Doctor Nash.'

I am obviously seeing yet another, different doctor. I walk slowly, aware that my gait reveals a less than happy disposition, and push on the door marked fourteen. My gaze is met by a smiling but distracted middle-aged lady. Dr Nash must be in her fifties. My first thought is of an iced gem biscuit; she has a round body and a pointy head. Her grey hair is tinted pink and pulled into a tight pile on the top of her head. She has a pair of green-framed glasses hanging on a chain like a child's swing.

'Hello, Tom.' I didn't consent to first names and she didn't tell me hers.

'Have a seat.' She is holding a sealed brown envelope. At least it's not displayed in the corridor like my inadequate exam results.

It feels like waiting to be sentenced, all eyes on the man in the dock. Will the verdict be not guilty, free to go home, make babies and live happily ever after, or guilty as charged, defective, below standard, not good enough, the end of my future plans, just like my father prophesied when he read my first school report?

She puts the envelope in her in-tray, retrieves her spectacles from their position on her ample chest and taps on her keyboard to bring up my verdict. She peers at the screen as if trying to translate from a foreign language.

I am not at the right angle to read the individual words, but I can see a couple of sentences. How can four hours of prodding of my private parts and taking samples and bloods and a hundred questions about the most intimate aspects of my life and relationship history amount to one short paragraph? My heart beats faster than feels comfortable. My breathing is shallow as I stare at her as she stares at the screen. Given GP consultations are only six minutes long, the sense that I have been waiting for an hour to hear her speak is probably unreliable.

'Tom, they certainly gave you the once-over, didn't they?'

I nod, silently trying to read her eyes.

'The reason your wife is not falling pregnant is because you have no sperm in your semen. Apparently, this is called azoospermia. I haven't heard that term before.' Lucky her. 'I am sorry to be so blunt. We should have found this out more quickly.'

She smiles in a way that is probably intended to look kind. She doesn't add anything but the screen turns off as she swivels her chair to face me.

I stare silently at the poster of lungs behind her head. She fills the silence. 'Infertility is a widespread problem and for one in five infertile couples the problem lies solely with the male partner. I am afraid it affects approximately seven per cent of all men, and is commonly due to deficiencies in the semen.'

Does she think it will make me feel better to know that in four out of five pairs it is the woman's fault, or is she reassuring me that I am not the only spermless man in the world? Either way, nothing is going to make this all right.

'Looking at your medical notes, it appears that there were some problems at birth with your testes. Your parents must have declined an intervention. Rest assured that there are lots of new treatments available, and remember, your wife is still a young woman, which is a real positive in a case like this. There is plenty of stored sperm for your generation and it is an easy procedure to insert sperm into a healthy female body and create a pregnancy.'

Decades of supressed rage surge inside me. Sweat bleeds from my forehead.

I imagine my parents being given a choice. *Your son's most defining body parts are damaged. This will ruin his life, his marriage and any chance he has of happiness. Would you like us to resolve it for him?* I visualise my father pushing his nicotine-stained fingers through his Brylcreemed hair and looking at my mother. *I don't think so, Rose, do you?* His voice would've given no choice but for her to defer to his expertise. *No, Victor, let's leave him faulty, shall we?*

'Tom. Did you hear what I said? Modern medicine has a range of solutions for problems like yours. Let's see if your wife's tests are normal, and I can see you both together to work out a way forward.'

I pull myself up, using her solid desk to stop me from falling. I thank her for her jury service. The purple arrows painted on the laminate floor kindly guide me to the exit and I stumble towards my vehicle without looking up. My body sinks into the seat and I weep like I should have done at my father's funeral.

My hands are still clutching a cheerfully coloured leaflet. It's now crumpled and wet. I see the title in my father's voice and hear it spoken with Leo's accent: 'Coping with Infertility'. They have left off the subtitle: What spermless men can do next.

I swing open my car door just in time to throw up.

As my arms and legs manage the car, my mind finds Siri's face when I tell her the dream is over.

This morning she'd tried hard to restrain herself. She'd managed not to mention the appointment until I had a hand on the door.

'Er – Tom Tom.'

'Gotta rush. Leo will be waiting to start the business meeting.'

'No worries. What time you at the GP?'

'Not sure.'

'How can you not know? Do you want me to call the medical centre?'

'No, I need to get to work and check my appointment card. I left it in my desk.'

'Okay, will you call me when you find it?'

'Sure.'

I'm glad I didn't commit to a time. I've missed four calls but she'll be on air now. She doesn't know I've been sentenced; she'll be chatting to her invisible audience, unaware of the situation. Then she's off tonight on a work trip to Amsterdam for Danny's fiftieth.

I slam my fist on the steering wheel. Come on, Tom, sort it out!

I am a liar; the honest part of my life is now a very small part of the whole. I could tell her I have had the all-clear. When she is given her clean slate, I could persuade her that we just need to go to Paris for a relaxing city break. I could say I know plenty of couples who get pregnant when they adopt or give up trying. Why not just keep pretending?

I had been hoping for happy news to soften the unemployment blow. So either the lies have to go on, with a few new ones added, or she might as well have it all and get the misery over in one swoop. The tunnel of light that Dawn's trust created has been snuffed out and the darkness is back again.

So how do I tell Siri I am unemployed and spermless? How on earth do I tell her the life plan is shattered, and we can give up sex altogether? A troubling theme in the back of my mind is whether Siri will stay if I can't fulfil her plan. She will remind me – for better, for worse, for richer, for poorer, in sickness and in health. Which is fine at a posh venue on a bright day. But who would say *I do* to worse, poor, sick and spermless?

I try and summon up Harry's voice of reason from the depths of my despair. He'd say, Tom, it'll work out, things always do.

But Harry, this time there really is no solution.

We can't adopt. Siri says all adopted kids have problems emotionally even if they're not visible at first. There is no way I am letting anyone insert some virile stranger's sperm into my wife. I couldn't love a child unrelated to me, and looking like *him*. I know what it feels like to be raised by a parent who despises you.

An obvious solution keeps edging into the periphery of my head. It wouldn't be easy for me but if I left her, she'd be free. She is wiser now; she could choose someone her age. some-one with energy and optimism. My chest hurts as I think of her hand in hand with a smart lawyer with a dark suit and pol-ished brown shoes. I need to vanish without trace. My family won't notice I'm gone; Siri will be free to pursue her dreams. It will be as if I was never there. I'm only stuck here because of her family, her job. The only place I feel remotely at home is in a shabby café with a bunch of misfits. It would break me to leave; it hurts so hard even to think about getting in the car and driving away for ever. But surely that's true love. If you love someone, you sacrifice yourself. You don't imprison them, take advantage of their guilt. You set them free.

There is some relief in finding a partial solution. But she won't even know how to pay the bills, let alone call a plumber or get the car serviced. So I'll have to tell her my plan. And of course, she'll protest, and tell me I am enough, but we'll both know I'm not. Years down the line we'll hate each other, con-sumed with our own variety of internal bitterness.

So I must leave practical instructions, go without saying, leave a letter, put Adam back in the fatherly place in her life. She'll hate me at first but, a few years down the line, she'll be remarried, two kids in tow, and the plan back on the road. Then, she'll want to call and say, you did the right thing –

thanks. You okay? I would be okay. I'd be free of pain, knowing I'd let her go.

My windscreen wipers are doing their best against the sudden rain. The rubber is half missing from one blade and is making a rhythmic squeak that sounds like someone giggling. Even the black plastic arm is mocking me.

Chapter 16

I wake up and the other side of the bed is cold. I remember that Siri accepted my refusal to go with her on the Amsterdam jolly without protest, which is unusual. Maybe she's also thinking about our going our separate ways.

There was some respite while I slept. But as I surface my mind is telling me there is a terrible puzzle to solve. Someone has combined three separate jigsaws and given all the pieces a cruel shake. I piece together one part but that throws out the other bits. I need some solid corner pieces to start me off, but they've all gone. Babies, the café, work, it's all disintegrating. Completing the overall picture, the happy ending, has become an impossibility.

I've been remembering a conversation with my first schoolteacher.

'Draw what you want to be when you grow up,' she'd asked her class of very small children. The others had rushed off to carry out the task but I'd stayed sitting cross-legged in front of her. Why had she asked such a silly question? She'd kneeled down to my level and asked, Thomas, what do you want to be when you grow up? A man, I replied. Laughing in her own wonderful way, she'd stood up and said, well, can you please draw what you will be doing as a man?

I'd drawn a detailed picture of a man in a brown suit with a briefcase. Like Mr Benn in that cartoon series I've mentioned – the one thing I watched with my dad. Next to my vision of 'a man' was a smiling lady with blonde hair in bunches. Between the two of them were matching girls and a cat. That picture had stayed pinned to my mother's fridge for the next few years before it vanished.

But now I give up on sleep, heave myself out of bed, and go next door to turn on my computer. While it's whirring to start up, I search for a CD to lift me. Doris Day, my mum's favourite, goes on. The first track, 'All Alone', sings out at top volume. I'm glad the lady downstairs is deaf.

As my hand seeks the mouse, the photograph next to it catches my eye. It's early last summer. Siri and I splashed out on an all-inclusive to the Maldives – our last holiday as a couple because the next one will be as a family, she'd said, when we were both optimistic, two suntanned bodies full of hope against an azure sky and white sands.

I'd managed to fob her off on the phone last night.

'You okay? You sound ill.'

'All fine here.' Good job she couldn't see I was already in my pyjamas at 6pm.

'Did you get the results?' I was surprised that wasn't her first question.

'GP was great, best one yet.'

'And…?' I could hear her breathing speed up.

'I was gutted. All results are back but the two important ones. She hopes they'll be back within a week.'

Why didn't I say a month, a year…?

'Oh well, I guess mine won't be back for two, so we'll

know by the end of the month. Better go, Eurostar has just announced the platform so everyone's moving.'

I'd kept the phone to my ear, not wanting to lose her voice.

The music soothes my thoughts. I start a new folder: 'Keep calm and carry on', I name it.

Siri will never cope without an instruction manual. Even free spirits have to pay the mortgage and the bills and service the car. I scribble a note to myself to update the life insurance, and write some headings: mortgage, bank accounts, insurances, bills, car, computers, printer.

I'm wondering whether to print out the final version to put in a colourful file or whether to leave it electronic. I decide to do both in case she loses the hard copy.

I add 'buy a colourful file' to my scribbles.

The door buzzer interrupts my flow; no doubt it'll be Amazon, although 10am is a bit late for them. I press save. I can finish that before she comes home tomorrow: one thing off my long list of departure tasks. Somehow, taking control has lifted some of my blackness. I try not to think about the thing I'm actually contemplating and focus on how I can leave her with a perfect survival plan. I suppress thoughts of what I will be saying goodbye to. Not even the bully's punches hollowed me out like this.

I spent the whole of yesterday evening in bed. I've never done that before. I couldn't believe my luck when I remembered she'd be going to St Pancras straight from work. Maybe Lydia's God *is* out there. I'd intended to shower and eat but had no appetite, so after an hour of trying to focus on football, I gave up and retreated to my cave. The painkillers I was prescribed for a knee injury knocked me out and I got plenty of coma time. Didn't wake up until this morning.

I realise I'm wearing Siri's pink fluffy dressing gown just before the door is opened with a key.

'Tommo, please tell me you don't spend the days dressing in lady's clothes. I know it's fashionable but...' Adam is wearing his best grin; it creases the lines under his wide eyes, making him look more like my wife.

He thrusts a Peppa Pig suitcase at me. 'Here you go, for Siri's trip.'

He's usually top of my 'people to see' list, but today, I am struggling to bear myself, let alone someone so upbeat. If he could see inside of me, he'd be ashamed to know me, let alone be related by marriage or anything else.

'She went yesterday.'

'Sorry. I'd forgotten.'

'No worries. Not sure this is what she had in mind though...'

'It's Indya's. I couldn't find anything else. Heather's away. I heard that racket from the street. Thought it must be coming from the old bird downstairs.' He turns Doris down to the lowest volume.

'Where did you say Heather is? Surprised she's not got you cleaning the house if you're off.'

He strides into the kitchen and opens the fridge as he speaks. 'She's at her parents'. Her dad's falling more, so her mum needs the help.'

'Don't you mind? I hate your sister being away and it's only been one night.'

'It's fine,' Adam reassures me. 'Heather says she needs more breaks. Fancy a beer?' he says, handing me one and taking one for himself.

He has a stain down his front. I can't work out if it's blood or tomato sauce.

'Rough night?' I point at his crumpled shirt.

Adam looks in the hall mirror and pulls up his collar. 'Think I look pretty good, for an old bloke.'

'You not at work?' I ask, recognising the hypocrisy.

'Work have put me on an action plan so home for three days while they write it up.'

'Oh Adam, why's that?' I feel a surge of real sympathy.

'They say I'm shambolic, forgetting stuff. I gave Alice, the apprentice, a compliment and she took it the wrong way. How come you're not at work?'

'Took a few days' leave. Think I have a fever. Don't want to pass anything on.'

Adam jumps onto the settee like a teenager and swings his legs up onto the far arm, shoes still on. It's a good job his sister can't see him now, reclining like this on her new velvet sofa. I'm trying to think about how to get rid of him. I can't say I was on my way out when I'm still in a dressing gown. And he clearly isn't worried about catching a bug…

'Adam, are you auditioning for Meelie's dance show? It's doing my head in.'

'What?'

'Your feet, they're dancing about like the proverbial cat on hot bricks.'

'Sorry… Heather keeps moaning I can't sit still.'

He sits up, keeping his eyes fixed on his feet until they are heavily planted on the oak floor. He continues to stare as if they are somehow separated from his legs.

'So, how's life then, Tommo?' He gets up and turns the CD player to Radio Sussex.

'Not so good, if I'm honest.'

'Let's see if Selma's on.' He's recently gone back to calling her by her real name which sounds alien. I can't equate that name with my wife.

'She hasn't been on in the mornings for nearly eighteen months. And she's away, remember?'

'Oh yeah.' He switches it off. 'How's life then, Tommo?'

'Not good, as I said two minutes ago.' My irritation is leaking. I want to be on my own but if he's going to stay, he could at least listen.

'Sorry, bit distracted. Dunno what's the matter. Not feeling myself.'

'Me neither.'

'What's up? Is my sister doing your head in? Baby stuff?'

'Yeah, it's not looking good. She won't cope if she can't have her own kids.'

'She'll have to.'

'That's what Harry said.' And so had Adam, back in November.

'She…' Adam's voice interrupts my unhealthy train of thought about him being a functioning drug user. 'I said… she needs to recognise it takes time and if she starts stressing, it'll reduce your chances. Heather took ages conceiving Amelia. Selma could never wait for anything. As a kid she'd sneak down in the night and rip open her Christmas presents. Mum had to keep hers hidden until the morning… Another one?' Adam is refilling my whisky glass. He opens another can of beer for himself.

I feel like weeping, which is embarrassing. How stupid to add alcohol into the mix: it makes me feel hopeless on the best of days.

My phone falls onto the floor as Adam shrugs his shoulders for the third time.

'Here, mate,' he says as he hands it to me. Then, 'What's all this? Should my sister be jealous?'

The screen shows I've got a voicemail message, a stream of texts and four missed calls.

'Just people at work.'

Adam gets up for the loo. He bumps into the door frame. He

is obviously not used to drinking in the mornings. I read the texts.

'Tom, where are you today? You said you'd be here.' At this moment, Lydia and I would usually be discussing some serious issue or another.

'It's nearly 11???'

'Are you not coming?'

'Tom! Tom???!!!'

Her last text reads, 'I'm going at 12, text me, Dawn's doing her nut.'

I switch it off as Adam tramps back into the room with the gait of an adolescent who's been asked to clear up his room. Siri would be furious if she could see the beer cans and a half-empty whisky bottle at midday.

'I'm starving. Got any food?'

'I'm not hungry, but help yourself.' He comes back with three rounds of bread and cheese. I wish I could eat like that and stay so trim. He opens another beer.

'I'm redundant.' The alcohol has robbed me of inhibition. I immediately regret opening my mouth.

'Nah, don't be daft – it takes two to conceive.'

I grab the opportunity to slightly change tack, relieved he's missed the point. 'Work is awful. Leo makes me feel completely redundant. But I don't want to give Siri even more to stress about.'

'We can't expect them to understand all that.'

'What?'

'Since Becca arrived, Heather couldn't give two hoots about me as long as my bonus covers her shopping cards. She's in the spare room most nights. She's a real witch, you know.'

'Come on, we love them really. I've never heard you diss your missus before. You'd best get home – the booze is talking for both of us.'

Adam doesn't take my hint. 'Find nicer company elsewhere, that's what I do.'

I'm horrified. We have drunk a fair amount and are definitely on the wrong side of sober but this isn't Adam talking.

'Siri is getting like Heather, moany and dissatisfied. They both need a good slap.'

My mouth drops open as if I'm a ventriloquist's dummy without a puppeteer.

'You gotta go, Adam. I can't deal with this. I just hope it's the beer talking, or you have seriously lost your way, mate.'

Ten minutes later the doorbell rings announcing his taxi. I open the door and push him out.

Am I so drunk and insane that I made up the past hour? I lean my head against the kitchen door. I have no means of a decent income, I can't give my wife a child and now this...

I go back to my computer, open 'Keep calm and carry on', insert the relevant links, and go back to bed.

'Tom, Tom, wake up, I'm home.'

'Oh... hello Siri... what time is it?'

'Twelve.'

'In the evening?'

'No, daytime. I texted you when I was on the train earlier today. I thought it was strange you didn't respond.'

Siri looks at the state of me, dishevelled and still stinking of whisky. But she gives me a tight hug and says, 'Tom, I know.'

Chapter 17

The front door wakes me up; please tell me Adam is not back. I must have fallen back to sleep. There is a note under my glasses – 'Love you, back at 1'.

'Hello, sleepyhead. Here you go: caffeine and carbs, the perfect post hangover solution.'

She plonks herself on my side of the bed. From the rebound effect, you'd guess she was ten stone heavier. A paper bag holds my favourite Bacon Bite from the bakery on the corner. She moves my glasses from the bedside table to make room for a brown takeaway cup containing a large, weak latte.

I hoist myself up, glad of the wall to lean back on. The old Siri seems to have returned. This is especially puzzling as the old Adam seems to have disappeared. My head is making confusing connections and taking me to some unusual places; she's told me that *she knows* but I haven't been sufficiently conscious to ask what she knows. Does she know about the test results? Adam? The job?

Siri pushes my thinning hair out of my eyes and places my glasses on my nose with a tenderness that's become unfamiliar.

'Tom, I'm sorry. I didn't know how bad things were. I hadn't realised Leo was so awful. I'm so obsessed with babies I haven't noticed how much you've been struggling. At least the tests are inconclusive. I guess that's the best we can hope at the moment.'

I slurp my coffee keeping my eyes on the duvet. I suspect my pupils are dilating fast and not from the caffeine. 'Who told you all that, honey?' I hope my voice sounds steadier than it does inside my mind.

'Adam – he texted me yesterday afternoon,' she says scrolling through her messages without looking up.

'Did he? What did he say? Read it to me – my eyes are still blurry.'

'He said, "Selma, big sorry, am in taxi back home. I gave him too much to drink to cheer him up. Your house is a tip but it was me not him. You need to be nicer, work is horrible and he's massively fed up but soz if ruined your homecoming".'

'I'm going to take leave this week. Stuff is getting on top of me,' my alter ego says without hesitation.

'Will Leo agree it?'

'He won't find out. Brian will cover for me if he pops in the office.'

I stay in bed with the curtains closed. I have managed to fix the blind by jamming an old credit card in the bottom so the darkness remains all day. I swig a mouthful of water to wash down the coma-inducing painkillers.

My mind is on constant fast-forward and rewind at the same time. Why did my dad hate me? Why didn't I save my mum? Why can't I be close to Gemma? Why did Leo pick me? Why didn't I claim unfair dismissal? Why can everyone else father children? What was Adam talking about? Have I got sinister motives for befriending a teenager? Peter's broad northern accent crashes into my head. How's your belly off for spots, lad? If only he'd been my father: kind, encouraging. Peter, I say, everything is ruined. No children, no friends, no family...

An emptiness engulfs me, presses down on me. The tablets give me the rest I crave. I wonder if Dawn or Lydia miss me… Probably not. I have left all their calls and texts unanswered. At least they don't know where I live.

It's my fourth day off and I am startled out of a deep sleep by the sound of the blind zooming up. Siri is standing by it with the credit-card wedge in her hand.

'What did you do that for? It's too light.'

'No more, Tom,' she says in my mother's voice. 'I have tried to understand how you are feeling, I really have, but this can't go on. You haven't washed. Or even got out of bed for more than ten minutes a day. You stink, the room stinks; this can't be helping you.'

'It's helping as much as anything else I've tried.'

'If you are feeling that bad, you need to look for another job – call up contacts, look at job sites, use your misery to motivate you, not swallow you up. I've had enough. It's so depressing to come home to you like this every day. You used to be fun. Talk to Harry for goodness' sake. Maybe you need some medical help.'

I resist the temptation to point out that she isn't much fun either. I slip the blind back down and reinsert the credit card that stops it flipping up and return to my stinking pit.

I can't move. I wonder if I have a disease: my body is heavy, I am tired.

'You said you'd get up and watch something with me.'

She's back already.

I feel a hundred years old as my legs try and carry my torso into another room. Siri puts a tray on my lap like I'm off sick from school. She sits down next to me, careful not to disturb my food.

When she's consumed by the programme, I take my plate

and scrape the food into the bin. I tear off some foil to place over it before I hit the lever with my slipper to close the lid.

After dinner, I sleep on the settee with my head on her lap. When she finally goes for a bath, my bear cave calls me back. I pretend I am asleep when she puts the light on and moves her body against mine. I don't even want that any more.

I hear the door slam. Siri has closed the door deliberately hard as she leaves for work. I'm certain she's hidden the credit card so I can't stay in darkness. In the bathroom, I catch sight of a tired, old, unshaven man. It takes me a few seconds to realise who it is.

Siri has propped a card in a red envelope by my bedside clock. I've forgotten Valentine's Day. Her card displays two jigsaw segments, one pink and one blue, the pieces are holding hands and the caption reads: *The perfect fit. I love you to pieces.* Inside, her handwriting says, 'I love you – please cheer up'.

There is a less neat note written on the back of a Lidl receipt. 'Going to Bexhill Theatre, its 80th anniversary, won't be home until 7. Don't forget to get up, and make yourself smell nice!'

The answer dawns on me, which brings a calm that's eluded me for months. Today is the day.

The thought of ending the deceit motivates me; my head is clear and the load is lifted off my back. She will have a Valentine's evening she won't forget, then I'll go; it can't feel worse than this.

I write a to do list to keep me on track. I am not a coward. I can see this through. It's for her good. Two months and she will be as good as new, or rather back to her former self, and free to fulfil her five-year plan: settle, babies, happy ever after.

Go into town, buy Siri ring

Buy file and dividers

Buy card, write letter and print off file contents

Call insurer

Bank

Buy fish-pie mix, milk, cheese, peas, potatoes, caramel, biscuits, cream, bananas

Clean flat

If I go now, I'll have plenty of time to do the errands and be back to prepare a romantic finale.

The cold air makes my nose run; being outside feels alien. Keep your focus, Tom. Free her up, true love opens the cage. There's no hurry. I'll go to the shops and then cook my signature fish pie with extra prawns. I'll leave her with a great memory, not one of a grumpy old man sleeping in a pigsty, reeking of old whisky.

When we moved here, one of the first shops Siri discovered was a small independent jeweller called Perrins.

'Good morning, sir. What can I do for you?'

'The eternity rings in the window. The blue one, bottom right?'

'Ah, yes. Give me a minute and I'll get the tray.'

With a small velvet box safely in my pocket, I mentally tick off item one. I've left the actual list in the car.

'Can I help you, Tom?'

'Mm, have we met?'

'At the school. You're Amelia's uncle? I'm her friend Ellie's mum.'

'Ah yes,' I say, none the wiser.

'Are you looking for anything in particular?'

'Just a card, but I'm okay. I'll give you a shout if I get stuck.'

I pick out yet another Valentine's card. *What do you call a lazy crayfish? A slobster*. Maybe I should get a card that's more explicitly Valentine's. I want to leave on a high note, everything as it should've been. But this one will fit with my fish pie supper and serve as an apology for my recent sloth-like habits. I grab the pink envelope.

'Good choice.' The yummy mummy shop assistant pops the card in a stripy bag. 'Women like a man who can make them laugh.' I try not to think about making Siri cry.

It's for her good. Set her free.

I visit the bank before dashing round to the supermarket to get the food. I grab a small trolley and throw in a blue file decorated with smiley faces and an A4 pad of paper. I want to write a letter to say the many things I've so far left unsaid. I've always been better on paper. Then I think of Dawn and Lydia and how I have let them down. Maybe I should create time to say goodbye to the café crew. What will Harry say? I decide it's best I go without a backward look or people trying to dissuade me. And if my mother could see me, she'd see a sense of purpose has returned to my stride.

It's for her good. Set her free.

It's for her good. Set her free.

It's for her good. Set her free.

When Siri comes home, the house is clean from skirting board to curtain top. I have even hoovered under the bed. I change into a clean shirt and work trousers. As I am lighting three tall candles, the door opens. I've missed that smile.

She comes straight to me and gives me a wholehearted kiss. 'Mm, you smell nice.'

'I've made an effort.'

I know I am doing the right thing for her.

It's for her good. Set her free.

It's for her good. Set her free.

It's for her good. Set her free.

A lovely evening ends with a banoffee pie, the only pudding I can make, and some baby-trying.

'It's so good to have my Tom Tom back. I've missed you so much.'

She falls asleep. I pull myself up on one elbow for a long look at her. When her breathing goes slow and deep, I kiss her cheek and breathe in her smell.

It's for her good. Set her free.

It's for her good. Set her free.

It's for her good. Set her free.

'Goodnight, my love, please forgive me,' I whisper to my wife.

I allow myself a few more minutes of indulgent watching. She flinches slightly as I stroke her arm and I see the new ring is a little too tight. For a fleeting moment, I wonder if I've made the wrong decision. I take two tablets to take away those thoughts and lie back on my pillow for one last time.

I get up first and make Siri a cup of green tea.

'Here you go, gorgeous girl.'

'Spot on. Things are looking up.' She smiles as she sits up, leaning against her pillow.

Soon, she's rushing round in her usual chaotic manner, throwing random things in her bag as she puts on a smear of lipstick without looking in a mirror. I watch her every move, the way she eats toast and jiggles on her shoes at the same time, the angle of her denim jacket slung over one shoulder, a purple cloth rucksack held between her knees as she peers into the mirror to insert long dangling earrings to match her carefree mood.

I kiss her well, drawing her perfume far up my nostrils as she disappears out of the door without a backward glance. My gaze follows her through the window as she pulls on the other half of her jacket and swings her backpack to its rightful place. Off she strides with such purpose. I stare like a little girl watching her daddy leave for work but knowing he's not coming back for supper. The tears fall onto my hand; my body heaves with an entire lifetime of sadness, disappointment and shame.

Pull yourself together, boy. Act like a man for once in your miserable life. Stop snivelling, take your hands out of your pockets and hold your head up.

First stop, a full tank of fuel.

I press my keypad to summon Radio 2. Radio Sussex wouldn't be manageable today. 'Here's Jessie J with 'Brave' to brighten up your morning.' I turn the volume dial as far as it will go, and push my foot down hard on the accelerator. The lyrics are personal, cheering me on…

I'm brave

Even when the fear is staring in my face…

You see, Dad. I stepped up.

Chapter 18

'Hello, I don't want to alarm you, sir, but you're in a very dangerous spot.' A man's voice speaks from behind.

Sitting here, I daren't move my body. My hands grip clumps of brown grass as I twist my head to glance over my shoulder. An older man in a pillar-box-red fleece is kneeling behind me. He has a sleeveless high visibility jacket over his jumper. I can't twist far enough to read the yellow writing on his clothes.

His right arm is reaching out to me, gently contacting my lower back with a light touch of his fingers. I didn't hear him coming. Perhaps he isn't real. My mind keeps playing tricks.

'Why don't you take my hand? Your position is very precarious.'

'That's my intention.'

The white cliffs are breathtaking, a beauty spot indeed. Hard rock cascades down like a frothy fountain. There are a number of wooden crosses planted along the green edge; they look as if they've been crafted by a child to say goodbye to a pet, each marking a death. Will I get one or will Siri feel that's too sloppy?

The man with less hair than me is edging closer, legs folded under him, like an amputee.

I take a quick breath and raise my palm at him, a policeman stopping traffic.

'Please stop.'

'I'm Marc Cole from the Beachy Head chaplaincy team.'

'Look, mate, the last thing I need now is a God-botherer, I'm sorry it's you on duty. Please leave me.'

'Tell me your name at least.'

'Kev.' The liar lives on.

'Kev, tell me, what's brought you here today?'

'If I'd wanted a chat, I'd have called a friend.'

Over the tips of my shoes I can see the seam where the shingly sand fuses with the sea. Today the water is clear enough to be the Maldives, our last break before children. Don't think about her. Let her go. Be brave.

'Many people have stood there, but got help and been glad.'

'I don't want help. Thank you though.'

The sound of pebble-sized rocks falling prompts my Samaritan to fall back to a sitting position. His hands are outstretched behind him; he could be on a winter picnic chatting to his kids about the kites in the sky.

'There is always hope, Kev. This feeling won't last, I promise you. Tell me why you're here.'

The wind is gathering voice. The man takes off his black cap and holds it to the ground secured on his thumb. My shirt is doing a decent impression of an abandoned helium balloon.

'You are not alone. Many come here, but they come back. Who are you leaving behind?'

'No one.'

'You'd be surprised. Whoever you are, your loss will impact people.'

'You don't know my life. Sometimes people need to be released from their burdens.'

I edge closer, my fingers entangled with brown tufts. They're rough under my palms.

The lighthouse in the distance is so small it could be an ornament, a reminder of a happy day at the beach. It stands as a warning: stay away, danger. The bullying waves assault its striped body, creating an angry foam around its base.

The light hurts my bloodshot eyes. I'm not cold even though I'm on the top of the world. It's liberating. I'm almost free of this relentless pain. The emptiness will soon stop.

'Kev, it often fails, you know. It looks a sure end, but it isn't. People get caught on the ledge, get life-changing injuries. So many say they wish they hadn't gone over.'

My mind falters. Is he right? Knowing me, I will screw this up. Typical, my dad would say; that wimp couldn't even die successfully.

My chest makes a sudden hiccup as another voice speaks out, a mumble from his radio. I can't hear what is said.

The rocks crumbling from the edge are irrelevant. I have a clear view for miles. An oversized gull swoops down, arms wide as it soars so close I could reach out and touch it. I lean forwards. As the sombre bird flies off, it swivels its head slowly to look back at me, opens its beak and whispers, 'Set her free, Tom, set her free.'

Chapter 19

Siri

'Hi Siri, it's Harry. You at work?'

'Yep, but not on air for another hour. You okay?'

'Yeah, I'm fine. You?'

'Good, thanks. Not seen you in ages.'

'Sorry, been busy. Have you spoken to Tom this morning?'

'Not since I left home. Why?'

'Probably nothing, but been calling him and he's not picking up.' Oh great, so now I'm Tom's PA.

'He'll be on a home visit. What's so urgent?'

'Nothing, just wanted to catch up. He usually returns calls in between visits.' I want to be reasonable but I can feel my exasperation coming to a head. What is it with men? Women don't expect other people to sort out every minor problem that arises.

'Sure he'll be in contact soon – he's probably calling right now. When did you last try?'

'Before you; it rang the first few times but now it's going straight to voicemail.'

'Oh, how long have you been trying then?'

'Not long. I'm between clinics. Sure he'll get back to me later. Hope your day goes well.'

'And y—' He rings off before I finish my sentence.

I could do without this faffing about. The first studio guest arrives in half an hour and I know nothing about alopecia. I've only just started reading through a heap of articles before I interview her. I have no idea what can be so important that Harry can't wait till this evening.

My phone buzzes to let me know a text has flown in. No doubt it's Tom; no one else texts mid-morning. I envy him having a job that gives time for these pauses. I've actually no idea why he gets so stressed. Leo only pitches up every now and again.

Blast, it's Eleanor.

'We still on for dinner at mine this eve? E.'

I'd completely forgotten I'd agreed to join her for supper. I'm shattered, just want to put my feet up and catch up with Tom now he's returned from being a grumpy zombie.

'Yep, all good for later, 6.30 still work?' Why can't I say no?

I'm gagging for a cuppa; my throat is still sore from chatting so much in Amsterdam.

I type a few words to Tom without looking and I race to the kitchen. It's a good job I do radio and can wear sloppy clothes and trainers.

'Morning.' Sarah, our producer, is looking vacantly out of the kitchen window; it's a tiny space and wisps of steam express the inner turmoil of the kettle.

'Tea?' She holds out my personal work mug. She obviously hasn't bothered to wash it and the stains from last week are creeping above the liquid. There is a smudge of lipstick on the handle; I hope it's mine.

My phone vibrates.

'Excuse me a minute, I'm waiting for a response from Tom. His bestie is after him.'

Sarah doesn't attempt to disguise an audible sigh.

'Yep, all good, see ya later at the Crown. E.'

'Him?'

'No, my friend Eleanor.'

'He'll be at work, won't he, like us?' Green tea slops onto my hand as I juggle my phone back into my trackie bottoms.

'I don't know. He's been off for a few days. I think today was his first day back. To be honest, I wasn't listening.'

'I never know what Dean's up to.'

'Tom's pretty good at keeping me in the loop. It's me that doesn't do so great.'

'Is he more upbeat? Less of the grumpy ole git of the last few weeks?'

'Yes, thankfully, I was getting totally sick of it.'

'I don't blame you. My brother-in-law was the same, went on for weeks, was diagnosed with depression in the end. Medication sorted it.'

'I'd started to think that he might be ill but yesterday it resolved, as quick as it came. He got up, even cleaned the house and cooked me dinner.'

Sarah is looking absently at her phone. 'What you doing on the show today?'

'Alopecia.'

'That'll be interesting, something I know nothing about.'

'Me neither, which is why I could do without playing *Where's Wally?* with my other half.'

My oversized chunky mug, illustrated with an old Mini, brings back happy memories – it was one of the first presents Tom gave me... *Old banger, been around the block... in good condition but bodywork needs attention, spare tyre included...*

'*Alopecia Areata (AA) is understood to be an autoimmune condition. The immune system which normally protects...*' The words are sliding into each other. Perhaps a quick nap... Apparently Helen Taylor lost her hair as a teenager. I wouldn't have coped with that. I used to love changing mine every five minutes. My phone vibrates again.

'Any word from your bloke? H.'

No.

Does Harry think I'm his pretty young secretary, at my desk, waiting patiently for his next command? Am I my husband's keeper, for goodness' sake? The clock tells me I'm running out of time. I'm on air at twelve. Helen is coming in fifteen minutes.

'*... the body from foreign invaders, such as viruses and bacteria, mistakenly attacks the hair follicles. This is what leads to hair loss. Alopecia Areata typically starts...*'

I shove the pages into the bin. I'll wing it. As long as she talks, I'll laugh in the right intervals and throw out a few back-channelling phrases...

There is so much we don't know.

Must have been hard.

That's courageous.

Will it ever come back?

It won't be the first time I've ridden by the seat of my pants.

In an unexpected flashback, my mind tells me exactly where my husband is. In my mind's eye, I can see him, lolling about on Adam's sofa. There is bad signal at his, and Heather's away. Lazy blighters. I bet they're half-cut watching sport surrounded by cans.

My watch tells me I have exactly seven minutes.

Much to my surprise, Adam picks up after four rings.

'Hi, it's Siri.'

'Hey, sweetie, you don't usually call during the day.'

'Is Tom there?'

'No, should he be?'

'He's not picking up his phone.'

'Glad I've not forgotten something. Is he with Harry?'

'It's Harry who's after him.'

'Not seen him since you were away. I was a bit of a prat. He was upset about his job.'

'Adam, I can't talk, I gotta go. Speak later.'

'Good afternoon! Welcome to BBC Radio Sussex in the afternoon. It's Selma Cleary with you until four. We've a great show lined up, including interviews from the Bexhill Theatre anniversary celebrations. Such a great time there yesterday evening, meeting wonderful people like Dennis and Marie who met at the theatre doors when they were children, still together after fifty years. More from them later... Did you see the programme on BBC Two on Monday night about older people being abused in nursing homes? What did you think? Do you have a relative in a care home? What have your experiences been? Give us a call and join our phone-in at two... Hey, thanks all of you for your welcome back texts. I was only out for a day... Now, let's indulge ourselves with one sloppy tune. I know Valentine's was yesterday, but we need as much love as we can get, don't we...? Now, in the studio today, I'm chatting to our lunchtime guest, Helen Taylor, from the Sussex Alopecia Support Group. Hello, Helen, welcome.'

'Thank you very much for inviting me.'

'So, Helen, you've told me you lost your hair at fifteen? That must have been very hard.'

'It was pretty awful, yeah. All my friends were experimenting, you know, with colour and things, and style, and meanwhile my own hair was dropping out by the handful.'

Marilyn is tapping on the glass, beckoning me to come out. My eyes meet hers through the transparent partition.

I shake my head and mouth, 'Not now.' She's not the brightest button in the box. She continues to gesture, beckoning and wobbling.

I shake my head. She continues to bend her finger at me like the witch from *Snow White*. I can't concentrate. 'So sorry...' I whisper to my guest. 'Let's play another tune. More from this inspirational lady in a few minutes. Here's the new single from Keane for a winter morning: "The Way I Feel". Enjoy.'

I rip off my earphones and march out to demand an explanation.

'What?'

Marilyn is unusually evasive. 'There are two policemen to see you downstairs, and they won't wait, or tell me anything...'

The police car is parked just a few metres from the office.

'I'm sorry to interrupt you at work, Mrs Cleary. We're looking for your husband.'

'Please take some breaths.' He puts a hand on my arm. 'Try and stay calm. We're just trying to ascertain his whereabouts. Can you first confirm that your husband is Thomas James Cleary?'

'Yes.'

The radio in the front of the car starts speaking; his front seat colleague rushes to stop it and speaks into his hand-held radio. It looks like he is talking to his chest.

'Go ahead.' He writes some symbols on his notepad and turns around to me.

'Can you confirm that your husband's car registration is GS04 BXE?'

'Yes. So where is he?'

'We don't know. But our colleagues in Eastbourne have found his car.'

'Eastbourne? Why would he be there?'

'We're trying to find out. Is he a walker?'

I do not want to be distracted by meaningless small talk. 'No, he cycles sometimes and plays football – well he used to… Please tell me what's going on. This isn't making sense. What do you want with Tom?'

'He isn't in trouble. Our colleagues at Brighton Central had a call from a Doctor Edgington saying he was concerned about his friend.'

'What? I know Harry has ideas above his station but calling the police because his friend won't return his calls is a bit much. Give me a minute and I'll call him.'

'He's been trying all morning to get hold of your husband.'

'I know, he called here.'

'Yes, but when Tom didn't answer, he went to your flat and found something that worried him.'

The bloke sitting next to me chips in. 'We understand Tom has been feeling low since he lost his job?'

'What? None of this makes sense. You must have got the wrong man. My husband works at a glass company. When I left him this morning, he was happier than me, and on his way to work.'

'Look, we don't know much more than you do, but we've been instructed to escort you home, and check he's not back, and look around.'

My mouth opens to reply but nothing is happening. My brain and speech have disconnected.

Eventually, the words drop out in a jumble. 'I'm sorry, guys, you've got the wrong bloke. The car must have been stolen. I'll call him…' I feel relieved and comforted by my explanation.

'Mrs Cleary, we are sure. We've checked your husband's details. They match his car and the personal effects that were left on the driver's seat.'

'He's probably stopped off for lunch. I bet his car is near a nice country pub, isn't it? That's why he's not with his car...'

'Also, this was in the car.' The younger PC reaches into his pocket, pulls out a cream envelope from a plastic freezer bag, and passes it back to me. I can't lift my hands from my lap.

DS O'Leary takes the envelope and hands it to me. The writing on the front simply says 'Siri' in Tom's unmistakable scrawl. It has been opened.

'I'm sorry, Mrs Cleary. In situations like this everything is important potential evidence. A colleague opened it to take photos before we could bring it to you.'

His mouth is goldfishing. I can't hear anything. I'm staring at the letter in my hand. My fingers won't stay still as they take the neatly folded piece of A4 paper out of the envelope. The paper looks like it's from a college notepad but the envelope is an expensive one; they don't match. A hand stops me. DS O'Leary has placed his hand on mine. 'Not here. Am I right in thinking you don't live too far from here? Let's go to your home and have a chat. I'm sure we'll find him.'

I nod and do as I am told. I am not behaving like a person I know. I am stunned but have the energy to run a marathon. Weird.

'Can I call Harry?'

'Of course.'

Harry's phone rings and rings. 'You have reached the voice-mail of Doctor Harry Edgington. Please leave a message.'

'Harry, where's Tom? What's going on? The police have come. I don't understand. Please call me.'

The journey that usually takes less than half an hour feels longer than the train across the English Channel. We pull up outside the flat, our flat. My mind, briefly distracted by the emotional discomfort of being with strangers in complete silence, shoots back to the present.

I replay my last sight of him. He got up spontaneously for the first morning in a week. He was washed and clean-shaven; he looked lovely in his blue shirt. He looked at me with such love and concern as he helped me check I'd got everything. He kissed me goodbye, laughed, and said, 'If you have everything, it'll be a first.'

The younger police officer takes the keys from me. He's very nice to look at and on a night out would've caught my eye. 'Here, let me help,' he says softly, guiding me by my elbow as if I'm newly blind. The house is cleaner and tidier than when I'm last to leave. At least I don't need to apologise for dirty breakfast stuff.

I am disoriented in my own space and can't decide what to do first, take off my coat or get a drink.

'Shall I make tea?'

'Thank you...' I'm usually good with names.

'Call me Josh. How do you take your tea?'

'Green. No milk please. Help yourself too.' I stumble over my words. What's the etiquette for offering hospitality to the men in blue?

I'm clutching the letter. My fingers feel stiff. I hadn't realised how hard I was gripping it.

'Here you go.' He hasn't made anything for him and his colleague to drink.

I sit down with the letter. The policeman says nothing but very carefully sits next to me.

Dear Siri, my beautiful, clever wife

I'm so, so sorry I've done this to you, but in a few years, you'll realise it was for the best, so please be patient and let me explain.

By the time you read this letter I will no longer be alive. I have tried hard to put that as kindly as possible, but I realise that no words will change the hurt I am causing. Please forgive me and understand I have done it for you, so you can be free.

'No...' My body hurts like I can't describe. It's bent me double without my permission. 'No, please tell me this isn't it. Please tell me Tom's not dead...'

'Mrs Cleary, look at me,' the young policeman says, with such kindness. He gets up and crouches in front of me. There are tears in his eyes.

'We don't know where he is. His car has been found at Beachy Head, so we believe he had planned to end his life but...' He waits until I look back at him. 'We have not had any information yet.'

'Beachy Head...? Oh... no... no... you said his car was in Eastbourne... Is it there? At the cliffs...?'

'It is in that area, but as soon as Dr Edgington alerted our colleagues, we put out an alert. Beachy Head is patrolled all the time by specially trained volunteers and our colleagues are there too. There is every chance they will find him in time.'

'I need to go. Can you take me? Please?'

'I don't think that's a good idea. By the time we get there, there'll be news, I'm sure. Let me take this letter – perhaps save it until you know more?'

'No, I want to know why. How could he do this? We're happy, trying for a baby...'

My eyes find his words again, but then dart back to the two uniformed men. How can this be? He got better. He bought me a ring...

Tom's writing becomes harder to read.

For the last three and a half months, I haven't had a job. I know that will come as a massive shock to you. I have become uncomfortably good at deception. I didn't mean to lie. It sounds pathetic but it's the truth.

Leo 'let me go' at the end of October. I felt so ashamed. I planned to tell you that day, that evening, but you seemed happy to see me for the first time in ages. We had a great weekend and it was like the old days. I planned to give myself a week to try to get a new job before I told you, but no one wanted me. I realise I'm no longer the Tom I thought I'd become, that I'd tried to be, but Tom the middle-aged man who is past his best.

My head feels heavy and my thoughts are grey. I'm sorry I can't explain it better.

It was our anniversary, then Christmas, then the fertility tests, and somehow it was never the right time to make you feel worse. When we started those tests, I thought I could get you pregnant and it would be okay. If the tests were clear, we could carry on trying. Siri, I'm infertile. I can't ever make it okay.

I wanted one last happy day with you. Thank you for saying that you'd stand by me whatever. I know you mean it but, in a few years when all your friends have children, the bitterness will ruin you, and us. I know I can't see you grow another man's child in your belly, knowing it won't look like me, but like you and someone else...

I'd planned to tell you about the results the day I got drunk with your brother. I thought Adam would tell me to stop. I wanted him to do that but he didn't.

Siri, I do think you need to talk to Adam. I don't think he's okay.

I couldn't bear to break your heart. You have great ovaries, you have great everything, Siri, and I have loved everything about you since the very first day I met you. But in time you'll find someone who deserves you.

I love you more than ever. Everything will be okay – all insurance policies are in place and I have transferred what's left of my redundancy into your account. There is a file on the computer desk. It contains everything you need.

Yours for ever

Tom x

I look up and see a file under the arm of policeman two. It has smiley faces on it. 'Please can I see it?'

He hands it to me. On the front it says, 'Keep calm and carry on, you'll be okay.' Inside it's perfectly divided into sections on every aspect of my life, all the things that don't matter. The only thing that matters is him. I refuse to believe he's gone.

How could he?

I can still visualise the first time I saw him, at a stupidly posh party. It wasn't my thing. My then manager, whom I was desperate to impress, told me I was going to a doctors' do. As soon as we arrived, I regretted going. I hung back as she circulated around anyone who looked influential or rich. I felt awkward and out of my depth. But then I caught sight of a gorgeous-looking bloke by the food. As I admired him from afar, I heard Eleanor's voice in my head. *Siri, he's balding and too short.*

This is true. Tom is only about five foot nine, shorter than my ideal, and admittedly even then his hair was showing signs of receding. But it suited him. He has smooth skin and the hair he did have was very dark. It was his face that appealed to me most. Even from a distance, I thought it looked honest, and he had eyes that laughed with his smile. I was instantly attracted. He was chatting to a woman who looked older than him. She was doing the thing women do when they are trying to impress a man, being giggly and playing with her hair. As I watched, she suddenly changed her behaviour completely, withdrew eye contact, shuffled about and darted off to another room. This is the man I am going to marry, I said in my head.

'What did you say to make her run away?' was the first line I ever spoke to him.

'You don't beat about the bush, do you?'

'No. Who are you and why are you here?'

'Tom. I am a practice manager at the GP surgery.'

'Really?'

'No, that's a total lie. I sell windows and that's why she scarpered when she found out.'

'Doesn't she need windows?'

'I think she'd like someone who could keep her in the manner to which she is accustomed.'

'I knew you were lying.'

'You did?'

'Yep, you were smiling without your eyes.'

'Mm... Without my eyes? Maybe that was why she found me so attractive.'

He laughed and told me I was much more interesting than Mrs Designer Dull. He told me his name was Tom Cleary and for the last six years we've argued about who spotted who first and the content of our first conversation. Tom insists his chat-up line was about his dead cat and I insulted him with a string of put-downs.

When he first asked me my name, I was reticent about telling him. It's embarrassing; my mother has always tried to convince me it's my father's legacy. I would have preferred it if he'd left me some money and given my brother the wacky name. Tom tried guessing what it could be and joked I was like some character from a children's book. I had no idea what he was talking about and had to ask Adam about it. I find it hard to admit I don't know something.

It was at that first party, after we'd negotiated several squabbles about politics, explored what was meant by the saying 'once in a blue moon' and battled over gender equality, that he said he would call me Siri.

'What?'

'Siri, you must know Siri, the creepy female on the iPhone. Anything you ask, she knows the answer and states it without shame.'

Adam loved that nickname and soon everyone was calling me Siri, apart from my mother and her sisters.

I didn't tell Tom my real name until he wore me down with endless name guessing.

'Selmeston? No wonder you're embarrassed!'

'I know it.'

'No way.'

He told me he and his friend Harry frequently use the pub in Selmeston. It's a tiny place and no one knows where it is. I told him it was a sign.

My mind jolts back to the present. Someone is unwrapping my fingers to take my cup.

I can't make out where the awful noise is coming from. Then I realise that the gut-wrenching wailing is coming from me.

Chapter 20

The police car stops outside the hospital main entrance and DS O'Leary gets out with me. His younger colleague puts up his hand as I turn my back to get out of the car.

'Bye, Mrs Cleary. Good luck.'

DS O'Leary, who I'm now calling Chris, puts his hand gently on my shoulder and steers me in the direction of the automatic doors. As they close behind me, I have never been so glad to see the two men in front of the reception desk. Adam and Harry. Harry is shifting from one foot to the other. I've seen him act like this only twice before – at our wedding, and the day before he was interviewed for a consultant post. Adam's demeanour is less familiar; he is leaning on the reception desk doing two of my mother's least favourite male things: lolling, and looking down the dress of the receptionist. The receptionist has sussed him out but he's making no attempt to modify his leering. It's not at all like Adam, today of all days.

'You look awful, sis,' he says with his arms outstretched like an American TV evangelist.

'You don't look so great yourself. I need to see Tom.'

'You sure you'll cope?' Adam asks, placing his arm firmly

round me. He keeps shrugging his shoulders. He must be more anxious than he looks.

Harry stands in silence as if he's not part of the dynamic. He hands me a tissue and I blow my nose. Adam is holding me like he used to when we were growing up, though he smells less sweet.

I explain to the receptionist who I am. She studies her computer screen without meeting my gaze. It takes her a long time to respond. 'Report to the east wing reception; they will talk to you before you go in. Do you know where it is? You turn right through the next doors, and then left at the end…'

'I know,' Harry snaps. It's so unlike him, not to be polite. He leads the way.

'Are you sure it was intentional?' Adam says.

'I don't think it could be any more intentional,' Harry says.

'I just wondered if it was some kind of joke that went wrong.'

Neither Harry nor I can think of an appropriate response so we walk the rest of the way in silence.

As Harry pushes through some double doors, we are met by a nurse. 'Hello, can I help?'

'We are here to see Thomas Cleary. Where is he, please?'

I have not seen Harry like this before: this must be Dr Edgington. The nurse, who introduces herself as Katrina, is very polite and quietly spoken and in turn introduces us to Leah, Tom's nurse, whom I warm to instantly.

'Tom's stable but heavily sedated so he won't be able to communicate with you yet. He's waiting for a psych assessment, and his blood pressure was very high for a while, so we are giving his system a rest while it recovers.'

'He is all right though? He won't be brain damaged or anything?' Adam pipes up. Harry responds with a hard stare

'We expect him to be fine. Marc Cole, one of the experienced chaplains, talked him down. He's a lucky man.'

'He won't feel lucky when my sister gets near him.' Adam is talking like Tom's a bit late for dinner. I have no idea what he is trying to communicate, but if we were alone I would be shouting at him to stop being an idiot and shut up. He has a strange twitch around his lips.

Leah leads us along a shorter corridor and into a private room with an empty bed. 'This is the room he'll be brought back to. I'm afraid I can't tell you when that'll be. The police are still with him.' She walks out and closes the heavy door by its metal handle. I climb onto the bed still clutching Tom's letter as if it's him, bury myself in the pillow and cry. Adam and Harry stand awkwardly at the end of the bed.

Leah comes in after a few minutes. 'Mrs Cleary, would you like a hot drink while the chaps wait here or go for a walk? There's a café in the foyer and a canteen on the top floor if you'd like something.'

I'm not thirsty. Am I being invited to go and chat to her on my own? Is this the bit where they find out what you've done to drive your husband to the cliffs? She ushers me into a small room with two chairs, yellow walls and a cheap box of tissues. The photograph on the wall is of Brighton pier after the fire in 2003 that left it a skeletal version of its former self. I wonder if it has been chosen to be symbolic.

'Mrs Cleary, I'm sorry that you've had such a horrible shock. What have the police told you?'

'That he was found on Beachy Head. They gave me his letter. They said it took two hours but eventually someone talked him down.' My lip starts to quiver again. 'I'm sorry, I don't usually weep all over strangers.'

'Please don't apologise. It's a shock, and you must have many unanswered questions.' Her talking gives me time to recover myself. 'That's right – one of the Beachy Head chaplains chatted to him. He's very shaken. You might find him very quiet. Try not to push him.' She thinks I'm a control freak. I bet she's thinking no wonder the poor bloke tried to top himself. Who wouldn't?

'I read his letter. I still can't believe he would do that to me. It's so out of character; he was so happy yesterday.'

'It's normal to be baffled. Relatives rarely see it coming. And it's normal to feel angry.'

'It's so selfish,' I say, without thinking.

'It does seem selfish, doesn't it? But when people try to take their own lives, it's because they feel desperate, and their mind convinces them that they're helping the ones they love, relieving them of a burden.'

'He's been lying to me about losing his job and he recently found out he can't father children, which he also kept from me. But this… he couldn't trust me. He obviously thinks I don't love him enough…'

'When people get very low, they can't think straight. It's like looking through dirty glasses. The good things are lost to them.'

'He has been down, but not depressed like you imagine. I should have known…'

'Suicide attempts make the other people feel like that – guilty, that they've been staring right at something and missed it. But it's so complicated. It's different from when someone is injured in some other way.'

'He wanted it, he wanted to leave me. What does that say about our marriage, about me?' Why am I telling her my intimate thoughts? I am not one for emotional outpourings when I'm sober.

'Did you know that suicide is the biggest killer of men between thirty and fifty – above cancer and heart attacks? Tom isn't alone. Most men who attempt suicide or succeed have no history of mental health issues. It seems they reach a crisis point and don't feel able to share their feelings or to find another solution.'

'Will he do it again?'

'I can't answer that; I don't know what brought you both here. He will have to see the psychiatrist before he leaves. They'll assess his mood and may prescribe some antidepressants, and suggest he gets talking therapy. It may be a good idea for you to go too... Things like this impact everyone involved.'

'Will he fully recover?'

'He will be sedated for the rest of today and we will keep him in for observation. His consultant friend is making sure we do everything right.'

'Harry has known him all his life – they're like brothers. It's his way of dealing with things...'

Leah's smiling. 'I didn't take it personally.'

'When will he come home?'

'Hopefully, tomorrow or the following day if all goes to plan. It will depend on when the psychiatrist comes in and whether they feel he's safe.'

Tears roll down my face yet again. 'I am sorry for being pathetic. I'm normally sane and pretty strong.'

'Don't be so hard on yourself – you have had an awful shock. It would be very strange if you weren't upset. You'll feel better when you can chat to him.'

I want to scream. Six hours ago, I was kissing my husband goodbye, the beginning of an ordinary day after a nice evening in our ordinary, mundane lives. Today I have spent two hours in the company of the police and am sitting in a room labelled 'Relatives' while being told my husband will have no ill effects after trying to kill himself. Tom doesn't get emotional; he is the strong one. How on earth can anything be normal again?

When I return to the room, Adam and Harry are still standing either side of the bed. Both have their hands in their pockets and look like schoolboys who've been caught shoplifting. Tom's things are now on the bed: the watch I gave him for a wedding present, his phone and the wallet he was given for his eighteenth by Harry's parents. It has TJC inscribed into the brown leather.

Harry speaks in an emotionless tone. 'I found the ward consultant. He said Tom's still with the police and a mental health nurse. They're deciding whether to section him.'

'What?'

'If they think he's still a risk to himself they can detain him here or at a psychiatric hospital until he's not in danger.'

'They can't do that! Where is he? I need to speak to them. Tom is not mental, Harry. You have to tell them Tom's normal.' Harry catches me, enfolding me in his arms. 'It'll be okay.' He strokes my hair, and I start sobbing again.

'Sorry.' The three of us manage to laugh and cry at the same time: my tears have created mascara streaks on his pristine shirt.

'It'll be okay,' he repeats. 'Tom's still a normal person. It's for his good. They need to make sure he's no longer suicidal.'

We all take our places around an empty bed.

My mind drifts to the radio station. Will my colleagues know what Tom's done? I imagine Marilyn talking to the other staff. *She's so hard to please, unreasonable, never satisfied. No wonder the poor bloke was driven to end it all.*

Harry's eyes are red with dark circles beneath them. He does indeed love Tom like a brother. When I think about Tom's family, I think of Harry before I think of Gemma and his mother. I should phone them, but I can't cope with his sister being judgemental. Besides, I'm not sure his mother would consider this enough reason to move from her chair. *So sorry, dear, but right now I have to watch the end of EastEnders*. I'm feeling spiteful.

Adam breaks the silence. 'Why would he do this?'

Harry repeats what Leah told me. This must be NHS party line for men trying to escape their relatives. 'Suicide is the biggest killer of middle-aged men, above heart disease and cancer; most men who do it have no obvious reason.'

'Thanks for that, mate,' Adam says sarcastically. 'I totally get it now.'

Adam is flicking a leaflet he has picked up. Harry is tutting and looking at Adam as if he wants to smack him. Adam is not stopping.

Right in the middle of his letter, Tom had told me to talk to Adam.

What am I supposed to be talking to him about? Adam is fidgety, snapping at whatever we say. He's been to the toilet three times in half an hour. My mind runs back to a comment Tom made a couple of months ago about Adam slurring his words. Tom and I'd had a massive row about it. I was sure he and Harry had been doing some ridiculous man gossiping, and I said, my brother wouldn't drink in the working day when he has to collect the girls, and it's none of your business, and Harry is just seeing dysfunction in everyone, and Tom said, well, he doesn't need to search too far for dysfunctional, does he?

I remember too many arguments ending like that this year. Adam's not coping, Tom's not coping, and I've been yearning so much for what I don't have that I've lost what I've actually got.

Chapter 21

Harry has gone home to make some calls. Adam is looking for food even though no one's hungry. I have only my husband's belongings for company.

I wonder what a dead person looks like.

A nurse comes through the door; it is clear from the look on her face that she'd expected the room to be empty.

'Hi, you must be Mrs Cleary.'

'Selma.'

'Hi Selma. Everything is going in the right direction. He's a very lucky man.'

'That's what everyone keeps saying. I don't feel very lucky right now. Are you sure he's okay?'

'He'll be fine. He's been sedated – he was very agitated when he came in.'

'None of it is like my Tom.'

I keep thinking he'll walk in and laugh at me for believing it all. *Really? You thought I would do that? I was at a meeting. My car got nicked.* We'd go home, glad it wasn't our drama, and eat pie and chips and watch television.

'Why can't I see him? Are you sure it's him?'

'We're sure. He's being assessed. We have a duty of care to

check all angles before he comes to the ward. If I were you, I'd go and get some rest. You'll need your energy for the coming weeks.'

She smiles at me, and goes out again. I lean back in the chair and close my eyes. I feel absolutely shattered but fired up at the same time, desperate to sleep but restless and as if I need someone to shout at. This is the first time I've been alone since I was 'arrested' at work. What did she mean about needing energy for weeks? Are they going to keep him, stop me seeing him? Last night he was my husband, my Tom, it was just the two of us. How did I get here, alone in a whitewashed room sitting beside an empty bed…?

A thought occurs to me. I pick up his phone. We've always trusted each other but if he'd succeeded in his mission, I would have inherited his personal effects and the phone would be mine. My fingers tap in the security code. I have one eye on the door. My inner voice tells me my behaviour is unacceptable, but I read the texts anyway.

'Tom, where are you?'

'Tom, you're bang out of order now.'

'For goodness' sake, you said you could commit.'

'Liddie's upset. She thinks you're staying away because of the baby.'

These are all from Dawn. Who is Dawn? Liddie? The baby? Oh, my goodness, how could I be so stupid? He's having an affair, he's got someone pregnant. He couldn't bear to tell me, knowing how much I want a baby, and he's taken the coward's way out, telling me in a letter he can't have kids.

Guilt is the explanation.

I actually feel a bit better. I thought it was my fault.

Yes, I think. Tom changed before Christmas. He was behaving very differently at the end of the year. He seemed distracted and, on a couple of occasions, he had said one thing to me and a slightly different version to Adam or Harry; then, when we were all together, he closed the conversation by accusing us of interrogating him. Liddie, his mistress, is developing in my mind: unlike me, she's voluptuous and kind with lots of children. She conceives without effort and lives in a large, clean house waiting to meet his physical and emotional needs without a thought for her own. But if she's his mistress, who's Dawn? Maybe he has two on the go. Or maybe Dawn is a counsellor and Liddie is the girlfriend. Maybe he has lied about fertility, or has a child from an old relationship. Every scenario is playing out in my head in a stupidly chaotic way. Nothing makes sense. This morning I was married to Tom, authentic, trustworthy and reliable. I'm now waiting desperately to see a man I thought I knew, but who actually is he?

The door of the room opens softly, yet again. How many times will they ask me if I'm hungry? My body makes a sharp twist ready to tell them where to stick their hospital muck.

Harry's head peers round the door, his mouth pressed into a weak smile. He looks better – groomed, and back in control. He's out of his suit and mascara-streaked shirt and wearing a warm jumper and some not-so-nice pale trousers.

'Hi, you look like you're about to go off on your summer holidays.'

'I wish.'

I get up and he gives me another of his long hugs before disappearing again without explanation. He returns with a chair from the relatives' room. He plonks it down on the other side of the empty bed and, like he often does, sits on it the wrong way around and leans over the back.

'How you doing, my friend?'

'Okay, thanks. Tom's not back. When he arrives, I may just stab him and finish what he started.' Harry opens his mouth but I speak first. 'Sorry, too much thinking time.'

'Can't be easy.' He draws his chair closer to the bed.

'I read his texts. They're all from a woman called Dawn. He's promised her some kind of commitment... she talks about a baby... it all makes sense now.'

Harry stares at the floor.

'I'm beginning to wonder if anyone knows him. Maybe he's telling different lies to us all and has women and children around the whole country. Isn't that what salesmen do?'

'Siri, stop. You're running away with yourself.'

'I am the safest person for me to run away with, Harry. No one else is making much sense at the moment.'

Harry looks me steadily. 'I know some things.'

'That he has another partner and a baby?'

'No, don't be ridiculous, woman. Dawn is the manager at the café where he helps out.'

'What café? What on earth are you talking about?'

Harry starts to explain. 'A couple of months ago, Tom confided in me. He told me he'd lost his job, that he was lying to you. He was heartbroken he was deceiving you – this is Tom, after all. He doesn't lie. He doesn't need to. He's straightforward and honest and has always been that way – even as a kid. Deceit doesn't come easily.'

'Really.'

'I know you're hurt. But it's been awful for him. He was made redundant at the end of October. He didn't even have a chance to say goodbye to his colleagues; he was humiliated. He wanted to tell you but knew you wouldn't be able to drop hours at work or have IVF if he was unemployed. The longer it went on the more frightened he was that you wouldn't forgive him for the lies, even if you could cope with his loss of income.'

'Does he think I'm that shallow?'

'It wasn't about you. He lost his way; he couldn't see what

was true and what wasn't. Lying was making him ill. He was having panic attacks in the night. When he still hadn't managed to tell you, he told me instead.'

'Did you also know he planned to end his life?'

'You can't be serious. He had black moods when he was in his teens. His father was cruel and bullying. But since he's been with you, he's been fine. I knew he was low but my oldest and best friend tried to kill himself because he felt alone. How do you think that makes me feel?'

'I'm guessing not as bad as me. Why did you call the police?'

'I don't know. I just had a sense. He always calls back. After I called you, I went to the flat. You need to hide the key in a less obvious place! Everything was normal apart from that file. Then I knew.'

Harry's tears are on his chin but I've no room for his distress right now.

'So why has he made a pregnant lady feel paranoid?'

'I honestly don't know about that. What I do know is that when he lost his job, he called and emailed everyone he knew in windows on the south coast, but nothing came up. He needed a base away from this area so he drove for miles, and stumbled on this café which turned into a bit of a safe haven for him.'

'Marvellous. So, I'm saving for fertility treatment and he is drinking our money away in expensive wine bars.'

'No, it's really not like that. The café is more like the community centre where I do a clinic. All his new friends have problems. Dawn's the woman who owns the café. I went there one time to meet up with him. It's an escape from reality for him.'

'Is he cheating on me?'

'He couldn't. I've known him since he was six and he just couldn't. He wasn't really talking to me, and I've been so busy I didn't call him.'

'I feel so guilty. I shouted at him for being selfish and childish, even though I knew he was worried and stressed. Then the next minute he seemed fine – he didn't seem depressed. He was happy yesterday…'

'Someone at work told me it's common for people who have decided to kill themselves to cheer up when they have made a plan. When they think they've found a solution.'

'How can he possibly have thought that was a solution? What about us?'

It's almost a relief when another male stranger comes in.

'I'm Oscar Reubens, one of the psychiatric liaison nurses working here. Tom is still being assessed. He doesn't want to see anyone this evening, but he says he'll see you both tomorrow.'

'What? He has to see us. He can't do this and then say that! Where is he? I'll talk to him myself.'

'Siri, sit down,' Harry orders. 'It would be good for you as well as Tom to have some rest, and then talk properly tomorrow.' He turns to Oscar. 'Will they section him?'

'I don't think so, but I haven't been in on the whole assessment. The police have gone now.' Then Oscar says to me, 'It would definitely be good for you to get some rest and a break.'

'I feel guilty leaving him.'

'He's in good hands.'

As we walk out, Harry has his arm round my shoulders. I allow myself to lean into him.

'He is in good hands,' Harry repeats as he takes my bag from me.

'We're not good hands, are we? He doesn't want us.'

'He needs some time to rest and think, get a clear head. I've taken the weekend off, got everything covered at the unit, so we can go and get food and sleep. Your place or mine, Mrs C?'

'I'm not sure Harry; I need a bath and sleep. I want to be back here early tomorrow in case Tom asks to see me.'

'You won't relax if you go home. You'll wind yourself up with thoughts of your wayward husband and his harems of women. Let's go by your place and pick up your things, and you can have a soak in my new bathroom while I cook your supper. No point in us both being alone and miserable. I can't help Tom right now but he won't forgive me if he finds out I left you on your own. This way we will both be fresh and alert for when he returns to himself tomorrow.'

'I hope you're right.' Doing as men tell me is a new habit I'd be reluctant to admit I'm quite enjoying.

Harry's bath is easily twice the size of ours. I could be at a luxury spa: the bath makes bubbles; a TV is fixed to the wall and a new white dressing gown hangs on the back of the door for me. My mind allows me brief moments of relaxation interspersed with massive heart jolts back to reality and sharp images of Tom alone getting ready to die.

My mind is tracking over the last year, reminding me of all Tom said and did to show how helpless he was feeling. Why didn't I see?

'Oi, Siri.' Harry's voice is a whisper through the heavy oak door. 'Supper will be ten minutes.'

I feel nauseous, not hungry, as I hide myself in the enormous fluffy gown, but in ten short minutes I am tucking into the fat-laden comfort food Harry has put in front of me. My body tells me I'm starving. I notice I am eating like Adam's children: too fast and with my mouth open. Harry and I enjoy the meal in companionable silence.

Chapter 22

It's still completely dark outside, but my phone tells me it's nearly six. I'm surprised to feel refreshed and well rested.

'I can't find any food in this kitchen,' I shout at Harry, who is still in bed.

'Mm, busy week. Sorry. There's coffee… and frozen croissants in the freezer.'

Harry insists on calling the ward before we set off. I'd phoned before I fell asleep last night and again as soon as I woke up. They told me the same thing when I called both times: Tom's stable, and willing to be visited by us both. I don't think Harry believes a radio presenter is capable of processing a medical update.

'What did they say?' I say, trying not to feel undermined. I'm not a doctor but I'm not stupid.

'He's stable. No changes overnight but they believe he'll make good progress today. He wants to see us.'

I can't resist a smug smile.

We follow the same route through the hospital as we took yesterday. I have lost the terror but can't decide what has replaced it. My body and mind are not yet connecting. I won't believe he's okay until I speak to him and he replies. It was good to be looked after by Harry; food and sleep were what the doctor ordered. I'm trying not to go over and over what Tom has been up to, and search in my head for 'my Tom' instead of the cloudy version who has been living with me.

As we approach his room, my stomach recognises we've been here before and I feel sick. I open the door. He's sitting up in bed, and looks straight at me.

'Siri, I am so, so sorry.' Tears are already pouring down his cheeks. I immediately break the promise I made to myself: seeing him feels too hard; the suppressed emotion of the last two days erupts and I cry too, in a way that is not acceptable in public.

'Nothing matters any more... *I'm* so, so sorry I missed how you were feeling,' is all I can say as I almost fall onto the bed. He holds me tight.

'Didn't expect you to be so bright-eyed this morning, mate,' says Harry, keeping his distance for a moment from the messy emotions around Tom and me. Then, coming closer, 'Shove over.'

The three of us lie on the bed squashed up like children, laughing as we remember a catastrophically bad canal boat holiday that required the same enforced intimacy. What a strange time to be having a belly laugh.

Much as we both love Harry, Tom and I are relieved when he makes an excuse to leave for a few hours.

'Who knows?'

'Only Adam, Harry and me. I haven't told your mum or Gemma – was that wrong?'

'Absolutely not.'

He talks about losing his job. About how he discovered the café with no toilet and the people there. About Dawn. About Lydia.

'I didn't mean to lie. After Leo tossed me out, I felt ashamed, and I didn't want you to worry. I only meant to keep it a secret until I got a new job. But it didn't come. I thought it would all be fine when you got pregnant; it was the last straw finding I was so-called *sperm-free*. Oh I hate that phrase… Then I got it into my head you would have a far, far better life if I left.'

'I thought you were having an affair… it was horrible.'

'I would never, never do that.'

'So this Liddie…?'

'Yes, Lydia. She is sweet, young, naive… but mature too. Her parents are Christians. She doesn't want to hurt them. We got close because we were both hiding something from our family. She's thought a lot about life's big questions, and that's fascinating to me. But of course it was never anything more than that…'

'Are you sure? You sound very attached.'

'Well I sort of am. You'll know when you see her. She's a child. It was nice to be the strong one for someone.'

'Is the father someone at college?'

'Sadly not. A middle-aged bloke, a friend of her tutor. She met him once. I was tempted to wade in, complain to the university… but I had enough problems of my own.' He looks straight at me and gives me the smile I fell in love with. It's beautiful.

I make myself as comfortable as I can lying beside Tom on the bed. He tells me everything he has been keeping to himself. I listen but say little. I am enjoying the sound of his voice, the nuances that are familiar but that I have stopped noticing: the way he swallows before he laughs, the crinkle of his forehead when he is serious, and the smile in his eyes.

By the time Tom has finished telling me about his café crew, I feel like I know them too. 'I guess I should be grateful to Dawn for guessing and calling you out? What's she like?'

'Hard to describe. She's not someone who'd be in our social

group. She got pregnant young, I guess that's why she mothers Liddie. Adam would describe her as broad in the beam, your mother would say she's a right nosy parker and Harry would say she's loquacious.'

'What does that mean?'

'Like you, she's good with words and has a lot of them.' I recognise the return of some banter. It's been too long.

Nurse Lisa Black is on duty this morning. 'How're you guys today? Dr Frost is not far away – he's the psychiatrist. He needs to chat to Tom and make a second assessment.'

'Why's that?' Tom mumbles in a tone that he usually keeps inside the house.

'Don't look so worried – it's just routine,' she says as she takes the thermometer out of his mouth and gives it a shake. She then unwraps the Velcro from his arm, folds it up and stuffs it in her uniform pocket.

'All good. You should be okay to go when the doctor's been.' She has a generous smile that lights up her face. A thin silver chain holding a delicate silver cross decorates a slim neck.

'Why don't you go and get some fresh air and let this boy have a sneaky snooze?'

I get the hint. 'Sure.' I rearrange my features to look like I enjoy being told what to do.

It's a bright, warm day that hints at spring. I find a quiet spot on a bench and there's enough sun for me to slip off my jumper. I dial the number Tom gave me. The morning air feels good as it fills my lungs.

'Hello. Can I speak to the manager, please?'

'I've told you twice already this week. No. I will not see you. I don't want to taste new coffee, tea or even arsenic cola. Go do one.' My phone goes silent and I realise the call has been terminated.

I am guessing this is Dawn, my husband's mystery woman. I call again.

'Hello. Is that Dawn? Don't ring off. You don't know me, but I'm Tom's wife.'

'Our Tom? So you must be Siri then. Well, where is he? He hasn't been here for ages. Has he changed his working area?' I feel myself bristle at this reference to our Tom. And she probably presumes I have checked his phone and am calling behind his back.

'Dawn, I know Tom is unemployed and has been working in your café.'

'Well, it's never quite happened actually; he's disappeared off the face of the earth. He's here all the time until I actually invite him to be here, pay him to be here, then he disappears. So, when you catch up with your husband, tell him from me, thanks very much.'

'You don't understand—' I try to stop her flow but fail.

'I haven't been to Carol's all week. She's beside herself – her mother's now got bed sores and she can't turn her on her own. Lydia thinks it's all her fault and is weeping into her chocolate cake…'

'Dawn, I don't think you under—'

'… and I am sick of Peter moaning about his broken computer which Tom used to help him with – as if that and Tom's disappearance are somehow my fault.'

'He's ill. He tried to kill himself.'

The line is completely silent. I know she's still on the line.

'I'm sorry – what did you just say? I think I misheard you—'

'Tom tried to commit suicide. He had some misguided idea that that was the solution to his problems. He's okay though…' A young bloke walks past me, pretending not to notice this hysterical woman who's speaking as if time is running out.

'Oh God. Oh no... Siri... are you still there? Siri? Are you okay?'

'Yes, yes. Sorry. It's been a lot to take in. I haven't got back to myself yet. I wasn't sure Tom would make it but he's okay... He went to Beachy Head. But he was talked down. We're at the hospital now.'

'Oh Siri, how terrible. I mean, your Tom... I know he's been fed up about the job and worried you would find out, but this... I can't believe it. Can I come?'

'Can I let you know? We're still waiting to see the psychiatrist. Please don't tell anyone. His family don't know. He feels ashamed.'

'I won't, don't worry. I'll say he's in hospital with pneumonia – that's what my ex said if he disappeared for a few weeks.'

'Thanks so much... Dawn, can I ask you something?'

'Sure, hun, anything...'

'Can I come to the café when Tom is better? I need to see you all and know for myself where he's been.'

'Course you can. We've wondered who you are and if you exist. Tea Cosy Café, on the main street in Middle Priory. Tell me when you want to come and I'll make sure we have the tea you like.'

I like this woman, I really like this woman.

'Dawn, thank you so much for looking out for Tom.'

'Clearly didn't do so well, did I?'

'Mm, you and me both.'

'Send our love, Siri, and take care of yourself.'

I walk back into the hospital with my head somewhere else. I pass the café. On an impulse I buy some unhealthy food for Tom.

'Did you get through to Dawn? Was she angry and shouty?'

'Yes and no.'

'The psychiatrist came while you were out. He reminded me of Basil Fawlty – he was all legs, and posh. He said he was leaving me a Beck's and would pop back later. I got excited waiting for the beer… He left this form. It's a long questionnaire – will you help me?'

I'm excited by two things. My husband has made a joke, and he has asked for my help. I realise that neither has happened in a while.

I read the title: 'BECK Depression Inventory (BDI)'.

'You have to decide how you've been feeling in the last week. I'm guessing not good? Here goes. Number one. You have to choose one of these options: I feel sad all of the time, I feel sad sometimes, I feel sad hardly at all, I don't feel sad.'

'I don't know how I feel. I don't feel sad at all, a bit ill, embarrassed and stupid but not especially sad.'

I read all the questions. Tom has to decide if he feels guilty, irritated, discouraged or a failure.

He then has to say if he wants more or less sex. We manage a giggle about that. 'It's become an extra job, hasn't it?' I confess.

The psychiatrist comes back just as Tom is pushing a sausage roll into his mouth. I've also got him a pink sparkly doughnut. Dr Basil apologises for interrupting. He picks up the form which is now covered in greasy pastry flakes.

'You haven't completed nine or twenty-one, Tom. Can I ask your wife to leave while we discuss?'

'My wife can stay; we don't have secrets.'

I can't help raising my eyebrows.

'Not any more,' Tom clarifies.

'So number nine. Have you ever had thoughts of killing yourself?'

'I guessed you might know the answer to that one.'

'Well, Tom, do you still feel like that?'

'I don't think I do.' I can see obvious tears in his eyes as they meet mine.

'And question twenty-one asks about your interest in sex. You've left that blank.'

'Right now, I fancy my doughnut. We are focusing on making a baby which has dampened my appetite, but you know what, doctor, I don't think that's any of your business...'

My brother returns at ten. He trips over my bag on his way to give me a hug, and then leans over to embrace Tom.

'What have you done to your leg?'

'Nothing, why?' Adam peers at his legs as if they're a new addition to his body.

'You are walking like the BFG. I noticed it yesterday...'

'Same old – stressed, work on my back, Heather on my back, nothing new, sis. Focus on sick boy here. It's a flying visit to ask if he wants to organise some sessions with the psychologist I saw last year. She's really good, you'll like her. You have to talk, Tom.'

Chapter 23

It's odd walking back into the flat. How can all this have happened in twenty-four hours?

Tom is unshaven and has swollen bags under his dark eyes.

'Go to bed and get some rest.'

For once he does as he is told.

In my favourite chair by the window, it's surprisingly bright and sunny and could easily be summer rather than not quite spring. I swing my legs over the arm in a futile attempt to convince myself I'm fine so I can find enough courage to make a few calls.

'Hi, Sarah. I'll need to take a few days off. I'll let you know more tomorrow. Sorry.'

'No worries, you okay?'

'Absolutely fine, yep, all good.'

'And Tom?'

'Yes he's great. All sorted. Sorry to let you all down.'

'You haven't. Everyone is sending their love.'

Is gossiping, more like. I can imagine the tiny kitchen stuffed with her, Danny and the others. They'll be huddled together in a sinister circle talking in hushed tones.

You will never guess what Siri's husband did.

No one can guess.

Only went and tried to top himself, didn't he?

No way. He doesn't seem the type.

Marilyn will be outside, with an ear close to the door, a vital file in her hand in case they come out.

I'm embarrassed by what Tom has done. That's an awful thing to say but if he'd been in an accident and broken his leg, it would be fine: everyone would send cards, I would secretly relish the attention and time off, and he could enjoy a few days of man pampering. Why is this so different? I've had messages from Mum, Heather, Eleanor and a couple of the neighbours. Everyone wants to know whether Tom's all right, but how do I know? I thought he was three days ago; in fact I thought he was happy…

Familiar hands massaging my shoulders wake me from a shallow trance.

'That wasn't a long rest.' I look up and see my husband, a tired version of the man he was last week. There is nothing very different about his appearance, but somehow I can't work him out. My feelings lurch between terror and a kind of silent rage.

'Couldn't settle,' Tom states without obvious emotion.

He returns quickly with two steaming drinks, pork scratchings, and a packet of carrot and pepper sticks I'd intended as a snack for my Zumba class.

'Thanks. Meat and two veg. We need to stay healthy.' I'm trying desperately to return to normality, but I'm unsure what I'm after, what that will look like. When I broke my wrist, I got a handout about which physio exercises to do, how many repeats were necessary and when I could return to playing sport; when Amelia fell off the climbing frame, Heather was told what to watch for, what the danger signs were, when to rush her back to A and E. So, where's my fact sheet? Why couldn't the lovely nurses Leah or Lisa or Oscar give me a fact sheet entitled 'What to do when your husband tries to kill himself'. How am I supposed to know when he needs blue-lighting back to their care? One of the nurses said, take your time, be kind to yourself, don't push him. Another one said, try and talk, ask the tricky questions, don't be afraid. What does that mean? We drink in silence.

I've done the washing up, made the beds, put a load of washing on; what can I do next to still my internal voices, shut them up?

'Since when did you become a 1950s domestic goddess? Sit down, try and relax.' Tom is stretched out on the carpet in front of me, his hands behind his head like he's sunbathing back in the Maldives with not a care in the world. I can't resolve this. Yesterday he was sitting on the edge of a cliff ready to leave me for ever. How can we ever return to normality? How can I possibly *relax*?

'What you thinking?' Tom bends his neck backwards to look up at me fidgeting from one position to another in the armchair. I can't find easy comfort, but at least I'm sitting.

'That you need to address your nasal hair.' I attempt to laugh but it comes out as a kind of snort.

He doesn't laugh. 'What are you really thinking?'

'You don't want to know.'

'We promised no more secrets, didn't we?'

My mouth blurts out the question I've been withholding, putting what seems an insurmountable wall between us. 'Will you do it again?' It prompts him out of his relaxed mode. I admire his muscular arms as they tense to raise him upwards. He leans his back against my chair, his shoulders and head resting between my thighs.

Then his arms reach behind my legs and embrace my calves.

'I don't think so. There was always part of me that didn't want to jump.'

Perhaps it'll be easier to speak the truth if we don't have to look at each other. 'How close did you come?' I attempt to control my tears, wanting to ask questions like he's just home from an interview that didn't go so well. I let my gaze take in his body, the slope of his shoulders, the lack of hair on the back of his head, trying to erase the image of PC Johnson sitting with the smiley-covered blue death file resting on his lap, Tom's exit plan.

'Very close. It seemed like the only way.'

'What made you change your mind?'

Suddenly, I'm wanting answers to questions too fast.

If only I could check back to the fact sheet. How do I talk to him without making him want to withdraw? What might push him back there? How can I ever forget, forgive him for ruining what I thought we had together, for smashing up the image that other people saw, Tom and Siri, a match made in heaven? From now on everyone will be thinking about what he did, what I drove him to, what he chose...

'You want the truth?'

Do I want the truth? Really, do I?

'Tom, from now on, always, however painful, you have to promise me that...'

'I wanted the pain to stop. Every day for months I'd wake up, feel good for thirty seconds and then my body would remember. The nausea came first and then a deep emptiness I can't explain, just nothingness. My head was full of competing thoughts that made no sense, whirring every minute of the day, no respite, old voices in my head, my father berating me, my mother crying, bullies at school, Leo putting me down. I wanted to be your happy-ever-after, take care of you, live until we were a hundred, surrounded by three generations of beautiful offspring.'

'So why didn't you jump?'

'The bloke up there told me I might screw it up.'

'What?'

'He said people go to those cliffs thinking you can't survive, but lots do, ending up brain damaged or paralysed with no hope of escape.'

'That made you come back, not me?' No, I don't want the truth. I want to hear it was me, my love, that brought him back from the brink, that it was the thought of me finding that stupid file, the thought of our wedding, the thought of our love...

'Don't cry my darling! I couldn't love you any more than I do. But I realised it would be so typical of me to make a mess of it and create even bigger problems. I had really thought you'd be better off. I even believed a seagull told me to jump. Then I thought of if I failed.'

'I'm trying hard to understand. But you were prepared to do that to me. I wouldn't have recovered, nor would Harry. How could you think that was a solution? If you'd got plastered and impulsively taken some pills, maybe I could have grasped your perspective, but you made a file. Who does that? You must have been planning it for weeks, changing bank accounts and insurances... How did you carry on like everything was normal, talking about the online shopping, where to go for our next holiday? It's the most selfish thing you could have done.'

Tom forces his way into the chair beside me. His T-shirt is damp and even his muscular hold does nothing to calm me.

'I'm so sorry, it's so hard to explain. My head was dark, consumed with black thoughts. I was a failure. I couldn't bear your disappointment. It wasn't just a low sperm count. I have no sperm, not a single swimmer, Siri. I can't give you my baby.

I wanted you to find someone to love and give you babies to complete your plan.'

'Tom, you are my plan. I want your baby because I want you; without you there is nothing.' I wrap my arms around his shoulders.

The talking stops. We reconnect. There are no expectations, no thoughts of reproduction. We just give each other love.

Chapter 24

Was Eleanor right? Maybe I should have married someone closer to my age. Watching Tom attempt to get into the passenger seat, it's like watching an elderly gentleman early in the morning. I have to look away. He's running on a slow setting at the moment. I'm trying to be patient.

'I'll drive.'

'It's pretty straightforward until the last couple of miles when you hit the tiny roads.'

'So, you said in your, your…'

'What?'

'Note, scrawl, scribbles…'

'Just say it. Suicide letter.'

'In your letter, you said something about speaking to Adam.'

He's silent for a moment. 'There's something not right. Lying awake last night I realised we've not been looking at him clearly, seeing who he is now.'

'What do you mean?'

'I was chatting to one of the nurses… She said, who's the chap with the film-star looks and luscious eyes? – she wanted an introduction! I told her he's my brother-in-law. She said, I bet he's not short of admirers. Don't suppose he's single? I'd accept divorced. I told her how Harry and I have always been jealous of his effortless style and people skills. After she'd gone I realised I was describing the Adam I first knew.'

'I don't understand.'

'I tried to speak to him the day after I got the results. I'd expected him to be kind and to offer to help in some way.'

'But he didn't?'

'He just wanted to drink. He didn't seem to be listening. He missed the point, and I lost my nerve, and didn't end up managing to tell him the whole story. His behaviour was completely out of character…' Tom tails off, his face serious, searching internally for more information.

'Yet he texted me and told me to be kind to you. I thought you'd had a heart-to-heart with him about work and me.'

'That's who Adam is, isn't it? The bloke who does right by me, you, Heather, everyone, but he's not like that all the time now, is he?'

'I don't know, Tom.'

'You don't know, or you don't want to know?'

'Don't Tom. Let's not argue. It's my first visit to meet your friends and I don't want to arrive feeling angry with you…'

I break off to check what the satnav is telling me and before I attempt to make peace with him, Tom is once again sinking into a deep sleep. His head jerks forward, startling him back into momentary alertness before he nods back off. This happens again and again but he's so exhausted he doesn't wake. The staff nurse's parting words were, you ought to take at least a week's leave, get your GP to sign you off.

'I'm sure Leo will understand,' I'd said. Tom hadn't laughed.

For today's visit to his friends, Tom had wanted to arrive for twelve-thirty; he says that's his favourite café time when everyone's usually around. He called it 'misfit family time'. I hope he didn't see my shoulders hunch.

They sound like the sort of people I would give a very wide berth. What do they think of me? A wife of whom her husband is scared – too scared to tell even about something as massive as losing his job. Will they resent me for barging into their world? It's more terrifying than meeting his family.

My breathing speeds up as I see the sign 'Welcome to Middle Priory'. I jab my elbow a bit too hard into an unresponsive body.

'Ouch.'

'We're here. Where am I going?' *Why* am I going? is the question I suppress.

'There! You need to take the next turning on the right to park.' Tom has perked up a little too quickly. Ha, it must be the thought of being with his besties. I can't believe he has done this journey several times a week to get away from our home. What am I doing here? I can't help feeling jealous. I've been oblivious to what's going on and he's been solving the world's problems with a pretty teenager.

In my nightmares, roses hang round the door of his haven. But the entrance to the café is poised precariously on the corner of a busy junction. A clunky bell makes an unusual sound as we go in, but I smell the comforting aroma of toast. Tom reminds me of a preschool child as he points to a yellow floral sign. 'I bought that.'

'Why?'

'Dawn moaned endlessly when customers barged in after closing time so I purchased an open and closed sign from the hardware shop at the top of the hill.'

'He's a right know-it-all, isn't he?' The slightly raucous voice suggests a man, but belongs to an attractive brunette with laughing eyes. 'Tom, it's so good to see you. Give me a hug. We've missed you. Lydia is meeting a social worker at twelve but has left strict instructions not to let you go.'

I furtively glance around for a target for my gaze; I'm the gooseberry with a romantic couple on a first date or a child at a party for grown-ups.

'Thanks, Dawn. You might as well say, welcome back, you lying mental person.'

'Ah, you know we love you – and what do you mean? Didn't I give you the keys to my castle after knowing you for five minutes? I knew I could trust you, Mr Cleary – I made you a cappuccino before you paid! And you must be Siri. It's lovely to meet you. We wondered if you were a figment of his imagination. Can I give you a hug too?' I get the feeling no is not an option. The familiar sting of tears is threatening my vision. Dawn opens her arms and holds me tight. 'We're so glad you're both here. Sit yourselves down and I'll make some drinks.'

Tom leads me through to what I thought was the storeroom but it turns out to be a small snug with a mix of velvet armchairs, three wonky old tables and three wooden chairs that wouldn't look out of place at the council tip. I'm struggling to see the appeal.

'Surprise!' Dawn shrieks as if pulling back a curtain on a bunch of unexpected guests at a secret celebration.

'What are *you* doing here?' Tom and I speak in unison.

'I've been a few times, haven't I?' a man dressed for the countryside says to Dawn. Harry is unashamedly positioned on what is apparently Tom's table. He wouldn't stand out at a point-to-point in deepest Surrey.

'Get that posh thing off my table.' Tom flicks Harry's tweed cap onto a chair.

'How come?' I ask, feeling like I've just arrived on an undiscovered planet that everyone else discovered years before.

'I took the week off, but with you two all coupled up, I needed some company. Dawn said yesterday you two might pitch up today.'

'Did she now?' I can't quite work out the fleeting glimpse that goes from Harry to Dawn. I'm guessing Harry has been giving her the low-down on me.

We went and sat down in the main part of the café and stayed there for three hours. I understand how Tom felt when he first met my relatives.

Cilla fired a rapid succession of questions at me. 'What do you do? Where do you live? Don't you think you're lucky having Tom? How's he feeling? Has he recovered?'

I start to answer but Dawn takes over. 'Pneumonia is like that – lasting fatigue, a long road, early days.'

I add, 'Dawn is spot on. The hospital warned us it will take a while to get back to normal.'

Dawn winks at me. 'I remember from when my son's dad had it.'

'How's your belly off for spots, fella?'

I look at Tom. I thought it was Cilla who had dementia.

'Not so bad, thanks.' Tom obviously understands the code. He catches my eye over the top of Peter's iPad which he's been given to sort. 'It means how are you?'

A young girl with bulky earphones hanging round her neck comes through the door with a brown satchel dragging behind her, and I know it's Lydia. I try to keep my gaze steady but feel giddy: this is Tom's confidante.

She looks even younger than I'd imagined. I'd have guessed she was in her mid-teens. She has naturally blonde hair, no make-up, very pretty – and definitely a girl not a woman, and thin, which makes her just visible rounded stomach all the more striking. My face flushes hot as she catches my eyes dropping to her belly. Tom hugs her tight and my stomach turns over watching him embrace a female in the biological state I long for. But I can see Tom has been telling the truth. He looks at home. He goes into the back room with Harry, leaving me with Dawn and Lydia.

I stick out my hand. 'You must be Tom's great friend Liddie.'

She ignores my hand and launches at me for a hug. I can feel her firm belly pushing into my flat one.

'He's such an old man, your bloke, isn't he?' Liddie says deliberately.

'Watch it you!' he shouts back.

'I guess so.' It's hard to see such natural banter between my husband and a female I don't know. I have to stifle the urge to say something a little bit spiteful.

Lydia rubs her hands together in a perfect impression of Tom when he can't open the sandwich bags.

'Did Tom tell you I'm pregnant?'

'Are you okay?' I ask.

'I think so. Tom and Dawn have been like parents.'

Dawn hands me a piece of kitchen roll to wipe my leaking eyes. It's so frustrating. What's happening to me? I'm not a needy studio guest, relieved to be able to spew out emotions on whoever is with me.

'Sorry, I didn't mean to be rude about him. He's young at heart. And I'm glad he's told you. My parents don't know what I've done. It's horrible, makes me feel sick all the time.'

'I'm sure if they love you, they'll understand.'

'I bet Tom has told you my family are mad religious folk. They're not, honestly. They're just genuine Christians who walk the Sunday talk. I know God always forgives, and they would too. I'm just not yet ready to be real with either them or God.'

She rambles on as if unaware her listener is a virtual stranger.

'Will the dad want to be involved?'

'He's married with kids; he knows about the baby but I don't think he'll be back in touch.'

It can't be that simple. I think of all the messiness, all the potential conflict and heartbreak. Who is the wife? Has he ever done this before? More than once? Often, even? But I change the subject. 'Tom said you're at college.'

'Yes, I was going to drop out, but Tom persuaded me not to. College have been supportive. My tutor has worked out now it was his friend who slept with me so it's all hideously awkward. He's leaving at the end of term though. I'm so embarrassed.'

'That's awful, Lydia. They're the ones who should be embarrassed, not you. If it was a student, I could maybe understand, but a grown man should know better.'

She shrugs, and I know that she is the one carrying all the guilt.

A voice behind me interrupts. 'Come on, you. I'm shattered. Lydia, give me my wife back please. She's my driver.'

'She's your replacement as far as I'm concerned. I have no idea what she sees in you.'

Tom laughs. What a good sound that is. 'Enough of your cheek, young lady.'

'Now I see what you mean about sounding like an old dad.' My mind doesn't know how to process the thought of Tom seeming like a dad when I'd have loved that for us. But there is no discomfort with her; this kid could fit into our lives. 'You and Dawn must come for supper some time.' Tom raises his eyebrows but looks like he's been awarded a prize.

'I'd really like that.'

Tom and I leave arm in arm. Harry stays behind engrossed in a conversation with Dawn about Carol's mum.

'He'll be there for the rest of the day. Once Dawn gets started, there is no stopping the flow. Even if Harry's pager shouts a medical emergency, she could keep him stuck. I've spent many an hour trying to escape her stories.'

We're nearly at the car when we hear the footsteps of someone rushing to catch us up.

'Sorry, sorry, wanted to ask when you might be back at work.' We turn simultaneously and there's Dawn, with cherry cheeks and out of breath. She apologises again. 'Sorry to ask… but do you reckon you can be back Monday? I have four potential customers on hold – I just can't manage the healthy meals and the café.'

Tom looks at me for a cue and I nod enthusiastically. 'Go for it.'

'See you Monday.'

'Can you make nine?'

'Now you're pushing your luck! Eleven is my best offer. I'm supposed to be resting.'

'Deal. See you then.'

Back in the car, Tom's looking at me expectantly. 'So?'

'I totally get it.'

'What?'

'Why you came here, why you stayed, and how you managed to separate yourself from your life at home and become a café person, not my husband.'

'Thank you,' Tom says quietly.

'But it's going to take some time to get my head around what else you did.'

Tom pretends he's fallen asleep, one of a number of strategies he's using to escape from difficult conversations. An unresolved silence plays for the rest of the drive.

Chapter 25

Tom

The alarm clock Gemma gave me for my birthday informs me it's only 6.45am. We left the price sticker on the top as it made Siri and I shriek with laughter for days. The original white sticker is now a faded grey and you have to squint to read what it says: 99p. The gift perfectly reflects how much I mean to my only sister.

My head feels too weighty to lift and my mind is puzzling over what day it is. I'm in my own bed, with our pinstriped black and purple duvet colour. The smell declares the bedding to be freshly washed and for once all four pillowcases match.

I sit up to receive the padded tray Siri is carrying. She carefully lays it on my lower half. Breakfast for me, two cups of strong coffee and some sugar lumps in a bowl with delicate silver tongs I've never seen before.

'Good morning, Sir Cleary. I see you have all the pillows for your throne.' She laughs but then ruins it with an insult. 'I'm afraid you still remind me of a man without a permanent home.'

'Thanks. Given up on green tea and insipid unleaded coffee then?'

'Yep, guzzling caffeine to make up for lost time. There has to be some prize for giving up on conception.'

My breakfast in bed is laid out as if for a hotel guest: a white china pot of jam and two rounds of granary toast, already buttered. In case I'm tempted by the knife, I wonder.

'Have I missed Christmas?' This new routine is getting a bit much.

'I want to make a fresh start, Tom... get back to how we were when we were first together.'

'Me too but breakfast before seven is extreme.'

'It's important to have intimacy time. How you feeling?' My wife holds the back of her hand against my forehead. 'You're a bit hot. Do you want some water? Shall I open a window?'

'Siri, stop! I haven't got a temperature. You've got to stop fussing.' We've had a good few days, but each one has started with a couple's breakfast like we're on holiday. 'You've got to trust me.'

'I do.'

'No, you don't. You're watching me like a hawk, cooking and cleaning like my mother, refusing to work. It's making me claustrophobic – you have to sort it out!'

In hindsight, I should have chosen my words more carefully.

Her voice is a high-pitched screech. I haven't experienced this since I've been home.

'Can I point out that your mother has never nurtured you?'

I open my mouth to say I was using the term 'mother' in a generic sense but before I can form any words, she erupts.

'I have to sort it out? You've been deceiving me for months, creating a virtual world, acting like a teenager and then, as a favour to me, you decide to top yourself.'

Her words are interrupted by a gut-wrenching sob. But whereas usually she would rush off and do some cleaning or whip her trainers on for a 5k, today she slithers up the bed and tucks her head under my chin.

The canvas of our wedding day hangs on the wall facing the end of our bed. It's not quite straight. Siri and I are gazing at each other, full of fresh hope and expectation. Harry's arm is in the air, a newly released bouquet is captured at the edge of the photograph and Adam is looking so young, so handsome, so proud.

'I need you to tell me more,' she says gripping my hand.

I explain everything, from the moment I walked out of my office to the moment in the garage when I purchased what I thought would be my last tank of fuel.

'The nurse said you're clinically depressed.'

'It's not that simple. I don't think I'm depressed, and Harry agrees and he knows me better than anyone.'

'Thanks.'

'Oh, you know I didn't mean it like that.'

'You need to take medication. I have to know you will be safe.'

'I haven't collected the prescription because I'm not going to do that, Siri. I understand you want to solve the problem for me. But you can't. It's me who needs to take responsibility now and work things out like a grown up.'

'But it's what the doctors told you to do when they discharged you. What if you end up…' I can see her eyes filling with tears again. It's a rare moment right now when one of us isn't crying, on the brink of crying or wiping tears away.

'I understand you're scared. Sometimes I worry I might do it again, but if we're going to survive this, we need to draw a line under it and trust each other again.'

My phone rings creating a welcome pause. Siri goes off for refills; my hand finds the handset under the mattress.

The display says 'Ad'. Underneath, in smaller letters, the

screen confirms 'Siri's brother'. I remember writing his full name in my contacts at our first meeting, a barbecue at his house; it was his birthday.

My phone is grubby but at least it tells me the day and the date. I press answer.

'Hey Tommy, you driving to work?'

'The work joke is wearing thin, Ad, especially before sunrise, on a Saturday. Why you calling now?'

'I just wanted to check you got my text about the address for Dr Funnell.'

'I did.'

'You need to go, mate. At least do a few sessions, just in case.'

'Don't worry. Siri is not planning to let me off that hook.'

Siri comes back huddled in an oversized dressing gown, skinny ankles poking out of the ridiculous elephant slippers I purchased as a joke for the family Secret Santa.

She mouths, 'Who?' I point at the photograph of her brother.

'Adam? Ask him to meet us.'

'Can we meet up for a chat tomorrow evening?'

'Good idea. We need a catch up. Just you and me?'

'Me, you and your sister.'

'Sounds serious. Am I in trouble?'

'Just be good to catch up. A lot has happened this last month.'

'You can say that again, Mr Rock Climber. I'll check with her indoors.'

'Shall we do the Black Horse at six? Tomorrow unless we hear otherwise?'

'Good plan. See you then. Bye.'

'Did he just say what I think he did?'

'What?'

'Rock climber?' Her face is forced into a classic Siri frown.

'Yes, his sensitivity dial has broken, or certainly been turned down a few notches.'

'I woke up early dreaming Adam was a pirate and Heather was furious. Maybe the stuff I avoid goes into my dreams.'

'Are you admitting that you've noticed changes?'

'Yeah, it's up and down, but there is something that doesn't hang together, isn't there? It was kind of him to help organise the counselling for you… but to get you drunk when you needed help… that's not Adam.'

'After you fell asleep last night, I got up to search through some old photo albums.'

'I didn't hear you get up. What were you looking for?'

'I dunno, couldn't sleep. I was looking at our wedding photos but also found some from when Heather first had Amelia. Remember how fussy he was about the way he looked – Mr Immaculate. Wouldn't go out in the evening without changing, always ahead of trend, voted best dressed fresher at uni. When he arrived at the hospital he had food down his trousers.'

'To be fair, Siri, the police had called to say I'd been involved in an accident.'

'I get that, but he's often unshaven, and he's walking funny. Watch him from behind – he lurches, maybe that's why he keeps falling. Think how many times he's been to A and E in the last four years, more than the children or my elderly mother.'

'Stress can do that. I thought I'd got dementia. I've driven to the wrong place, forgotten what I was saying. When you're constantly thinking about other stuff, you do all sorts of odd things and you can't hear other people. You're in your own head all the time.'

'Maybe we should confront him, say what we've noticed, suggest he goes to his GP?'

'Let's see how he is tomorrow. You ought to get going if you're to be in the studio by twelve.'

'I can't believe I agreed to cover a Saturday. Bet you can't wait to get rid of me.'

Before I can answer, my face leaks an unacceptable answer and a pillow is hurled at my head. Cold coffee from an upturned mug spills over the clean bedlinen. Neither of us cares.

Siri has gone to work, a huge relief to me and her producer.

In our bedroom is my new work attire. I'm ashamed to notice myself feel a flutter of excitement. A courier arrived yesterday holding a parcel addressed to me. On the reverse, the return address was the café.

Siri carried it through to our room and we perched on the end of our bed hunched over the package like it was Christmas morning. We both gave it a shake, I squeezed it, and Siri tried to guess its contents. I couldn't think what Dawn might post. Inside was a see-through bag containing what looked like a white linen tablecloth. The label stuck on the plastic said 'Men's size medium'.

I pulled it out. Siri took the wrapping, still in parent mode. It was an apron. On the front was a multi-coloured illustration of a man with rosy cheeks wearing a tall chef's hat with a floppy top. He was flipping pancakes. The writing above the cartoon declared: 'This apron belongs to Tom, the manager'.

The bell clatters. It still needs fixing. This familiar space throws up a new feeling of uncertainty. The sense of relief is enormous, but two worlds merging is a strange experience. It's not dissimilar to when your old friends meet a new group; it should feel positive but the new pressure is on you as the common denominator to ensure they blend.

'It's Billy!' a familiar voice shouts from the back room. I can only see Dawn's back view; her head is buried in the fridge.

'Do you now have eyes in the back of your head?'

'Nah, Liddie saw you coming down the hill. She's very excited.'

'Where is she then?'

'Gone upstairs to the office to get something, I think.'

Black leggings are running too fast down less than solid wooden stairs, closely followed by a black hoodie and finally a blonde ponytail swishing in time with the pace. Before I can shift my discomfort at the prospect of being confronted with her expanding midriff, Lydia is in my arms hugging me as if she'll never let me go.

'I have missed you so much, old man. I have loads to tell you. Your mate Harry came in three times last week. When Dawn sees him she's like an excited guinea pig.'

'I'm not sure what that looks like. I haven't paid much attention to the emotions of vermin.'

She giggles. 'We've always had guinea pigs, much to my dad's disgust. He says they stink. When they're happy, they squeak and clap their ankles together like Dorothy from the *Wizard of Oz*... It's called popcorning...'

'I learn something new every time we speak.'

We sit at my old table. Dawn has obviously been busy; it's stopped wobbling and the carpet has been cleaned.

'So, what else have I missed?'

Lydia thrusts a small flat parcel at me. But it's hard to pull my eyes away from her middle, to not think about the unwanted life growing in there. The tears are coming again. This happens so frequently now I hardly notice.

'You can open that, you know.'

I carefully undo her parcel. It seems to be a flimsy piece of paper wrapped in pink tissue and sealed with a gold heart shape. I am guessing it's a handmade card to welcome me back. It takes me longer than it should to recognise the grey picture with a thin white edge round its perimeter. At first, I think it's an old photograph: it's grainy and unclear. But the blurry white areas are unmistakably a baby. Two light grey ovals fused together and ten obvious toes. I swallow and try hard to push down the sob that threatens to erupt out of what feels like my whole body.

'Liddie, it's beautiful. It's your baby.' I force a smile. Can she see my anguish?

'Tom, it's your baby.'

There are tears running down her flawless skin.

'Lydia…'

'Tom! It's the answer. You must be able to see that. I promise you it's what I want… I feel almost as if you've been given to me just for this, even though I don't deserve it. It would make it okay, and it would make things okay with you and Siri. You can see that, can't you… please, Tom—'

'Lydia, it's beautiful of you. I don't know what to say… but no, no, I can't, I couldn't…' I'm crying. I can hardly hear my own words. Her childlike trust, her faith – and her faith in me. How could I even begin to take this on, now? I look at her face, shining with tears, imploring me. 'No, Liddie, I can't…' I whisper. I can't, I can't. I lay the scan photo down on the table. Somehow I reach the door of the café.

All I can hear is Dawn's voice, very far away. 'Tom, you can't just flipping…' Then utter silence.

Chapter 26

'Hello, mate. How you doing? Can you hear me? The signal's not great.'

'Yep, all good, you?'

'Just checking, you and Selma still on for this eve?'

'Yep, all good, we're on our way now.'

'Me too, see you in a bit.'

Siri places two half pints of Coke on the sticky table.

'We not drinking?'

'I didn't think alcohol and depression were a good mix. It's a depressant. You okay, hun? You're still very pale.' She looks at me with the face of a concerned parent. It's the expression she currently wears most frequently and it's doing my head in. How can I recover our relationship, forget what I did, when she's constantly peering at me like the mother I needed when I was five?

But I just say, 'Where's your brother? He should've been here first.'

'Yeah, we said six; it's nearly seven. Maybe he's forgotten.'

'But he called—'

As if he's been outside waiting for a formal announcement, in swaggers Adam looking like he has showered in his clothes.

'Is it raining?' Siri asks.

'Sorry, guys, I was halfway home before I realised I should be here.'

He looks at his phone and realises that there is a voicemail from Heather. The handset is put on speakerphone and deposited upside down on the sticky table. 'Again! Thanks for that. I presume you are somewhere else. I'm at your daughter's school in case you're wondering. Call me.' Heather's exasperation is all too evident.

He flips his phone over, deletes his wife and attempts to peel off his cardigan. Siri goes round to help him shuffle himself out of the arms.

'It's boiling in here.'

'Think it's just you. Are you not going to call Heather? She sounds cross.' Siri sits back down and pulls her coat tighter.

'She's always cross.'

'Sounds important. Is it Amelia?'

'Another parents' evening, no doubt. I will pick up some flowers at the garage on the way home.'

Siri throws her brother the scowl of disappointment. I know it well.

'I'm soaked through to my pants. I forgot I was meeting you here, went to the Berwick Inn by mistake. I ordered a drink then realised where I was meant to be. I left my umbrella behind. Need the toilet, back in five.'

He stumbles up. He is walking like he has been on a fairground ride: it looks very strange.

'He's not got a coat,' I comment.

'I know – shorts and T-shirt seem a bit optimistic even with a winter cardi.'

'What's he doing in there? He's been ages. Should I check on him?'

'Give him five more minutes. You don't think he's snorting cocaine, do you?'

'Siri, you have been watching too much TV.'

When Adam returns, he seems steadier. Probably not cocaine.

'You want your usual, Adam?'

As I lean against the bar waiting to be served, I watch my wife with her beloved brother. There is no mistaking their matching raven hair and round eyes. Adam is jiggling and shuffling like he needs the toilet again.

I notice my hands are trembling as I attempt to carry a tray of three precariously positioned pint glasses a few metres across a crowded bar. I don't want to meet my wife's eyes when she sees I've defied the no alcohol rule.

'Here you go. If you take yours, Adam,' I say to his back, 'I can put these down on…' Inexplicably, Adam staggers to his feet but misjudges the space; his elbow rams into me and three drinks go flying. Adam goes crimson, and turns towards the door.

'Sit back down, Adam, and settle down.' I copy Harry's calm authority but my mind tells me it lacks his charisma. 'I'll go and get some more drinks. Look, the barman is already on his way over to clear up.'

'Tom, we don't need more beer. Get Adam a Coke as well.'

'Adam, are you on drugs?' Siri splutters before he has a chance to sit down again.

'What?' Adam looks horrified by his sister's accusation. He's a good liar if he is, but who am I to judge? His hand flies to his head as if we're talking about an outbreak of head lice.

'Siri is just concerned, mate. You seem different – you're all over the place and a bit distracted. If something's up, we want to help.'

There is a brief silence. He looks at the wall. 'I'm pretty sure

I've got cancer.' His body is too stretched out for the pew. He looks like he's trying to get comfy in bed. I wonder if he's going to slide off the seat. He doesn't seem able to bend.

We were thinking work, the kids, money, drugs, drink, but neither of us had thought ill.

'Have you seen a doctor?'

'Yesterday. She was non-committal. I've Googled the symptoms. I think it's brain cancer, sis, or a tumour, or possibly motor neurone disease – that thing Stephen Hawking had.'

'What makes you think that?' I keep my voice even, defying the inner shake that's in my belly.

'How many times have I been at Minor Injuries this year? On my last visit, the nurse bandaged up my hand avoiding eye contact, then gave me a leaflet. She said, there's no reason to feel ashamed, Mr Markham – it happens to men too. Can you believe it? It was a leaflet on male domestic abuse. She thought Hev was beating me up.' He throws back his head and laughs for longer than would be expected even with a joke that was actually funny. Siri doesn't join in.

'It could be stress, couldn't it?' I say. 'Look at me. I drove home one day instead of going to the supermarket, and had two bumper crashes before I realised my mind was completely elsewhere.'

'I've had my final warning. The police insisted I made an appointment with my GP.'

'The police?' Siri and I are doing a lot of synchronised responding at the moment.

'It's why I went to see the doctor. I was driving to see a new client. I was looking at the house names and didn't see a junction. I went straight across, nearly crashing into an old bloke.'

'Oh no! Was he okay?'

'Yep, he was fine, the postbox less so. But the police turned up and breathalysed me.'

'Adam, you'd been drinking. How could you?'

'Thanks, sis, glad I can rely on your loyalty when times are tough. No, it was lunchtime.'

'Ah, that's okay then... sorry.'

'Well, they didn't believe me either. They said my behaviour was consistent with an altered state of mind, so they took me to the station for a drugs test. Before you ask, that was negative. The police doc was called. I had to stay in a cell. He said my symptoms have a neurological feel.'

'What does that mean?' I ask, gently pulling my wife back so she's a more appropriate distance from her brother's face.

'Something to do with my brain.'

'So did the GP think it was something serious?' I ask, hoping the police doc was in a hurry, keen to find a plausible non-criminal explanation and get on his way.

'She agreed that something isn't right, but she wasn't prepared to guess. She hit my knees with a hammer, asked me to touch my nose without looking, walk on a line. It felt easy, but when I opened my eyes, I was way off.'

'You need to see a specialist. We can pay. You can't leave it there.' I can hear the parent tone returning to Siri's voice.

'Don't panic, sis, it's in hand. She's sending me for a scan and more tests... But Heather won't cope if I have something wrong with me. I'm not insured for critical illness. We'll lose the house and the girls will have to go to the comprehensive school.'

'Adam, don't go so fast.' That's what Harry says to me when everything feels insurmountable.

'You need to wait for the test results. People are always calling into the programme to say a GP has screwed up. They're not specialists.' The intensity of his sister's gaze leaks a fear I've seen a lot of recently.

'Please don't tell Heather or Mum.'

I open my mouth to reassure him it's probably all routine stuff, but I've made a promise to stop lying.

Chapter 27

'Tom.'

Siri's voice breaks through my dream about a white van cutting me up on an aircraft runway. In the depths of the night, my mind is doing strange things right now.

'Tom.'

'I'm coming,' I shout back, my voice hoarse and tired.

'Have you eaten my homemade granola? There's hardly any left.' A grumpy lady follows me to the toilet. I catch a glimpse of my prominent forehead in the bathroom mirror. They say worry increases hair loss. I hope this psychologist calms me down.

'I thought you once promised to give me all that you had. Doesn't that include oats?' I reply over my shoulder.

'I made that cereal to last me all week. You need a new dressing gown. That old thing is awful. Your mother would be horrified.'

'Fortunately, my mother and my dressing gown won't be catching up any time soon.'

'Why does she even want me to come? It's not me who did it.'

Siri has put on the yellow gloves and is scrubbing the toilet bowl with bleach.

'What?'

'The psychologist. Why do I have to come with you?'

'I'm not totally sure. But at my initial assessment last week, she asked you to come for my second appointment to give what she called an observer's perspective.'

'She thinks I watched from the side-lines while you got increasingly depressed and did nothing. She thinks I don't care.'

'She knows you care, because I told her. She just wants your view of how I was, leading up to the crisis.'

'You say crisis as if it wasn't anything to do with you.'

'How would you like me to describe it? My suicide attempt, the day I sought help from Beachy Head, an afternoon at the cliffs…? Apparently it's routine in cases like ours to meet a partner.'

'I don't want to be a case.'

'Better than being a nutcase like your old man.'

'Ha.' At least, she's laughing at my jokes again even if it's with fake glee.

'Can you please let me get out of the bathroom before you spread that everywhere. It stinks and I've only just woken up. If we're going be on time, I need to get ready.'

She pulls off the gloves and shoves them back behind the pipes, marching off to wherever she came from.

I know that really, being Siri, she wants to come with me. I guessed it was hard for her last week, knowing I was there without her, without her prompts, without her opinions. But she's defending herself, trying to detach herself a bit from my mess; when she can't influence a situation, she tries to pretend she doesn't want to.

So last week I had my first appointment with the psychologist, Dr Lucy Funnell. I knew exactly what Gemma and Leo would say about me seeing an *–ologist.* In that conversation, the speakers would be interchangeable.

Poor Tom, never a coper, was he?

Heard he has now gone properly off his rocker.

Yes, he's off to see the mental doctor.

Perhaps she'll lock him up.

Probably for the best.

The appointment was at her home. She said she was moving to a new building as of the following week. Dr Funnell was more normal than I'd imagined: no sign of a white coat, and I sat in a regular armchair. My hands failed to discover the switch to recline it into a psychiatrist's couch.

My mother would describe Dr Funnell as having worn well for her menopausal years.

'Call me Lucy,' she commanded. 'And may I call you Tom?'

I told her to go ahead.

'So, Tom, tell me why are you seeking help now.'

'I'm not, exactly. I've been persuaded to.' It was Adam and Siri who'd insisted.

'Are you always so obedient?'

'No, but I visited Beachy Head, so I'm down on Brownie points.' She was the first person not to looked shocked by that shameful disclosure.

'Do you feel able to tell me what has been going on in your mind over the last few days?'

'I have constant disaster movies running in my head, playing over and over on a loop, every time I close my eyes. The images dance on my eyelids like a permanent live stream.'

'What happens at the end of these movies?' she asked.

'I'm an amazing film producer. I create a variety of endings, testing each one out many times to see which one is most likely, looking to create a Gantt chart of actions – if this happens, I can do that, if that, try this…'

'This all sounds very familiar.'

'It does?'

'Oh yes. The human mind is always looking to catastrophise, to transport us in a TARDIS, whizz us back to regrets and forward to the next *Titanic*. It's exhausting when our flawed minds don't let up, isn't it?' With her head postured at an unusual angle, she diagnosed my childhood as 'perhaps emotionally impoverished?' At the end of the session she presented me with a wide range of negative thoughts that had reportedly leaked from my narrative. *I'm a failure. I was never going to amount to anything. I have to protect Siri. I will screw up. There is no point to my life. Harry is so successful. I can't keep a job. I'm spermless… infertile… jobless. Can't even kill myself. Not good enough.* She labelled me a classic over-thinker.

'Very common,' she said. 'I'm the same.'

She showed me a couple of slick ways to better manage my ill-disciplined mind.

'Bring your wife next time,' she instructed as I left. 'It'll be in my new office in Old Church Road.'

Our joint appointment is in a modern office block in the town centre. The plaques on the outside wall indicate the block is home to several businesses – ASB Law, Old Mill Dentistry and Mind Your Head Psychology. At least if we're seen going in, people might think we are consulting a divorce lawyer rather than a shrink. As we go in, I pull Siri from behind me as if she's a child trying to stay hidden behind her mummy.

A lady behind an intimidating desk awaits while two men in suits pretend they are not interested.

There is a brass sign bent like a tent labelling the secretary as 'Jane Leap'. She is small but wide in an oddly disproportionate way. She's not someone who would naturally be associated with sudden movements, let alone leaping.

'Hello, do you have an appointment?'

'We're here to see Lucy Funnell at ten.'

'Please take a seat.'

I feel she is watching me. Her narrowed eyes follow me into the plush toilets and watch me as I come out with the soap down my T-shirt. Who puts the handwash at such a stupid angle? Her gaze follows me from side to side. She watches me look out of the window, then examine the photograph of the Empire State Building.

My mother used to say, sit down, you're making my head spin with your pacing. Wearing out the carpet won't solve the problem. My head reminds me what an appalling son I am. I haven't visited her since we saw her at Christmas. She has no idea who I am, the boy who went to the cliffs, infertile, unemployed.

'Sit down, Tom.' Siri joins forces with Ms Leap.

Lucy Funnell opens the arthritic door to her office; its slow movement wouldn't suggest it belongs in a modern building or that it moves once an hour. Jane Leap looks up at Lucy from her report and her eyes point to me as if Lucy won't remember I'm the bloke she saw a few days ago.

'Come through, Tom. Good to see you again. And you must be Selma.' She gestures for us to sit down. 'Tom, thank you for being so open in your initial assessment. I feel I know you quite well already. And thanks for coming with him, Selma.' She looks at Siri who is preoccupied with annihilating the piece of tissue in her lap.

'Call me Siri, or it'll get confusing,' Siri states without any head movement.

'How've you been this week, Tom?' Her empathic nods are overly enthusiastic at times. 'Were you able to practise getting present using your five senses?'

'Tried, but didn't succeed. My mind wanders and I give up… sorry.'

'Don't be sorry, practise anyway. Minds run about like ill-disciplined children. We're all the same.'

'You need to practise what she tells you, Tom,' my wife unhelpfully chips in.

I hang my head like a naughty schoolboy.

'It must be a hard time for you both.' She searches unsuccessfully for Siri's gaze.

'It's better now we're both back to work,' Siri reassures.

'Great,' Lucy says. 'So, how could we use this session to help you both move forward?'

'I have no issues of my own, thanks,' Siri answers quickly.

I take a very deep inhale of oxygen and open my mouth slowly. 'Er, can I bring up something? A major issue has come up for me.'

'Of course, Tom.'

Siri's head jerks upward with such speed that Lucy simultaneously moves backwards. What on earth did I say that for? The intensity of my wife's stare is that of a hungry owl looking for unsuspecting prey. Her neck has twisted, her eyes wanting a boxing match. My inner temperature is rising, small beads of sweat are building up under my hairline ready to perform a humiliating trickle down my nose.

But I take a deep breath and tell them about Lydia's unusual offer, keeping my eyes on the picture above the psychologist.

'And what did you feel when Tom told you this, Siri?'

'I haven't mentioned it,' I jump in.

'Why's that, Tom—'

'Yes, that's what I want to know! I thought we were now

trusting each other, over-sharing even. A pregnant kid has offered you a child, two whole days ago, and it's slipped your mind?'

'Sorry. There hasn't been a right time. You've been very busy – manic.'

'What's that supposed to mean?'

'Well, it's what you do, isn't it? When you're upset or anxious, you run about like a headless chicken, cleaning, running and taking on too much work.'

'Maybe because my husband takes to his bed or descends into a morose silence.'

'Can I please press pause?' Lucy asks in a quiet, tentative way. We both stop mid-sentence. I've forgotten she's there.

'Siri, I can understand you're upset at not knowing such an important event has happened. What you're both describing is how you both cope with negative emotions. If one partner is an avoider, and the other an over-thinker, needing to confront things head on can create a clash.'

'So, run that past me again.' Siri ignores the third party.

'Lydia wants to donate her baby to us. She can't keep it but doesn't agree with abortion.'

'Tom, is it your baby?' Siri looks as if she's been hypnotised.

'Your husband's infertile. Remember that minor issue in our history.'

'Oh yes. I thought maybe a healthy young partner might have solved the problem.'

'My basic understanding is, without sperm, a man can't get anyone pregnant. The other major flaw is I didn't know her at the time of conception.' My wife slumps down into her chair, stretches her legs in front of her and stares up at the ceiling.

'Why does she want to give her baby to you?' She talks upwards to the room.

'She is young and naive and has recognised she has something she doesn't want, but we do. We bonded over lying and hiding. I feel sorry for her – she's lonely.'

'What did you say to her?'

'I cried and ran away.'

She sits back up and laughs into my face. 'And you say I'm not a coper.'

Lucy coughs. 'Tom, can I ask why you didn't feel able to bring this up outside of this room?'

'I don't know really. I dismissed the idea as, well, sort of just impossible. I thought, Lydia will change her mind – you can't pass babies about on a whim, can you? When it all goes wrong, as it inevitably will, it will be "period day", but much, much worse. There won't be a next month to pin our hopes on this time.'

'I can see it's not straightforward. Siri may well get hurt or disappointed. Is it your role to protect your wife from emotional distress as if she's a child?'

'I guess I'm a wimp when it comes to these things.'

'I notice the self-bully again,' Lucy observes.

'Or the truth,' my wife adds.

'I'm afraid we need to wrap up. I can see you are a strong couple. You have a lot to talk about. You'd be welcome to come back as a couple or to book individual appointments. It was nice to meet you, Selma. Good luck.'

The noise of the street is a nasty contrast to the frosty silence sending a chill down my spine as I run to keep up with my partner.

'I'm sorry,' I mutter when I catch up, reaching for her hand. The silence continues as we start the drive home. Should I cut my losses or be brave and reignite the fire?

'She's calling me relentlessly.' My mind speaks out as Siri indicates to turn onto the dual carriageway. She always drives when she's angry. After an unnatural pause, she responds.

'Maybe because you're refusing to answer? Tom, shouldn't we at least talk about it...? Tom...?'

I pretend to be asleep and she plays along.

Chapter 28

'Morning. I thought you'd disappeared again.' Dawn embodies a less-than-patient head teacher when she's not impressed.

'Sorry, just need thinking space.' I can feel my gaze drop to my feet, my default pose.

She points her head towards Lydia's back whilst frantically buttering bread and chucking in bits of turkey. 'She's clearly doing the same thing – she's not moved from your chair for two days.' She adds, 'Hear her out, I don't think she's as naive as you think. And when you're ready for some work, let me know.'

'Thanks Dawn. I'll be in properly tomorrow. I promise.'

She shrugs. 'Go and talk to Lydia. That's more important.'

'Hello Liddie. Hot chocolate by way of apology for rushing off.'

Lydia looks through me as if I'm the last person she expected to see. 'Running away you mean. You say it's Siri who can't face the tough stuff.' Her eyes stay on a doorstep of a book.

'I'm so sorry. There's a lot going on in my head just now.'

'Yeah, well, you're not the only one who has issues, you know.'

'I do know. Sorry. How are you?'

'Well, I haven't changed my mind.' She closes her book, her body loses the tension and the smile returns to her eyes.

'It was very funny. Philip heard me say the baby was yours. He thought – proper yours. I told him you're infertile so that would be an immaculate conception.'

'Thanks.'

'You want a baby. I have one I can't keep. It makes total sense.'

'I'm overwhelmed, Lydia. I understand what you're trying to do. It's amazing, and thank you. I will never forget it. But you can't do this. Babies aren't pets; you can't give them to someone else. This child belongs to you, your family, and although it may look simple now one day you will regret not keeping this child, I know you will.'

'Tom, don't patronise me. I've thought about this more than anything in my life. I don't want a baby, but I don't want to kill it, or hand it to strangers. You and Siri will be amazing parents and it's not fair that you can't have one. I've looked it up and spoken to a social worker at Dorset House. There is something called kinship adoption – I can give my baby to someone I know, and after a few years, they can adopt it.'

My thoughts are whirring, swirling, elements muddled and tangled. It's not right, I can't do it. But then, it's such a marvellously simple solution to my problems. I'm infertile, teenager gives me her kid, what's not to like? Then back again and my mind becomes the speaker for the prosecution. She's so young, she's sure to change her mind. Siri will have decorated the nursery, booked maternity leave and a christening at a grand hotel – and then Lydia will instantly fall into mother love and run into the sunset. That will surely break my wife for good.

'Tom.'

'What?'

'Are you listening?'

'No, probably not, I've...'

'Yeah, I know you've got a lot on your plate. I said, have you asked Siri what she thinks?'

'Sort of. She wants us to talk properly to you. Perhaps come for dinner next week?'

'I'd rather do it at Dawn's if you don't mind. The social worker said to protect myself by distancing from you, or it'll be too much to part with the baby, you and the café.'

'Sure, we'll do whatever works best for you. I'm so sorry, Liddie, I've got to go, I promised Siri I would drop a birthday present to Eleanor.'

'That Eleanor?'

'Yep, the Eleanor I can't stand. I won't be crossing the threshold. I promise we'll be in touch with a date to chat, okay?'

'Yes, please.'

'Tom.' Dawn's voice travels from the other room.

'I'm on a tight schedule.' I deliberately keep walking towards the door.

'Heard that before!'

'It's the honest truth. You have four minutes and thirty seconds starting now!'

'We need to sort this out. We've got a stack of orders coming in for the diet food. I can't keep up. Can you open up every day, and close Monday and Wednesday—'

'Probably, but I'll be in tomorrow to talk about it.' I blow her a kiss and shout over my shoulder, 'Your time's up, missus!'

'Talk to Siri,' Lydia shouts over Dawn, who is still speaking.

'Yeah, Tom, talk to Siri,' Cilla adds as I close the door on them all.

My backside hasn't hit the car seat when my phone rings.

Ad's name flashes up. I'm not sure I can cope with him right now. Bluetooth chooses for me.

'I had my scan results.' A voice comes from the clock space.

'That was quick; you only had it a few days ago.'

'GP pushed it though. I got in on some two-week rule. Can't fault the NHS, very efficient. The staff were lovely, even the receptionists. I got coffee before and after. Gorgeous-looking nurse...'

'I'm glad. People say MRI scans are traumatic. Was it okay?' I'm deliberately not asking about the results.

'It was fine. It's a closed-in hole, quite small, but you get earphones for the noise. Closed spaces have never bothered me like they do Siri. I reckon she's claustrophobic.'

I try hard to keep my voice casual. I end up sounding squeaky and odd. 'So, what did the scan show?'

'It was clear. No evidence of a brain tumour or stroke and I haven't got cancer.'

'Ah, mate, that's fantastic. Siri will be so happy. I guess it's just stress. I saw Lucy Funnell. Do you want me to see if she can fit you in? We could ask for a BOGOF.'

'What?'

'Buy one get one free, idiot.'

'I'd hoped it was stress, but the consultant said he is pretty sure my problems are neurological.'

'I don't understand. You said the scan was clear?'

'He caught me as I was going out. I only had a scan appointment so it was a fleeting chat. He said he was not being deliberately elusive, which is what I accused him of being. They want to investigate genetic diseases.'

'I don't understand.'

'Neither do I really. Apparently, there are some neurological diseases that can cause the changes I have and don't show until adulthood.'

'But your mum and Siri are healthy?'

'They want me to talk to Mum about family background.'

'Did he mention any specific conditions?'

'Yes, hang on a minute. I wrote it down.' The line goes quiet and I wonder if Adam has ended the call by mistake. 'Huntington's disease. I've never heard of it, have you?'

'No, mate, can't say I have. Did they explain more?'

'I've got an appointment next week at the movement disorders clinic. Meanwhile I'll do a bit of research.'

'Well don't scare yourself again. A problem with moving sounds much better than brain cancer, so I guess it's relatively good news.'

'Yeah, that's what I thought.'

It's frightening how I can drive miles and have no recollection of the journey. I can't help the transient thoughts, the images of myself walking around the shops holding a pudgy leg either side of my head, kicking a ball with a blonde-haired boy with blue eyes. The happy thoughts are quickly elbowed out by more realistic questions. What if it looks like him? Will Siri actually be angry with Lydia for treating a baby so casually? How will we cope if Lydia changes her mind? Will her parents find out, kidnap it and force it into church?

What did Adam say he might have... Hunting, Huntingman, Huntingon...? What if Adam can't be treated? What if Lydia takes the baby at the same time her brother is lying in a hospice, alone because his only sister is too heartbroken? I pull over and try to calm my head. I feel dizzy and nauseous. Perhaps this is what Lucy meant by being so hijacked by the inside stuff, your thoughts, your memories, that it makes you ill.

When my foot hits the pedal, a film about me going back to the cliffs catches me by surprise. This time Marc Cole is crying as I fly off towards the gull...

I climb the stairs to the flat more exhausted than I should be. Siri opens the door before my key touches the keyhole. 'Hi,' she says. 'I heard your footsteps. You look tired – long drive?

Hard day at the office? How were sales?' She stands on tiptoe and plants a kiss on my receding hairline.

I ignore her. 'It was good to see everyone.'

'Has Peter decided between Windows and a Mac?'

'I don't think Peter cares. He just likes chatting about things Cilla can't understand. I've promised Lydia we'll meet her.'

'Cool, we need to. I was talking to Sarah at work who said I'd be entitled to maternity leave. She's got some baby clothes left over from the triplets. She said by the time we have ours, Seren, Sam and Joel will be eighteen months. It'll be a perfect hand-me-down gap. I have no idea how she copes with working despite having three. She said one will be a picnic.'

A sigh escapes my body. I didn't intend it to be audible.

'I know, I'm getting carried away, but—'

'You have to hold off until we've discussed things with her much more extensively. There's a social worker involved who'll assess us. There'll be lots of intrusive questions and what I did might go against us. I know it's really hard but we have to stay real. Don't tell anyone else.'

'You heard from Adam?'

'Yes, spoke to him in the car.'

'He left a message to say the scan was clear but they're doing more tests. They think he might have something genetic.'

'Yeah, but it's to do with movement, so that's better than a tumour or motor neurone disease which is where my head has been going.'

'Did he seem all right?'

'Yeah, he seemed to be taking it in his stride.'

'I'll call him after supper.'

'I'm sure he'll appreciate that. He's going to tell Heather and see if the four of us could have a meal with your mum. How long is it for food? I need the loo before we eat.'

'I will put the veg on. Be out in ten minutes max!'

I lift the toilet lid, and pull down my trousers so I'm not lying.

I type 'Huntingon's disease' and tap the screen to activate a search. 'Showing results for Huntington's.' I thought that was a place; maybe I misheard. As I read, I deeply regret upgrading to a super-fast connection. The first site I find belongs to the Huntington's Disease Association. There's a long list of available fact sheets on eating and swallowing, behavioural problems, psychiatric problems, involuntary movements, choosing a care home… I click on the one titled 'A Guide for Young People'; the children's leaflet should be easy to understand.

The first paragraph makes it plainer than I want to see.

Huntington's disease (HD) is an inherited disease that affects the brain, resulting in changes in behaviour, thinking and emotions. These changes happen over a number of years. Symptoms can start at any age but in most people the first symptoms start before they are fifty years old.

'Tom, how long are you going to be? Dinner's on the table.'

I flush the toilet to authenticate the show and unlock the door. As if placed to deliberately freak me out, Adam and his picture-perfect family stare back at me. Amelia has new front teeth making her mouth too big for her head but the three girls look cute in handmade matching dresses. Heather and Adam are above them looking at each other as if they're alone. Becca is looking up at Adam to intervene, whining that Amelia has too much room. Meelie has her legs wide open but doesn't care.

The sentence I tried not to read floods this scene. *If someone has Huntington's disease, each one of their children has a fifty per cent chance of inheriting the disease.*

Chapter 29

'Tom.'

'What?'

'Hurry up. We're supposed to be collecting Adam and Heather in less than an hour.'

'Siri, I'm waiting for you. I've been ready for twenty minutes. I'm in the sitting room.'

My mind draws me back in. There must be treatment for whatever's wrong with Adam. I'll research it. There are lots of diseases that are partially genetic; Mum's cleaner, Susie, had genetic breast cancer but neither of her daughters have it.

'Just coming. I forgot I hadn't dried my hair. Now I can't find my purple necklace.'

'We're going to your mother's, not Buckingham Palace.'

She rushes in, fiddling to insert her earrings, a bag balanced under her arm.

'I want everyone to see how well we're doing, that everything is okay.'

She thrusts me the car keys without comment, a biscuit crammed into her mouth. I have no idea why she spends ten minutes doing her teeth and meticulously applying lip colour.

'Don't you know how to get to your mum's house? Leave the satnav off. It's annoying.'

Siri ignores me and presses go. The satnav announces, 'Starting route to twenty-two Station Road.'

A beep announces a text. Siri instantly reaches for my phone. 'It's from Lydia. She's asking when we can meet her with the social worker. Have you not got back to her with the dates?'

'Yes, this morning.' I leave out that I called deliberately early, knowing she wouldn't be up. I left a message promising a formal meeting in the next couple of weeks.

We met with Lydia a few days ago, and against my better judgement we've agreed to meet formally with the social worker. A secret fear that's gaining centre stage is that, in the presence of a child, I will become my father. I can't say that out loud to anyone, not Harry, not Lydia, let alone my wife. My mother frequently says that my father was a loving and friendly chap before they had kids.

'Great, shall I text or call?' Siri briefly looks at me for an answer but then taps in the number and holds the handset to my face.

'Hi, Liddie. Sorry it's taken me so long.' I search for my window-selling voice.

'Yeah, why has it?'

'My brother-in-law is ill. Things are difficult. But Siri's keen to meet and talk about how we can support you.'

'I don't want support; Dawn gives me support. I need you and Siri to take the baby at the birth. It says so in the book my midwife gave me.'

'Woah, Liddie. We've not agreed to take your baby! What book says it's reasonable to give away your baby as he comes out?'

'Obviously it doesn't say that…'

'We need to talk properly, Liddie. You have to stop this. I'm sure the social worker will agree – and why are you calling the baby he all of a sudden. I thought you'd named it Stella.'

'The second scan showed it's a boy.'

'Congratulations... a son.'

'Tom, he's yours. I won't change my mind.'

I realise the phone is dead.

'We need to meet her. It's not fair to her otherwise. A boy... you wanted a son...' Siri is staring dreamily out of the windscreen.

'Stop. We can't go there. Please don't, or I'll put a halt to it all now.'

'Tom, you sound exactly like your old man.'

'Can we please get today over? We need to find out if Adam's seriously ill before we commit to the baby idea. He might need help with the girls if he has to have surgery or something.'

'We can do both. You don't even have a proper job.'

'Thanks for reminding me. I don't want you to get your hopes up. It will be like before but a hundred times worse if she changes her mind, which there is every reason she will, especially if her parents get a sniff of a grandchild.'

'She trusts you. We need to help her whatever she decides. I'll have to cope.'

A timely tap on the passenger window interrupts us. 'Hello, hello.' A comedic face is pushed against the glass. Siri slides down her window to give her brother a peck on the cheek.

'Back or front?' she asks.

'Don't mind.'

Heather is shouting from the door. Even my wife now agrees Heather's 'positive encouragement' has tipped into bullying.

I open the rear door for my sister-in-law. She's unusually flushed, and her skin looks blotchy; typically it's hidden under layers of make-up. She pulls up her expensive-looking suede skirt to get in next to her husband, revealing equally smart shoes.

'I can't believe you've done that. So stupid. Why on earth did you have the key at work? The idea is to keep it at home in case anyone gets locked out. That's why it's called the spare key.'

'I said I'm sorry. What else can I say to shut you up?' Adam's voice leaks a rising panic.

'What are we going to do now, Adam? I've taken the girls to Julie's and told her there's a spare key under the stone. Now there won't be, will there?'

The journey is good: no traffic or hold-ups as there often are on the A27. Inside the car, the climate is less positive. Heather is making a huge deal of sorting out what in reality is not a crisis; anyone else would text Julie with a simple change of plan. Instead, she calls Julie, Adam's office, and his mother – and humiliates Adam in every conversation. I'd be furious and I can see Siri's body tensing in the seat next to me, but Adam seems oblivious.

As the traffic light changes to red, I glance in my mirror to review the back seat. Heather is peering into a small circular mirror, creating her face. Adam is silently staring into the back of Siri's headrest; he looks alert as if watching something intently but there's nothing there to look at. His hair is messy and longer than he usually lets it grow. His mum won't appreciate his stubble. His shirt is ironed and clean but his clothes are not put together how Adam's should be. He was scouted for a model agency a few years ago. Siri says all her friends fancied him when they were teens. I could understand why. Now he's lost something imperceptible. He's in constant motion, his legs keep catching the back of his sister's seat, juddering her body.

I'm surprised she isn't moaning like she does when Amelia does the same thing.

We arrive at Adam and Siri's mum's in plenty of time for lunch. She opens the door and invites us into the bungalow with genuine warmth. She is dignified and elegant, obviously the mother of my wife and brother-in-law.

Siri's family have an interesting heritage: her great grandfather was black and he and his wife had twins, one black, one white – considered freaks at the time. Siri's grandfather was white but with his father's beautiful skin, pitch-black thick hair and his mother's green eyes. Margaret and both her children share these features. It's an unusual look and most definitely what first attracted me to my wife. Siri's mother is wearing an outfit that wouldn't look out of place on someone forty years younger and she looks fabulous. She welcomed me at our very first meeting but she's hard to read. I'm not sure I'd know if she didn't like me.

Siri and Heather have disappeared into the kitchen by the time Adam coordinates his limbs out of the car. It's not hard to read what Margaret's feelings are now; her smile evaporates as she hurries down the path to greet her son. She helps him stand and find his balance before wrapping her arms tightly around him. This expression of emotion is not typical for my mother-in-law. There are tears in her eyes as she gives me a hug, a little longer than usual. 'It's so nice to see my boys,' she says with transparent affection, and I wonder what she knows.

She fusses over everyone, hanging coats that could stay on chairs and adjusting napkins. She is postponing something she doesn't want to face, something none of us wants to face. We all sit round a table with the finest china, a three-tiered cake stand and a large pot of tea. Maybe I should've dressed up.

'What have you young folk been up to? It's a shame the girls stayed with Julie. How are they, Heather?' Margaret chatters as she hands a plate of perfectly symmetrical ham sandwiches, divided like she is expecting the children. Adam piles his plate so high, the food bonfire topples and a cream scone ends up face down on the previously immaculate beige carpet. Heather and Siri both give him a look but he seems unaware. His mum fetches a dustpan and brush. 'Never mind,' she says as if it's a visitor's child who has dropped food on the carpet.

'They're thriving, thank you. Amelia is class captain. Indya is starting to read while none of her peers even look at books yet. It must be because we've read to them so much…'

'I read to them most,' Adam sniffs, strangely defiant.

Heather ignores him. 'Rebecca's health visitor says she has superior fine motor skills.'

If we had children, we'd treat them like people, not trophies. I can tell by Siri's face that she's also unimpressed.

'And how are you, Adam? How's work?' Margaret asks with the concern only a good mum can muster.

'I've been signed off for a few weeks; they say I'm not myself at the moment.'

Adam is definitely not himself. He looks tired and answers questions with one or two words. The women chat about some recent TV programme. Small talk. We are filling time to avoid saying what we're all thinking. Until Siri takes the bull by the horns.

'Mum, did Dad get ill before he died?'

'Adam asked me that on the phone.'

'And?'

'He wasn't here much, Mum. Neither were you for that matter.' Everyone turns to look at Adam; no one expected him to speak. He wears the same blank expression.

'I don't think that's entirely fair. But we were often not home at the same time, if that's what you mean.'

'Mum,' Siri asks. 'Did Dad have any problems like Adam is having?'

'No. I can't remember him hurting himself or having any difficulties walking.'

'What about his personality?' Heather pipes up.

'Albi was what people describe as colourful, a character...'

'Do you mean gay, Mum?' Siri chips in.

'Oh no, dear. Gay men are usually so kind, aren't they? He was a very self-centred man. He loved Adam, and later you, but on his terms. He was the same with me. He enjoyed parties and wanted to be out. He'd always say, life's too short, Margaret. We had bills to pay, responsibilities. He was used to money, he was a successful lawyer and my parents gave us more than we deserved. But he spent money in excess. I didn't realise how much debt he was in until he died.'

'What did he spend it on?'

'I didn't ask and it was all cash, so no bank statements I could check. I trusted him.'

'What did he die of?'

'A brain haemorrhage. There was a post-mortem...'

'Did you find out after he died what he got up to?'

Siri sounds like she is doing a radio interview rather than dragging up difficult family issues.

Adam looks uncomfortable. He can't seem to stay still; he's like a hyperactive child. Margaret is being more open than I thought she would be; she's usually a fairly private person, and has always been cagey about her husband.

'I think he used prostitutes when he was away – and he gambled.'

Heather looks horrified. Siri gasps.

'Times were different, sweetheart. Looking back, he was perhaps more outlandish before he died. He would've loved to have been an actor. He was always a little frustrated by the mundane, which included the things normal people do, so any changes in him were perhaps more subtle than if he'd been a regular family man.'

'What sort of changes can you see, with hindsight?' Siri is determined to interrogate her mother; it's as if it's she who is ill, not Adam and maybe his poor little girls. I can hardly bear the thought of their beautiful faces fidgety, contorted.

Help. I need to stop thinking. It'll be fine, Tom. The doctor probably just mentioned Huntington's to Adam as a worst-case scenario and he got muddled. He's so like that at the moment. Here we all are, writing his will for him, and it'll turn out he's got a problem with his spine that can be fixed by summer.

'I guess he was impatient, often bad-tempered, a bit unkind I suppose. I thought he was drinking. He'd always enjoyed a tipple, but he was unsteady more and more often when he came home. Looking at Ad, perhaps I misjudged him. It's an awful thing to say but when he died, I was relieved. He'd started to pick on you kids.'

'Hey ho, I guess I might as well follow Tom's example then. Bring on the relief for you all.'

'Oh, darling.' Margaret shoots her hand up to her mouth and rushes to her son. She perches on the arm of his chair, her hand gently placed on his shoulder. 'I didn't mean that for a single minute. Your dad wasn't very nice, even when I married him. I should've left earlier, but I had you two and it wasn't the done thing. So… where have we got to with this infuriating business?' It's as if she's asking about an extension that is a little behind schedule.

Adam shrugs as if it's nothing to do with him; his leg jerks upwards kicking an imaginary ball. Everyone tries not to look, but he doesn't seem overly irritated by the puppeteer who controls his limbs without permission.

Heather coughs as if interrupting naughty children, caught

in a room off limits to them. 'The neurologist said he's pretty certain it's Huntington's disease. He wanted us to get some clinical background...'

Siri butts in. 'What's that?'

'What Margaret has told us, facts about your father.'

Siri's frown goes back down to the tissue in her hands. There are tiny snowflakes all over her lap.

'Adam has a blood test in ten days to confirm, but with the issues he has, what Margaret has said and the fact it's been going on for years, I'm in no doubt. Huntington's is what it is.' She pushes away Adam's hand as it seeks hers and inhales more oxygen. 'Siri can have the pre-symptomatic test whenever she chooses but the girls can't be tested until they're eighteen.'

A cold hand grips my heart and squeezes harder and harder. I can't breathe. My head has been pushed into water and held down. My eyes dart to Siri who is still analysing the patterns in her skirt.

'Siri? Why would she be tested?' I don't want this question answered.

Siri's eyes meet mine. 'Doh, did you not realise I too have a fifty-fifty chance of having this?'

Doh... She speaks as if I've forgotten to collect the shirts from the dry cleaners or left a cake in the oven. *Doh* is not what you say when you realise your husband has no idea he's married to someone on death row.

It's supposed to be our happy ever after. I will stress and weep over Adam, the girls; somehow, I've only been thinking of him passing it downwards.

'Did you know?' I ask my wife.

'Of course I knew. Where did you think he got it from? A virus at work?' The clipped tone is familiar and I know it's my cue to shut up.

I'm a selfish fool. It's karma. Just when I thought life was beginning to look good again.

'Will you get tested, sis?' There seems to be a goading quality to Adam's question. Our synchronicity continues but what comes out of our mouths is very different.

'Of course not,' Siri explodes.

'Of course she will,' my father's voice declares.

Without looking at either of us, her mother says, 'I don't think there is any need for the test. What's the point of worrying yourself into an early grave over something you probably don't have anyway?'

It's hard to pay attention to driving. Siri opts to go in the back and chat to Heather; she says her brother will find it easier to sit in the front. 'You can do man chat with Tom,' she says.

As I slow to pull up in the driveway, all three girls are waiting expectantly in a line behind the window. The door bursts open and they cascade out, energetic youngsters keen to get home when the school bell has chimed.

Amelia helps her daddy pull his legs out of the footwell and swivel round, then she and her younger sister take an arm each to pull him up. I see two young carers.

Heather raises her hand to say goodbye to Siri. 'See you soon, no doubt. Thanks for driving, Tom. Sorry it wasn't much fun.'

'Jump in the front,' I say to my wife, 'or I'll feel like a cab driver.' I get out of the car, pretending to help Heather with her lightweight bag.

'You said this has been going on for years?'

'It has – six, maybe longer. Certainly since I was pregnant with Becca.'

'Why haven't we seen anything?'

'I think Siri has, but it's been mostly personality stuff – the obsessions with a rigid timetable, a constant bad temper with the girls, dropping things and tripping. I guess all that can be passed off as life. The grimaces, shrugging and reflex kicking have only started in the last few months. I guess that's not so easy to view as normal.'

She pats me on the arm. I can't ever remember Heather touching me; she's not a demonstrative person. 'I guess you and I have to stay strong, Tom; it's not going to be easy.'

As we drive away, Siri starts to cry. 'Tom, I won't be able to bear it if Adam dies.'

I do my best to comfort her. She doesn't mention her own predicament. I can't believe she knew and hasn't said anything. Too many jigsaw pieces are slotting together and I am frightened of the picture that's forming. I'm also aware that death is not always the worst-case scenario.

I'm relieved the day is over when Siri turns off the light and her breathing tells me she's asleep. I send a quick text to Lydia. 'Sorry, lots of bad family stuff going on. You are in my thoughts. Will be in touch soon. Send love to everyone and don't do anything I wouldn't do! TC.'

Chapter 30

'I wish we hadn't agreed to go through with this.' I know I sound like a miserable child.

'We haven't agreed to go through with anything, Tom.'

Siri is driving too fast for the weather and I am wishing I hadn't gone out for lunch with Harry. It was last minute: Siri was working and Harry called to say he had a slot between meetings and did I want to meet for half an hour. Half an hour became two hours and although Harry wasn't drinking I had two pints as well as far too much food. Big meals in the middle of the day wipe me out. By the time I stumbled in, Siri was already home and irritated.

'We have to present ourselves as responsible people and you turn up plastered.' She sounds like Heather.

'Hardly plastered darling. We don't have to be there until three-thirty. I had two pints. By the time we get there I will be as sober as you.'

'But you said if I went to work, you'd make me some lunch and be ready.'

'I did. And I was.'

'Toast and jam wasn't what I needed! And you stink of beer. I'm shattered and I didn't want to have to drive.'

'I don't think I'm over the limit.'

'I'm not risking you getting caught for drink driving on our way to meet a social worker.'

I don't say, Beachy Head and inherited time bomb might be more likely to scupper our chances.

I'm pleased she's becoming less committed to arguing to the death: the conflict fizzles by the time we reach the end of our road. She grabs my hand when she's safely round the corner.

'You look nice,' I offer in response.

'You can't worm your way into my good books with a shallow compliment, Tom Cleary. Once upon a time, maybe.'

So I know I'm forgiven. The tide has finally turned in our relationship. We can argue without it becoming spiteful and personal. At the end of last year, we'd stopped liking each other. We were constantly competing, grabbing any opportunity to throw a punch.

'Have you met a social worker before?'

'Not sure I have. Don't they have greasy hair and wear flared trousers?'

'We shouldn't mention the possibility of Huntington's. I'm already terrified of being analysed without her knowing I might be off my rocker in ten years.'

That's the first time she has properly acknowledged the ultimate large elephant in our improving relationship.

'If she's astute, she'll realise you're already off your rocker.' A punch lands on my belly.

My eyes close. The alcohol and food I have consumed are taking effect.

'Great, you get drunk, forget I need lunch, and now I get to drive in silence.'

I can hear a muffled voice in the distance; I think Siri is upstairs.

'Tom, we're here. Wake up.'

'What, where here?' I remember where we are and why. 'Sorry, I think I fell asleep.'

'You don't say, old man. You've snored your way through a whole hour. Scintillating company to keep my mind off the real issue.' A comb is thrust into my hand. 'Use this. You have bed hair. And wipe the dribble off your chin. Sometimes I have to dig deep to remember why I said I do.'

Dawn is waiting when we arrive, holding the door open. 'The social worker has arrived. I've sent her into the back room with Lydia.' Dawn is whispering so quietly I have to lean in.

'Tom, you stink of a business lunch.' She fumbles in her apron pocket.

'Open wide.' I obediently do an impression of a fish and she pops in an Extra Strong Mint.

Dawn leads the way. A woman who looks young enough to be my daughter is sitting with her legs crossed at the far side of the table, a pile of damning-looking reports in front of her. Lydia is next to her and Dawn drags two further chairs to squeeze us round the table.

'Shall I stay or go?' Dawn asks.

'I'm not sure we need an advocate now I'm here.' This professional clearly hasn't met this café owner.

'I was asking Lydia. Would you like me here, love?' Dawn excludes the woman from her gaze line.

'Yes please,' Lydia responds with an uneasy smile.

Dawn grabs a further chair and creates a second row behind me. I shuffle my chair along so she can join the magic circle.

'Welcome. I'm Annaliese Frost from the child and family service. You must be Tom and Selma.' She obviously doesn't realise she's the guest.

'Call me Siri.'

Skinny jeans rather than flares. Annaliese hands round a piece of paper with 'Agenda' typed at the top followed by 'Re:

informal meeting for baby Gerrard. Due date 14.8.' I realise I don't know Lydia's surname.

The list of topics is intimidating. Item 1 is Lydia's capacity to decide. Annaliese has a deep voice that, by comparison, makes me sound like a girl.

'We're here to talk about the issues relating to a potential kinship adoption of male baby Gerrard. When Lydia contacted our department, we were concerned that she's only just eighteen. The first decision we need to make is whether she has the mental capacity to decide what happens to her baby. This involves looking at four criteria: her ability to understand her decision, to remember what she has decided, to weigh up the issues and to communicate her choice.'

She looks across at Lydia who is staring at her trainers. 'We have met on two occasions and I'm impressed by your maturity, but I want to check a few details. Is that okay?'

Lydia is as quiet as when I first met her. She nods without looking up. I wish I could do the same.

'Lydia, can you explain to us why you feel unable to keep your baby?'

She continues to study her feet.

I try to help. 'I think she feels too young and that the pregnancy will hurt her parents.'

'Thank you, Tom, but I'm speaking to Lydia.'

'I regret sleeping with the man. I have a strong faith in God and my behaviour was not in keeping with that. I can't give a child anything, and I don't want my parents to be hurt.' Lydia is still avoiding looking at anyone.

'Do you feel your parents are going to punish you?'

'If I go home, my family will sacrifice me on the church altar,' she says without a hint of a smile. Annaliese – I have forgotten her surname – is suitably horrified.

Before the social worker can formulate a response, Lydia

looks up. I have seen that look, I know we are about to get drenched by an angry monologue.

'No. God won't punish me because he's not like that. He's a loving God, I was joking about being sacrificed, you know...'

Annaliese is still wearing a serious face; she is not going to crack a smile. While I'm finding it hilarious, Dawn and Siri are hard to read.

'If you feel God looks on you favourably, is it your parents you're worried about?'

'If I told them, they'd look after the baby and me, but I don't want that for us. Tom understands.'

'And what about the father? Does he know he has a son? Is he willing to be involved?'

'No.'

'Did you invite him to have a role in your son's life?'

'He told me he was married with three children and couldn't support me. He gave me money to kill it.'

Annaliese digs into her scruffy-looking bag. I bet it smells musty like my parents' house. She pulls out a document and flicks through it without explanation. Then, as if someone has released the pause button and pushed play, she says, 'I'm happy Lydia knows what she wants and I'd be happy to support an initial kinship adoption but—' I knew there'd be a 'but'. My mind is shouting, but Tom is a paedophile, but Tom is mental, but Tom's wife will go mental, but Tom had a bad father as a role model so Tom will also be a bad father...

'Tom.'

'What?' Annaliese, Dawn, Lydia and Siri are looking at me.

'Would that be okay?' Anneliese says.

'Would what be okay?'

'It'll be fine, I'll talk to him and call you Monday,' Siri agrees

I have no idea what has been agreed but everyone is very relaxed. Dawn goes downstairs to see Annaliese out. Siri's arm is casually slung around Lydia's chair and they're looking at the scan picture on her phone. My heart skips a beat. I dare not look.

'What will be fine? What did I miss when I was hooked?'

'Hooked?' the girls say at the same time.

'*Ology* jargon. It's when your head hooks you in and you lose track of the present.'

'Siri and I agreed you will go and live at Annaliese's for the rest of my pregnancy so she can check you out.'

It takes me a few seconds to notice their giggles. 'Joke, old man.' Lydia is openly laughing at the horror on my face. I'm glad that they can't see what's coming up inside of me. What have I started? Nothing ends well for us.

My father's red face enters my mind without my consent. I see his hand raised in the air ready to slap or punch whichever one of us got in his way. Will I be like that, so resentful of this child who isn't mine that I punish him for being born? Will Siri be able to love a child she hasn't conceived, given birth to or breastfed? Isn't that how women bond with babies? What if neither of us can do it? It'll have to go into care. None of these film endings are happy ever after.

'She said she'll come to the flat to do proper checks and we'll need to have interviews separately and as a couple. But she can't see why we can't have the baby.'

Siri is crying tears of joy when we get back to the car. My tears are not far behind, but they're tears of terror.

Chapter 31

'Aunt Selma.'

'Yes, Amelia?'

'You're on the radio in the kitchen and you're here.'

'It's mad, isn't it? Yesterday, I went to work and they recorded me, you know, like Daddy records you at your dance shows?'

'Yes.'

'So that's how I'm here, and there. Let's turn me off, shall we?'

It's lovely to hear an authentic natural laugh come from my wife. She takes hold of Amelia's hand and leads her out of the room. I can hear the two of them giggling about being able to turn off a person. My mind plays other scenarios where she might be switched off.

The first time Siri was given her own show we all gathered together to listen – Adam, Margaret, Harry, Eleanor and I crowded into our front room. We had been ordered by Siri to meet at 7.45am, although Heather was given a late pass to sort out the girls. We all had breakfast together and it turned into one of those memorable family times – last-minute, unplanned, fun and unforgettable. Siri had left at 5.50am to be in the studio by seven, leaving over an hour to do a thirty-minute journey. She was due to start the morning show at ten, taking over from Danny Slide. Danny's voice changed its tone at 9.55am. 'You are in for a treat, listeners of Sussex. We have a new morning presenter. Let me introduce you to Selma Cleary. Hello, Selma.'

'Hi, it's great to be here. My friends call me Siri.'

The room cheered; we high-fived each other, imitating Danny, sharing the excitement that little Siri had achieved her childhood dream. We were still there over four hours later for a celebration late lunch and champagne, and Margaret and Adam glowed with pride when she came in to a shower of confetti and cheers.

My wife is now one of the most popular presenters. Her listening figures have exceeded those of her longstanding predecessor, and her dream of becoming a producer in five years is a definite possibility. Siri's voice kept me company when I was on the road, between stints flogging windows to unsuspecting victims. I would chat back to the radio as I completed my sales reports sitting in the car or ate my lunch. It's still a surprise when I switch on the radio and hear my wife…

While I've been reminiscing, the mood has changed.

'Amelia, stop it. I've asked you five times.' Siri usually has endless patience with these girls but not today. The giggles have evaporated.

'I want Mummy.'

'Well, you can't have her. She's at the hospital,' Siri snaps, without taking her eyes off the book Rebecca is reading to her.

'But she'll be back very soon,' I add, in what I hope is a softer tone.

'No Floppy, up Floppy, down Floppy,' Rebecca reads with enthusiasm and confidence. She's oblivious to all that's going on.

Lucky, lucky her. I wish I was able to switch off my knowing. Every time Siri and I talk at the moment, we argue; it's worse than the infertility. At least we could delude ourselves that sex was upping our chances of winning, but this fifty-fifty. I've never been a betting man, waste of money, but I know these odds aren't good. Siri looks so much like her brother. I've read endless articles and watched countless YouTube videos – about being tested, the first signs. If Adam's been ill for so long, maybe Siri has it already.

I'm insisting she gets tested but she won't agree, says she doesn't want to know. I can't bear it, the constant watching, overanalysing. I don't want to be a carer. I'm such a wimp. I won't cope when she changes, let alone when she's dribbling and trembling. She'd hate that. Dignitas was mentioned on some of the websites. We need to talk. I have to know what she'd like. Or is it what I'd like, what I can't cope with?

'Uncle Tom.'

'Uncle Tom.'

'Uncle Tom.'

'Tom!'

'Why are you shouting at me?'

'Your phone is ringing.' Amelia is thrusting my phone into my face.

'It's Mum,' she says. 'I answered it.'

'Hi, Heather.'

'Are the girls okay?'

'Yes, they're great.' Siri shakes her head and raises her eyebrows as Amelia climbs back on the couch and starts to bounce. Siri shouts at her.

'Is someone upset?'

'A minor hiccup,' I lie.

'Amelia's definitely picking up the tension. Indya goes into herself but Meelie has always been sensitive to high emotion.

She's the only one who is old enough to miss him. Anyway, train is just pulling in so we're ten minutes or so away…'

'No rush.'

'Please rush.' Siri comes in, shutting away Amelia who is kicking and screaming on the kitchen floor.

Adam's getting worse. His walking and odd movements are the same, but he is becoming more peculiar in the way he treats everybody. It feels as if he is falling out of love with each of us, one by one. Today he's gone with Heather, or should I say Heather has taken him for what they've described as a confirmatory and diagnostic test. They'll take his blood. We all know the result will be positive.

'Mummy's home!' Amelia has been listening for the car. She used to be excited when it was Daddy coming home.

Heather is without her make-up again and she looks younger, more vulnerable. Adam barges in behind her doing what Becca has started to call crazy dad dancing. A year ago, he'd have scooped her up and tickled her for teasing him, but now he doesn't respond at all.

He grabs a can from the large American fridge but doesn't extend an offer to anyone else. He plonks himself down hard onto the couch and Indya's tiny frame almost bounces off the edge. His leg kicks her and her face winces but she doesn't complain. He seems unaware: his leg goes out several times. She appears paralysed. I sit down the other side of her, shuffle closer and scoop my goddaughter onto my lap. I hold my breath. If he feels undermined, he throws a fit, shouts and even throws things, but his eyelids look heavy. Amelia goes to him, takes the half-empty can and chucks it into the recycling.

'Good girl.' Heather flicks a tiny smile.

When Adam's head hits his chest, Heather beckons us through to their spacious dining room. This is where the outside caterers spread out delicacies to impress the local ladies. The table is piled with files and paperwork.

Heather flushes. 'I'm sorry, it's such a mess. It's hard keeping up with all the admin. I'm going to have to rejig the finances and change the insurance and wills.'

'Looks like ours on a good day, doesn't it, hun?' I reassure.

Siri is not in the mood for banter.

The large bay window looks out onto a private estate enclosed by an electric gate: it's an expensive area. All the girls are in a prestigious private school.

'What's happening with Adam's work? He won't be able to go back, will he?'

'They're still working it out. They've been having complaints from staff and customers about mistakes – and some sexually inappropriate behaviour. He was off on a disciplinary, but I took in some information the doctor gave me about Huntington's and disability discrimination, so they're looking into it. We'll get a payout, I hope, to tide us over.'

'And then?'

'Who knows, Tom? I'm taking each day as it comes.'

'How did you get on at the hospital?' Siri asks.

'Okay, I guess. Nothing unexpected. They said they're fairly sure it's Huntington's; they think his father was definitely the carrier but he died before he developed symptoms, so no one knew it was in the family. We went through the checklist of symptoms with the doctor and it makes sense. I realise I've missed a lot.'

'Is it certain then?'

'No, they can't be certain without a test but it's straightforward, just a blood test. We'll have to go back to the genetics centre in London.'

'And the girls? Will you test them if he has it?'

'I can't. It has to be their decision. If we'd known it was in the family, we could have tested them in the womb.'

'Indya looks most like him... does that mean she is more likely to have it?'

'No, each child has a fifty per cent chance of having it. They could all be negative or all be positive. It's like gender – with each pregnancy, you go back to the same fifty-fifty odds. I've stupidly read too much information on Huntington's disease forums of people who have first lost their partner to the disease and then watch as each of their children gets ill and dies. Quite frankly I can't think of a disease with worse implications.'

Heather is doing her best to conceal the agony. I'm trying to be kind but my attention is consumed with what this means for us. She quickly recovers herself, pushing a floral hanky hard against her wet eyes.

'I'm sorry, Siri, it must be much worse for you. I keep forgetting... How are you coping?'

'I'm fine, keeping busy. But we have had some good news.'

'Fabulous, we need that. Another promotion?'

'Tom and I are having a baby.'

Heather is still. 'Have you had the Huntington's test?'

'No, I don't plan to, ever.'

'You must, Siri, you could pass it on. Surely it's bad enough our girls will have to go through it? Why would you get pregnant knowing...?'

'I didn't. Tom's infertile.'

'But it's you who's a carrier. It'll be the same with any man.'

'Thanks!' I chip in, knowing Siri is being deliberately evasive. 'There is a young woman in the café. It's hers.'

'Oh, my goodness. But you're infertile?'

'Do you think I'd be sitting here, still alive, if I'd fathered a child elsewhere?'

'No, probably not. What then? I don't understand. Adoption?'

'Yeah, sort of. Essentially it's an accidental pregnancy and she wants her son to have a good home.'

Heather gives us both a warm and long embrace. 'We certainly do need good news.'

Chapter 32

'I just can't see how that's going to work.'

'Tom, don't raise your voice. It's what Adam's asked for, and if Mum and Heather are happy, you can't interfere.'

'I can understand he wants everyone there, but it would make far more sense if he and Heather go in and speak to the doctors and we meet them afterwards.'

'Adam wants us all with him and the doctor has said they can accommodate that, so you need to accept it's going to happen that way.'

'Why not invite Harry, Eleanor and Dawn for good measure?'

'Tom, shut up!'

So Siri, Adam, Heather, Margaret and I are all on the train to London to be with Adam when he gets his results. I have no idea what the doctors will really think. We are late for the meeting: Adam needed the toilet at Victoria, and Margaret insisted on buying some snacks to get some loose change.

We arrive in the hospital and make our way to the right waiting area. A man who looks like an older version of the milkman from my childhood, grey and wiry with a kind face, arrives and asks us to follow him to his office. Adam calls directions from the front in a voice appropriate for a school trip.

Professor Lyndon Johnson is the neurologist and the clinical lead for Huntington's at the National Hospital. 'Please, take a seat everyone.'

There is a scuffle for chairs. We sit in a row. Professor Johnson shakes each of our hands as we introduce ourselves.

'Hey, Mr President,' Adam says in a voice too loud for the room.

'Thank you, Adam. Yes, a few patients have made that link. This is Kerry. She's the specialist nurse and will be here for the rest of the afternoon to answer any questions you have.'

'I'm sorry there are so many of us. You must think we've come on the crazy bus.' My attempt at light-heartedness falls very flat.

My mother-in-law produces an audible sigh that is unlike her. 'Adam wanted us all here, Tom.'

'It's fine. Really. Everyone is different and many families come in a group… So, Adam. How are you keeping?'

'All good, thanks, especially as the gorgeous Kerry is here.'

Heather flushes pink. 'That's not entirely true, is it? You're twitching more in your face and arms, and your bladder is weak.'

The doctor says gently to his patient, 'Adam, are you prepared for your results?'

'Sure thing, buddy.'

For goodness' sake, Adam, my mind shouts. You're not in a sitcom. Margaret pats down her skirt and looks at the creases, then concentrates on smoothing them out.

'Adam, before I open your results, I need you to confirm your full name and date of birth.'

'Sure. Twenty-fifth of December 1980. Adam Richard

Markham. No 'arm done eh, doc.' Adam moves his head to catch the eyes of his audience as if he's doing stand-up.

'He's making a joke out of his initials. It's a well-rehearsed one. Sorry,' Heather says, raising her carefully plucked eyebrows.

'Thank you, Adam. And I want you to know, all of you, that whatever happens, there's a lot of available support.'

Adam is looking out of the window distracted by the rubbish collection going on outside. My hands are trembling. The fear is rising from my legs upward. I can't catch anyone's eyes. It's like a parody of the Oscars. I expect him to rip open the envelope and reveal the winners, starting with third place. I can't bear to gaze at my wife. I know the results are not going to be good – we all know – but what I also want to know is what will happen when it's our turn? Does Siri have it already? She stumbled over the doormat yesterday and there are two broken glasses on the draining board. How subtle are the early symptoms? She *must* have the test. We can't possibly take Lydia's child if in two years' time Siri will be mumbling and shuffling like an old woman and tantrumming like a toddler. Adam's hand shoots up as if to answer a question but then goes straight to his ear and back again. I look at my brother-in-law suddenly as he is: he's lost weight; he's a shell, a husk of a person. A sob fights its way up from my chest.

I couldn't be a carer. I'd let her down. We'd let this child down.

'Adam.' The doctor quietly gets his attention. 'I'm afraid your test results leave no room for doubt: your CAG repeat is fifty-four. I'm very sorry to say this is a clear positive result, and you have Huntington's disease.'

Adam continues to stare at the bin men; he is unresponsive.

'I will get my secretary to make some tea and for the moment I will leave you in Kerry's capable hands.'

Not sufficiently capable though. She can't take away my wife's risk, she can't rescue us from the horror of watching three beautiful children understand they have a potential death sentence. What if they all have it? Fifty-fifty sounds optimistic in some contexts, but in this one it means that all of Adam's children could have this crippling, perverted, horrifying disease.

No one says anything. Kerry looks at my wife who's not revealing what she is thinking or feeling. 'You understand, Selmeston, that you also have the same chance of being positive. While you are here, would you like to make an appointment to talk about a predictive test?'

Margaret speaks first. 'There's no point in Selma having a test until the girls can have it.'

'What?' I demand, shocked at the force of my own voice. 'That makes no sense. Amelia can't be tested for ten years. If Siri's positive, she could have established symptoms by then.'

'It's up to her, Mum,' says Adam unexpectedly.

'And me, it will impact me too. I need to know. I need to know a little bit about what the rest of my… our… life—'

'Shut up, Tom.' Siri curls her lip. Sometimes it's sexy; today it's not. 'A few weeks ago, your plan was to jump out of your life leaving me to pick up the pieces. Perhaps now you can see what it feels like to be on the ignorant and helpless team.'

She pushes aside her chair. It flies backwards, narrowly missing the person carrying a tray of cups.

It is Heather who restores order. 'We were pretty certain Adam would be positive, so this is not a big surprise. He is calm, the sun is out, so I suggest we walk and eat. There are many issues that need careful consideration but nothing can be decided in haste.'

Margaret, Adam and Heather get up. Siri takes Margaret's

hand. I am relieved we are going, but I have no appetite; surely they don't want lunch?

Kerry hands Heather a file. 'This has information about local services that can meet Adam's clinical needs. There is an East Sussex branch of the Huntington's Disease Association. The contact details are in the pack.'

'Thank you – actually I am already in touch with them and going to the family support meetings.'

I am the last to leave the room. 'If you need anything, just call. Here's my card, Tom. When you have a chance – when you feel ready – you can give me a call and we can talk. There is no pressure for your wife to be tested, and we're also here for anyone who has an HD-positive relative.'

I came here with someone I still wanted to believe was a normal bloke and I am leaving with an HD-positive relative, possibly another one on the way. Heather is right: nothing has changed with this confirmation, but everything has changed. Hope is gone. I recognise this fear, the same fear that overwhelmed me when that other medical verdict robbed me of an imagined future, so recently. Adam hums the tune from *The Dam Busters* as the automatic doors close behind us with a thud. To observers, we must look the same as anyone else enjoying a day out in the early spring. I see Siri waiting at the side of the building. Margaret comes towards me. Adam and Heather are standing waiting in the sunshine as if we're all on a family outing.

'Siri and I will find our own way back. We'll call you this evening, Margaret.'

'I need to speak to her,' she insists.

'Please give us some space. I promise I'll be in touch and we can all talk properly.'

'Hey, hun.' I pull her towards me with what I long to feel is a strong, dependable husband's arm.

'I don't know if I can do this, Tom. I can't bear to look at him. His symptoms disgust me... the thought I could be next... Maybe I've got symptoms already. Oh, I can't cope with the idea of people analysing me as if I'm an exhibit in a freak show... *Did you see her drop that? Oh, do you know about her brother?* I slipped up on lots of words this week...'

'We can do it together. That's what we agreed when I came out of hospital, you and me against the world.'

'Yeah, but that's before you knew I'd be crumpled up in a wheelchair...' She attempts a smile.

'At least it'll be me that's driving though... Ouch, that's domestic abuse, you know...'

Siri allows herself another half-hearted smile, but the stricken tone returns. 'I don't want the test, Tom. I know that's selfish but if I don't have it, I can stay hopeful.'

'But if you're negative, you'll have genuine hope, and we can enjoy family life without worrying.'

'But there is a fifty per cent chance I will be positive. Then we spend from now to for ever, overanalysing. For every new year, we will wonder, is this the one? Every scrap will end with both of us asking, is this the irritability? I don't want that. I'd want to end it all.'

'I thought I couldn't go on in February, but I'm here...'

'Tom, if Lydia or the social worker get a sniff of this disease, that'll be game over. I don't want the test.' She looks away. 'Maybe... I can make an appointment to see Kerry for next year. Then we can enjoy the baby's first six months.'

'Sounds like a plan.'

'Just to chat with someone, though. I'm not promising I'll go for the test, Tom. I can't.'

I remove my arm from her shoulders and take her hand in mine. 'Remember this ring?' It's still too tight on her finger;

there's a small mound of pinched-up flesh on each side of the metal. 'I promised I'd love you for ever, and I will, whatever.'

'Yeah, but when you made that promise, you knew you only had to tolerate me until the next morning.'

I ignore that one. 'In my first appointment with Lucy, she said I spend too much time in my TARDIS mind, in the past, regretting my family weren't like yours or Harry's. Or I'm in the future, second-guessing and catastrophising. She showed me how to pay attention to the present. You can do that by choosing one of your five senses and focusing on just this moment and just this sensation because here there is no regret about the past and no fear for tomorrow.' Suddenly, I am hungry. 'So, right now, take a deep breath and inhale the smell of red meat smothered in garlic mayo. Let's go and pursue a happy death by food poisoning from that dodgy-looking van.'

Chapter 33

The crunch of the gravel throws me back thirty years. My bedroom window looks much the same: black frame, diamond patterns obscuring a pleasant view. I shiver as I remember the ice on the inside even in the spring.

I'd spent so much time looking out, wishing I wasn't in there, dreaming I was someone else's child, hoping tonight was the night when he'd come back full of love.

My father drove a large intimidating vehicle with tinted windows. I think it was a Daimler but Harry says it was a Jaguar. It made a great noise grinding into the small stones on the wide driveway as he accelerated himself towards the house. If he saw me at the window he'd look away. As soon as I heard him coming, I'd take a sneaky peek. Would this be the day he'd change, come home as the dad in the movies, present under his arm, shouting, where's that beautiful boy of mine?

The film star stayed away. The car door would swing open, and out he'd get. No present, just a brown leather case with a brass clip on the top. It was usually dark by now, and he'd lock the car with a hand on the roof to steady himself. I'd watch him stagger a few steps, but then I'd rush back to my cold bed in case he saw me. I'd dive under my flimsy eiderdown, hoping I wouldn't hear the shouting.

'Tom.' Harry's hand is on my thigh. When we were younger, I'd thought perhaps he was gay. But then I met his father, and I realised he'd learned the touching at home. I didn't realise men touched other men to express kindness.

'Sorry, I was miles away.'

'I know. I'm not sure this is a good thing right now. A lot has gone on. You're not quite back to yourself. And your mum won't be looking out. We can just turn around and go to the pub, sort the world out like usual.'

'Sounds nice, but I have to. If I'm going to be a dad, even if it's not a biological one, I need to understand.'

'You will not be him, you never were. That was the problem.'

I've been ruminating more and more about what your DNA can do. It's the invisible killer, unobserved, but silently plotting to drag up your history, repeat patterns when you least expect it. I'd had a dream about hitting a baby. He was sitting in his car seat. He was crying, red in the face, tears squeezing from his eyes. I raised my hand, pulled it back, paused, then smacked my fist in his little face. The seat made an audible thud as it fell upside down onto the hard stone floor. Its contents were gone and there was silence.

I'd woken up with sweat rolling off my head and chest and my heart thudding. When I came to my senses Siri was staring down at me. 'Tom, Tom! I thought you were having a heart attack.' She held me while I sobbed.

I want to be the dad that Adam is.

Was.

I turn to Harry. 'Maybe, but I want to make sense of it all.' I know Harry doesn't get it: he didn't want me to come here.

'All right, but listen. If at any point you've had enough, just say, Mum, I forgot to ask about *Coronation Street*, and that'll be my cue to jingle my car keys.'

Two smartly dressed men trudge up to the large entrance, trees on either side, of the family home everyone desires. We could be Jehovah's Witnesses or, more likely, ordinary blokes flogging windows.

The door opens more quickly than I expected and the inside smell hits me like I've been punched in the face. It's a smell without description, and it's old and well known.

I put a hand on the door post and lean forward to give Mum a cheek kiss. She steps back to let us in.

'You didn't say he was coming,' is the greeting my mother offers.

'Good to see you, Mrs C.' Unusually Harry doesn't reach out for a welcome hug.

'I wondered if you were still alive,' she mutters as she follows her velvet slippers over the stone floor of the kitchen. My insides produce a cough; I realise I haven't taken a breath since stepping over the threshold.

'I presumed you didn't want food.'

Harry catches my eye and gives me a wink. I attempt a smile.

Gemma is sitting opposite us. She's gained a catastrophic amount of weight since I last saw her, although I realise it has probably been four years. Her hair is grey and frizzy: she looks ten years older than she is. The deep vertical lines above her mouth are much the same, and her badger face hasn't changed.

'Hi,' I say awkwardly as if meeting a child I've been forced to play with at the park while my mother chats to her mother. I don't know where that thought came from. As far as I remember, we never went to the park.

'Hello, Gem.' Harry is himself.

'What are you, matching security guards?' she snaps without looking up from her knitting.

'Just thought I'd make an effort to look smart.' I'm five all over again, justifying my choice to arrive smart casual, defending my right to share the oxygen.

Harry was right. I have enough on my plate. Why did I come? I wanted to try being authentic, to share with my family what's happening to me. Now I'm here I know there's no way I can say, Adam is dying and I'm trying to bully my wife to find out if she's in the same basket, if I'm going to be washing her, changing her sanitary towels…

'How's that kid you live with?' Gemma asks as if she can read my mind. I always thought she could.

When I was little, she was like a second mummy, holding my hand, feeding me chocolate buttons, inviting me to play dolls' houses, but as she got older, the anger she developed towards me expanded. What are you looking at, cretin? she'd say if I looked up at the wrong time. I hate that word. I remember looking it up in a dictionary. The small green book gave me a quick response. A stupid person.

Looking over my shoulder, my year two teacher had said, there are more uplifting words in there as well, you know. Why don't you look up wonderful, generous, helpful? She'd put her hand on my shoulder. I could still feel the delicious sense of her squeeze as she walked away. I loved all my teachers in primary school.

When I come to, Harry is mid-story. 'Siri and Adam are fine, both working hard. I have a new job and Tom's just been headhunted to be a manager in Surrey, haven't you, mate?'

I nod.

'Mum, Gemma, I've come bearing good news.'

My mother is looking expectant.

'Siri and I are having a baby in November. Admittedly, not in the—'

'Thank goodness for that,' Gemma butts in. 'When Mum

mentioned your trying wasn't working, I thought you were infertile.'

'I am. We're adopting. Apparently there was a problem with my piping at birth.'

I look to my mother but she stays quiet. Her face is expressionless. I'm tempted to confront her about my inability to reproduce, but what's the point?

'You're not having a baby then, are you? You're taking in a reject someone else doesn't want. There'll be good reason for that. It'll have problems. You'll regret it. Adopting parents always do. On *Loose Women*, that Denise was saying adopted kids are always screwy. Apparently half of them get sent back…'

'Ours won't be sent back, I can assure you.'

'It's great news, isn't it, Gem? Uncle Harry and Auntie Gemma. I can't wait.' Harry's enthusiasm doesn't draw much attention.

'It's good you can knit,' I say, needing to rescue him. 'The little one is going to need some blue cardigans. It's a boy.'

Now that Gemma's taken in my news, maybe she'll show her love for me suddenly, that she cares, that she's sorry our father soured the family, apologise for her part in my pain.

Instead I see that look. She's jealous. What? Surely she can't be jealous? She always said she'd be sterilised at puberty, that she didn't want a child of her own.

'All about Tommy. It's always all about sweet little Tommy.' Gemma's mouth compresses into a tight line, malice in the crooked raise of her brow. Spite pours out of her mouth, hitting me harder and harder as her voice increases in volume. 'You are so like him – weak, pathetic. I'm surprised you haven't copied him and blown your own brains out. The amount of times you've screwed your chances up, no wonder you ended up marrying someone too young to recognise the difference between a real man and a fake.'

An icy chill runs through me and I feel sick. I could scream, I could cry, but I do what my mother is doing. I smile.

'What do you mean about your father's death, Gemma?' Harry asks the question I was trying not to raise.

'He killed himself.' My mother's voice is flat, empty. And this revelation from nowhere about how he died leaves me unmoved. With all the hurt and sadness of the past weeks, all the anguish about my infertility, about Adam and Siri – the fact that my dad succeeded where I failed actually gives me some comfort. Perhaps I'm less like him than I thought.

But with my mother, and my sister, nothing has changed, nor will it ever. Why did I allow myself to hope that they would understand, want to be part of a new Cleary generation where we could renew ourselves, create a loving space for a new boy? Why did I cling on to the hope that Mum might suddenly turn to me, maybe smile, maybe say, I'm so sorry, Tom. That Gemma could be the sister I dream of, the sister who used to take me to the shop and hold me up to reach the sweets, her younger brother, already too heavy for her tiny arms?

And I think of Adam and his relationship with his sister, with his mum, the incredible bond they have, relishing each other's company, knowing that they are always there for each other, speaking every day, enjoying huge family get togethers. How is that they're the ones who are being punished while my family are allowed to carry on in all their narrow mean-mindedness?

How different would my life have been if I'd been nourished by family love? My father ignited the anger and pain, then my sister carried on the relay. She thrives on her loathing of me and she, my mother's golden child, is visibly strengthened by putting me back in my rightful place as the pariah of the family.

She sits back, as if she's just finished the last course of a very satisfying banquet. She licks her lips and wipes them with the back of her hand.

Harry is standing. 'We have to go. Tom needs to be home by midday.' He is walking to the door.

'Bye, Mum.' I reach down and touch her hands. They are moving rapidly as if trying to find the right position to pray.

'Bye, son.'

Perhaps my ears hear her say, I'm sorry, but I'm unsure. I think it's the seagull again.

As I use the heavy knocker to close the front door, its loud clunk draws the line.

'Come on, my friend. Family is not about genetics. It's about shared values.'

He holds open the car door for me, like he did the day my dad died, the day I was punched in a street brawl. Before the passenger door has closed on me, I wake up. I'm not part of that house, with its envy, spite and damage. I'm Thomas James Cleary, the little boy who was transformed in the hands of Harry's pa and ma, the cheeky one who was genuinely liked by his teachers and by his team at work, and who has a warm, inclusive family. Siri, Adam, Margaret, Harry, and now Dawn.

Harry looks at me with puzzlement. 'Well, I didn't expect you to come out of there smiling...'

Chapter 34

'Tom, Harry, do you children want tea or coffee?' Dawn's offer is laden with sarcasm.

'Tea please,' I answer. Harry's kindly offered to host this unusual meeting at his expansive flat: Lydia wanted it to be on neutral territory and Dawn's front room is a bit of a squash when we're all there.

'Strong coffee for me,' Harry says.

'Flippin' heck. This so-called special hot tap isn't working. Why can't you have a kettle like a normal person?' she shouts.

Siri is busying herself searching for five appropriate chairs. She's placed them in a circle, like I imagine they are for group therapy. I'm tempted to say, I'm Tom and I'm unemployed and infertile. Annaliese, the social worker, agreed that she would monitor us at arm's length as long as we made some concrete plans in writing so that she had something for her file. She's met with us on four occasions and concluded we are safe. She's explained to us that in order to keep this child long term, we need to apply to get parental responsibility. After three years we can apply to formally adopt.

We've chatted openly to everyone about Lydia's desire to donate her baby to us. No one has been negative apart from my family. Margaret accepted without question our decision to take care of a stranger's child. I'm sure there is unspoken relief that Siri hasn't managed to conceive an additional HD-positive relative. The infertility has changed from an evil monster to a kind friend.

'All right, old man?' Lydia asks.

'Yes, thank you, fatty,' I reply to her from my hands and knees.

'Yes!' shouts Harry as his car runs into the winning flag on the track.

'Can you believe them?' Dawn says over the top of five matching mugs. 'Harry claims the most expensive Scalextric set in Hamley's is your boy's first present.'

'It's Siri and Tom's boy,' Lydia corrects, playfully digging her trainer into my leg as she moves to give Siri a hug.

'Say hello to your mummy,' Liddie says, pushing her belly against Siri's.

I have to look away. I'm going to miss this kid when she goes.

'Come on, you two boys,' Dawn orders. 'I am officially calling this meeting to a start.'

'I can see you as a social worker,' Harry quips as he drops heavily onto the seat next to Dawn. 'You ever thought of retraining?'

Dawn uses Siri's favourite non-verbal prompt, the sharp elbow into the rib, to take her revenge. Then, she shuffles a pile of A4 sheets and hands one to each of us. It has a title and agenda points just like the formal meetings.

'Really?' I moan.

'It needs to be done properly. There is a baby in there who we all want to protect, and if we don't have a frank conversation now, and things go wrong when he's born, you could all be very hurt. Lydia, do you want to start? I think we first have to agree that this is your birth child and it will never be too late to change your mind.'

I grab Siri's hand. 'We totally agree,' I nod and Siri joins in.

'Yeah, Lydia, if when you see him, you regret what you've promised and need to keep him, Tom and I will help you. We won't make a fuss.'

'It's what I want. I won't change my mind.'

'I'm sure you won't, Lydia, but we all need you to know that you can,' Dawn reiterates. 'I've had three babies and I can assure you birth isn't easy and you will be cascaded by hormones that may alter your feelings.'

I don't want to hear this. I look at Siri who is clearly thinking the same. Her hands have found a tissue and as usual she is piece by piece ripping it to shreds. I put my hand back on hers: she has no conscious awareness that this habit occurs when she jumps in her TARDIS. Will this kid change her mind? I can't see why not; even people who do surrogacy for the money change their minds. I've watched endless documentaries about how it works and how both the giver and the receiver react at the birth. Siri walks out of the room if I play them when she's there. She's much better than me at ringfencing issues. It's easy at the moment for Lydia to disconnect from the foetus, I think, stashed away as it is in that private space, and not imagine him as a little boy. But when he's placed in her arms, a warm, breathing part of her, what then…?

'I want the baby to be given straight to you both.'

'Lydia, you don't need to rush it.' I can hear panic even in Siri's voice.

'I know it will be hard, but I have been reading about surrogacy and it says the quicker you hand over the baby, the better it is for everyone.'

'I have told her that she needs to stay with me and rest for at least two weeks.' Dawn is in mother mode. 'I've warned my girls.'

'I will, and then I'm going home to my family. I want to be there for the end of the summer holidays. I've told them I'm homesick. The college has said I can transfer my course to Northampton Technology College.'

'Okay, let's move on to the actual birth. Lydia will let me know as soon as she goes into labour. As you know, she is spending less time at the café. Annaliese says she needs to look to the future and start reconnecting with people near her family, obviously without mentioning the pregnancy.'

'Are you sure you don't want your family to come for the birth?' Harry pipes up. I want him to shut up. Obviously, if they come, they'll take their grandson. You'd have to be pretty unfeeling not to.

I imagine my grandmother turning up to Gemma's birth. My mother says to her, oh, by the way, Mum, I'm giving this baby to the two people you will have seen just now in the corridor, you good with that? Absolutely fine, my grandmother says. Great, says my mum. Then we can all get home before *Britain's Got Talent* starts on the TV. We don't want to miss the final.

But Lydia's family are normal: they would be horrified, and, I realise with a pang of guilt, heartbroken, to know their first grandchild is going to strangers, especially heathens like us.

'... and I'll call you two,' Dawn is saying, nodding her head to Siri and me. 'Lydia, what do you want at the hospital, when you're in labour and giving birth?'

'Well, I want you there, obviously,' and she looks at Dawn. Dawn's face is transparently proud; she peeks a quick look at Harry. 'I also want Siri and Tom to be there for as much of it as possible, to see their baby enter the world.'

'I'm not entirely comfortable with that,' I say.

Harry laughs and does an impression of my father standing outside the door, smoking a cigar. 'Oh no, not a place for men in there, old boy.' Then he says, 'Go with the flow, Tom. You'll know what's right when the time comes.'

Lydia is focused. 'I want Siri to take the baby and for you and Tom to go somewhere else as if you've just had it. I want the experience to be as close to the real deal as it can be.'

Siri's eyes instantly moisten at Lydia's kindness. Seeing her moved is the straw that breaks my resolve to stay a little bit detached from it all. I cry every time Siri says 'our son'. She has lost most of her reservations, and the preparation for the home-coming, the christening and the child's admission to school are a distraction from Huntington's disease, and the rapid deterioration of her superhero bro.

'The last item is his name.' Dawn puts her agenda on the floor, looks up and folds her arms. 'Over to you.'

I think about Sussex place names. 'What about Lewes?' I suggest. It's a joke. But as I say it, the name Lewes Cleary has a nice ring to it.

'I vote Alfriston, Alf for short,' Harry contributes.

Dawn attempts a return to the serious issues at hand. 'What about a Bible name, Lydia. That would be a small link to your own beliefs.'

A rash starts on Siri's chest, slowly creeping up her face. The red flag. Her heart is overflowing with emotions she is keeping hidden. We've talked endlessly about how we manage all this. Do we tell him when he's three, or wait until he's fifteen? What about Mother's Day, the term they do family trees – *take a photo of your parents and look for similarities*? There's an overwhelming number of hurdles to overcome.

'That's a nice idea.'

Siri asks for suggestions. 'I don't know much about Christianity,' she admits. 'Tell us some names.'

'There are the Old Testament ones like Boaz, Noah, Elijah, Reuben or Jacob, or the New Testament names like Matthew, Mark, Luke, Paul...'

'Is that why people say Matthew, Mark, Luke and John?' Dawn asks.

Harry can't keep the horror off his face. How can someone be so uneducated, he'll be thinking.

Lydia answers without a glimmer of superiority. 'Those four are the ones who wrote the gospels. They're the main source of information for the historical evidence for the life and death of Jesus Christ.'

'Any of those names float your boat, Siri?' I ask my wife.

'I like Reuben. What does it mean?'

'No idea,' Lydia says.

'*Reuben is a boy's name of Hebrew origin meaning behold, a son.*' Harry reads from Google.

'I like that... Reuben Cleary.' I say it slowly, listening to how it sounds. My tears threaten to ruin me yet again.

Siri says, 'Let's settle on that for now. You okay with that, Lydia?'

'Yep, I like that too. You and Tom can think of a middle name in private and surprise us when you hold Reuben.'

The sensitivity of this kid never ceases to amaze me. People three times her age couldn't be as kind and aware as she's been. I've experienced more sacrificial love from her in months than from my family in a lifetime. I can see my wife is equally touched as she excuses herself to wash up the mugs. She has surprised me too. I'd have never believed she would cope so well this year. Maybe I've done what Dr Funnell told me to, allowed her to be a grown-up.

'I think we have a plan. Let's get you home with your feet up. You look like you might pop.' Dawn takes Lydia's elbow and helps her off her chair. She pecks Harry on the cheek. 'Thanks for the hospitality.'

I catch Lydia's eye and we both suppress a smile.

Chapter 35

I'm woken by the ringing of our landline. My heartbeat quickens. Is this it? Is today the day I will meet Reuben, my son, the day I will become a daddy? Or will I be devastated beyond what we can bear if something goes wrong or Lydia changes her teenage mind?

'Morning, Tom.' I recognise the crisp voice as my mother-in-law's and I try hard to cover my irritation.

'Good morning, dear Margaret. What can I do for you?' Why do old people ring so early at the weekend?

'Is Selma up?'

'Fat chance of that.'

'Can you both come over? I need to speak urgently with you. It's very important.'

'What on earth's the matter? I don't think this family can cope with more bad news. Are you ill?'

'No, Tom. Don't panic. Honestly I'm fine, everything's fine. It's just that what has happened with Adam has made me think very hard about many things. I may not be here tomorrow, and there are lots of loose ends I need to tie up – finances, wills, and things Siri needs to know now that Adam is… changed…'

'Ah, Margaret, I do understand. What does Siri need to

know? Tell me. She's still fragile. We're on tenterhooks a bit – our baby could come any time.'

'I know, Tom, which is why I need to see you, today or tomorrow. I don't ask often.'

'I'll check with Siri. I know Harry's coming round to cook for us tonight, but I don't think we're doing anything tomorrow afternoon…'

Margaret has her front door open before I turn off the engine.

'Come in, lovely people. The kettle is on,' she says as she turns to lead the way.

I've puzzled over my mother-in-law's decision to downsize and move to such a rural area at her time of life, but as I pause to watch her link arms with her daughter I can see the appeal. I listen to the sounds of the countryside, and notice that the cries of the sheep in the nearby field are more like a roar than a bleat; after a pause comes a timely response from a single bird. It's as if they are chatting. I find a fleeting sense of peace despite my inner turmoil. For a moment I watch the bird perched on the hedge; its tail is bigger than its body, its beak upturned, eager to speak.

'Come on, slowcoach.' Margaret comes back to find me poised with one foot on her first step.

'Ah, sorry. You don't hear all this in town.'

'Beautiful isn't it? Can you hear the long-tailed tit? It's a very distinctive call. It reminds me of someone saying, do you see.'

'Well, I noticed it was talking to the sheep. But I would only recognise a robin to look at.'

'That'll be the Christmas cards,' she laughed. 'Come on, we need to talk.'

I follow her into a small but tidy sitting room. Siri is sitting on the sofa with a handful of crisps, one hand cupped underneath the other to catch the crumbs.

'Have you no manners, young lady?' Her mother reprimands her offspring, but with a smile. 'Why do you think the table is laid with fine china plates?'

I squeeze in next to my wife.

The end flaps on the little dining room table have been extended for the occasion. On the table the centrepiece is a pretty white milk jug decorated with poppies. A matching three-tier stand is piled with enough cake for a crowd, and is surrounded by small bowls of peanuts, crisps and olives. There are three places set with cup, saucer and plate. This lovingly prepared spread wouldn't be out of place at an expensive tea-room. My mouth waters, but I know better than to suggest we eat before chatting.

'It's only us, Mother. No royalty expected.' Siri looks at me and raises her eyebrows.

'Ah, but when you get as ancient as me, you never know when it will be your last cuppa and if my last brew was from a mug it would be unbearable.' Her chuckle never fails to make me do the same.

Siri jumps straight to the point. 'Why have we been summoned then, Mother? Do you want your inheritance back to go on a cruise?'

'If only. I'm afraid it's far more serious.'

I sit up straight. A heavy sigh leaks from my tired body. Please, no more bad news. The sounds of outside are no longer sufficient to calm my gnawing fear.

'You're not ill, are you?' I ask again, wanting to run away.

'I'm not ill. Don't panic.'

'What then?' Siri snaps, wiping food grease onto a tissue. I grab her hand for a squeeze, willing her to be kinder in her tone.

'You don't need the test for Huntington's disease.'

'Margaret, with all due respect...' There's an edge to my

voice that hasn't yet been heard in the presence of my gracious ma-in-law. 'Please don't start this again…'

'Mum, I know how hard it is for you to sit back, but it's my body, my life, and no, at the moment, I don't want the test, but in the future I might want a baby of my own.'

I try not to reflect on what my wife means by a baby of her own.

She is staring at her daughter with an intensity that is making my heart beat faster. Has she already seen the same symptoms in Siri that she's seen in her son?

'What?' Siri sounds equally freaked out. Her hands are ripping at the tissue faster than ever.

'I said you don't need the test…' Her voice tails off and she shuffles back in her armchair, dropping her eyes.

Siri opens her mouth. I can see she is working herself up for a fight.

'Why, Margaret? What do you know? What have you seen that we haven't? You can't just say that and back off. We have enough uncertainty already.' My voice is becoming rough, louder.

'You and Adam have different fathers,' she says, and she puts her hands over her face as if hiding from us.

Siri and I look at each other.

'Mum, what do you mean, we don't share a dad?'

Margaret's head turns unconsciously to a photo of Adam on the sideboard, her eyes brimming with tears.

'Oh, my goodness, he's my father, my brother is my father!'

'Don't be ridiculous! I know you failed your maths GCSE but he was ten when you were born. Albi is not your father – but neither is Adam!'

'I have no idea what you're talking about.'

'Well, be quiet and listen then. Your father was away a lot. He was up to no good. One of the contracts managers at work showed an interest, and I was flattered. I knew he was playing games, and that it was wrong, and it wasn't serious, but I went along with it. When I started to go off coffee, he was gone from the area...'

'Did he like coffee?'

'It's how I knew I was pregnant. The same thing happened with Adam. I lost my taste for hot drinks.'

'Does Adam know about this?' Siri's questions so far seem cool, detached.

'No one knows, because I'm deeply ashamed. I hardly knew the man. I was fed up, lonely. He was a married man who was homesick and in need of company.'

'So you're saying he was my father. Not Albi.'

'I'm as sure as anyone can be.'

'So if Albi wasn't my father, I can't have the disease.'

'I know, that's why I'm telling you. And if Adam wasn't ill, I would have taken it to my grave.'

'Did Albi know?'

Siri is continuing her radio interview, but I'm reeling. She may not have this deadly disease. Oh my goodness, this is extraordinary. My wife may not be Huntington's disease vulnerable? Why won't she stop and process that news, experience some relief?

'Albi didn't say anything, but we hadn't slept in the same bed for weeks. Perhaps he didn't care, or felt it was what he deserved. It was different then; people didn't talk. He treated you the same as Adam, when he was here: you were the centre of his world. But he wasn't here much. No one else suspected and you and Adam look so like me and each other.'

'Are you sure Adam is his?'

'Thank you, madam! I'll have you know I was faithful to Albi apart from that one mistake. I don't regret it – I have you, a much-loved daughter. I've felt desperately ashamed and guilty for deceiving you and Adam, but I thought it was best for everyone if I kept quiet. Adam's diagnosis has changed everything...'

As silence descends in the room, it's as if God has turned up the volume outside. The sheeps' cries have changed; they are wailing, as if demanding a rescue plan. My mind is racing, but I have no idea what's going on for my wife. Her head is down; the tissue is still being frantically dismantled. There are no clues to what's coming next. My thoughts are coming thick and fast, a relentless chain; does this mean my wife won't have Huntington's? Is she really only Adam's half sister? This is – isn't it? – wonderful news.

But is it actually? Now she could have her own children. Will she want IVF, someone else's baby? Shut up Tom, this *is* good news; your wife had a possible death sentence, but now she's free, alive.

Margaret searches my face. Hers is still flushed, but hard to read; her lip is quivering, but there are no other signs of the deep pain she must be feeling, until tears finally seep over her lower eyelids. They are hurriedly brushed away with the reverse of her hand.

A small voice comes out from the person next to me, a deflated, tiny sound I don't recognise.

'Thanks for telling me, Mum,' Siri whispers, 'but...' and there's a pause as she takes a further intake of breath, and I realise I'm holding my own breath, and open my lips to inhale; it's almost a gasp. 'Do you realise I've been having suicidal thoughts, knowing what could be coming to me? I've wondered if Tom had the right idea. I've thought of taking Adam for a drive and crashing us both into a wall, united in a dramatic escape that the local newspapers would relish. Yet, you've known from that day we came here as a family, with Adam, that I'd be okay. You kept me hurting, and Tom, all that time...' Her speech is getting faster. She squeezes the tissue remnants inside her right hand. I have never heard her speak to her mum like this. They're so close.

Margaret uses both hands to wipe her wet eyes. She gets up from her chair and comes towards us. She lifts up the hem of her skirt as she bends to one knee in front of her child.

'I don't know what to say. I'm so, so sorry. Please believe that.' She places her hand on Siri's arm, and gently encourages her daughter to lift her head, placing her finger under her chin. 'Please look at me, Selmeston.'

'Don't call me that! Is that the place you committed adultery...?'

Margaret gets up faster than should be possible at her age. She looks like she's been slapped. It would've hurt her less if her daughter had indeed slapped her.

I appeal to her sympathy. 'Siri.' But my wife isn't going to be dialled down just yet. She gets up, giving her anger more fuel, and shouts at her mother, who is now using the doorframe to support her.

'You watched me break my heart at the hospital, the day Adam got his results, and you said nothing. How could you? Get up, Tom.' Siri springs up. 'We're going.'

Margaret pleads to Siri's back. 'I wanted to tell you but I didn't know how. I worried you'd be like this, think me immoral, be hurt you didn't know, or even want to find your real father.'

'Maybe that should've been my choice to make and not yours. For goodness' sake! You had a one-night stand. Get over yourself.'

'Siri.' I try to mimic Harry's calm authority. I put my hand up to stop her. She's going to say something she'll regret. I know too well how that feels.

Margaret speaks in a whisper as her daughter swivels away

from her offered embrace. 'Siri, please don't do this. My only son is dying before my eyes. How hard do you think that is?'

'As hard as thinking you're next.' Part of me expects to hear the familiar theme tune of a well-known soap. And Siri leaves me to face my mother-in-law. Margaret has tears running down to her chin. I realise I've never seen her cry until this afternoon.

'She'll come around,' I reassure her, enveloping her in a hug that is genuine and warm.

'I hope so. I can't lose two children, Tom.'

'You won't, and you're going to gain a healthy grandson very soon. I'll call you when he's here so you can visit. He'll love you as much as the girls do.'

The thought of Margaret having taken a lover is going to take some while to process. I feel for both these women but I can't contain my sense of joy and hope as I bounce down the outside steps.

'Are you okay?' I can see the struggles in Siri's head as she grapples with the car door. I forgot I had the keys.

'I don't know how much more I can take. I'm so angry with her.' She ducks under my arm to fall heavily into the passenger seat.

I get into the driver's seat, and slide it back away from the steering wheel so I can pull her close.

'I get how it must feel. I've also been breaking my heart at the thought of my wife ending up like Adam and dying before my eyes, but try and understand how it's been for your mum. The news about Adam is awful. Then she's got to find a way to talk to everyone about something so personal she's never told a soul.'

'But leaving me to watch Adam get worse thinking I was next. What sort of mum does that?'

'One who is grieving and isn't thinking straight.'

'She's been my rock. I've always trusted her.'

'And you still can; these are exceptional circumstances. We've all been under such awful pressure and we're all gripped by such sadness.'

We sit in the car for some time. My is wife is silent and unusually willing to simply lie in my arms, defeated by having too many emotions to untangle. When her breathing tells me she is becoming sleepy, I withdraw my aching arm and push her gently back to her own seat.

'I know you're right, but I can't get rid of how I feel,' she finally confesses, adjusting her seat and ready to lie back and sleep on the journey home.

'You don't have to, but imagine how you'd feel if something happened to her before you had the chance to make it right.'

'Let's go home. I'll mull it over while we drive, maybe call her tomorrow.'

'Siri, pop back in and give your mum a hug before we go. People do things to protect those they love. Sometimes they get it wrong.'

For once she does as she's told with no backchat.

Chapter 36

Even before she gets back in the car, I can see by the bounce in her step that she's made up with her mum. She has the ease of someone younger than me. I realise how much I love her.

'What are you staring at?'

'My wife. You okay?'

'I think so. I feel I shouldn't be, having just found out my father is someone I'll never know – but then I didn't really know the first one. It's just such a relief about the disease, that I'm clear. It's hard to take it in after all the horror of imagining what the future might be…'

'I feel the same. It's been so completely awful thinking you could have the same future as Adam. That sounds really selfish, doesn't it?'

'Not at all. I feel selfish, and I feel guilty.'

'Why would you feel that?'

'It's not fair for Adam that I should go free.'

'It wouldn't help Adam for you to be ill, and the real Adam would be ecstatic you're not at risk.'

'Should we tell him and Heather?'

'I think we need to let the dust settle for a while. Really, it's your mum's story to share. I'm not sure Adam could take in that sort of news at the moment.'

I wait for a response but Siri's snoring in the passenger seat, looking wrung out.

We're not far from home when she wakes up, alert straight-away.

'Let's stop off at the Kumari and get a curry.'

'How can you do that? Wake up from a deep sleep and demand food? I haven't recovered from Harry's three courses last night yet.'

'I know, but we've had a lot to manage and we deserve a treat.'

The curry house is empty so I allow myself to be cajoled into ordering lots of food, lots of fat and carbohydrates. My card is in the machine when a loud bang on the glass makes Khaled take a fast step away from the counter. My hearts leaps into my mouth. I turn round, and I see my wife, frantic and banging on the window with her fist. Her other hand is holding a phone to her ear. She puts her hand over her mobile and mouths, 'It's Lydia. Her waters have broken.'

I run out of the door.

'Tom, your food.' Khaled runs after me and shoves it through the door as I'm closing it.

I push my foot onto the accelerator. The fatigue of ten minutes ago has evaporated. Maybe this is what becoming a dad is like. Siri feeds me poppadoms as I drive. 'Be careful, Tom. After all we've survived we can't die in a car accident.'

Dawn is outside the hospital on her phone. 'Thank goodness you're here! She's nine centimetres dilated already.'

'Almost there,' Siri translates.

Lydia is half sitting up against a pile of pillows, her legs holding up a sheet as if it's a kids' homemade camp.

'Go up the smiling end and hold her hand,' Dawn shouts to me.

'You okay, kiddo?'

She grips my hand harder than it's ever been gripped. She whispers between clenched teeth, 'No, Tom, of course I'm not okay.'

Dawn holds her other hand. I don't know what to do. Siri is awkward too. I want to save her that. After all, if it wasn't for me she'd be lying in Lydia's place.

'Pant slowly, Lydia. You're doing so well,' the midwife badged up as Noreen says in a gentle, hushed voice.

'Are we ready?' Maryrose, the other midwife, asks as she puts another half-roll of kitchen towel on the bed.

'Indeed we are,' Dawn says in an inappropriately animated way.

'Siri,' Lydia manages to huff between open-mouthed dog pants. 'Look out for his head. I want you to be the first person to see your son.'

'Push,' the two midwives exclaim at the same time.

Chapter 37

Our son is born at 6.09am on 17th August.

The midwife says he is small but not unusually so for the baby of a young mum. He is both healthy and ugly.

Lydia was amazing. She had no pain relief. 'The young ones always do well,' the midwife tells me outside the labour room. I hadn't thought I'd be able to watch, seeing her in pain, and coping with Siri watching a labour rather than having one. I'd thought it'd be too much, but it was the most incredible experience of my whole life.

'Tom, he's here!' Siri throws herself in my arms and sobs and sobs. I fear she'll never stop.

A bundle of yellow blanket is placed in my arms. Poking out of the top is a pitch-black head. Lydia needs stitches and we go to the day room with the baby while the doctor does his stuff – I try not to think about it. The day room is almost empty as it's still early. We sit together and I hold a parcel that doesn't move. We worry he isn't breathing: he's so still and quiet.

'Hello little man, the image of your mummy.' A tousled-haired lady in a dressing gown pulls back the yellow wrapping to take a peek. She's right: I expected the baby to be as fair as Lydia. I don't believe in miracles but, if I did, this would be it. He looks as much like Siri as a baby could. His black hair reaches beyond his ears.

As I say, I can't honestly describe him as beautiful. He has blotches on his face, skin flakes in his hair and his eyes are shut tight. He looks like an old man. But I loved him the moment he was placed in my arms. I had worried about Siri giving birth to a baby that wasn't mine, and yet my heart is breaking over a child that doesn't share biology with either of us.

The bundle screams and waves his arms and legs as Noreen uncovers and weighs him.

'What a beauty. Babies with lots of hair look so much nicer, don't they? What have you decided to call him?' she enquires, looking from Siri to me, the baby's parents.

'Reuben Harry,' Siri says without hesitation. Her smile is the widest I've ever seen. I don't know if the midwife knows our situation but if she does, she's saying nothing.

We take him back to see Lydia. My heart breaks for her, doing all that, and having nothing at the end of it. Lying on the bed with a blue teddy bear that Dawn has bought for her in her arms instead of a baby. My mind goes into overdrive. Will she want him back? Now I've held him, I can't bear to have him ripped away. I look at my wife, a natural already with a tiny body cradled in the crook of her arm.

As the door opens, I see Lydia turn away and lie on her side with her back to us. I go round to face her but Siri stays back. I give her a nod of agreement. I bend over an exhausted-looking child with bed hair and a nightie covered in cartoon animals. She looks barely older than Amelia, not old enough to kiss a boy, let alone give birth.

'You're one amazing kid, do you know that?'

'You're okay for an old bloke,' she flips back at me.

I can't help myself. 'You still sure?'

'Totally, but I know it's best to hand over immediately, less painful for everyone. I don't want to see him. Can you take him out so I can say goodbye to Siri?'

'You are a brave young woman, Lydia. We will make sure this little boy knows about the amazing young person who gave him to us. I can't thank you enough.'

'I told him you'd love him,' she says.

'Will you be okay?'

'I think I will. I won't forget what has happened to me or my baby. I just feel it's meant to be. It makes me happy that a bad situation turned out well for you.'

'You can always visit, you know.'

'I won't. I want to go back to my old life, start again.'

'Well, if you change your mind, get in touch. We'll tell him the truth about who he is. Is there anything we can give you to say thank you?'

'Yes,' she says with a certainty I hadn't expected.

'Anything.'

'Take him to the evangelical church in the high street. I want him to know there is a God who loves him.'

'Deal,' I say, feeling slightly terrified about what I've promised.

'Goodbye, Tom.'

I left Siri to say her goodbyes.

Chapter 38

'It's not your son, though, is it?' Siri's phone is balanced on her knee whilst Reuben sucks noisily from his bottle and pushes noisy wind out the other end. I understand already why Dawn laughed when I described having a new baby as romantic.

'Thanks for that, bro.'

'Whatever. Shall I get Hev?'

It's been a very long night but she wanted to call her mum, her brother and half of her contacts list before grabbing some sleep. Her beautiful olive skin looks like snails have crawled from her forehead to her chin; if shedding tears was an Olympic sport this year, we'd be gold medallists. The phone is on speaker as she insists I get to hear every call.

Eleanor shrieks louder than Dawn. Margaret cries.

My mother's telephone goes straight to voicemail.

Heather takes the phone. We can hear Adam mumbling at her.

'Hi, I'm sorry he said that. He can be very cruel.'

'Heather, it's fine. We know it's not the real Adam. He is telling the truth; he isn't trying to be unkind.'

The real Adam is a term Margaret uses a lot. She's pointed

out that, when we talk about the 'old' Adam versus the new version, it sounds like he's changed deliberately.

'The saddest thing for me is he would have been thrilled for you both.'

'We know that. How are you Heather, and the girls?'

'Hanging in there. We have a routine and they accept their dad for how he is. I'm desperate to see your little boy. Can I come to the hospital?'

'We're home already. Dawn is with Lydia at the moment and the plan is she'll take Lydia home when the doctors have given her the once-over. The staff have been fabulous and have treated us like his real parents from the minute he was born.'

'Parents are the people who love and care for a child; you are his true parents. Can the girls and I come over?'

'Of course.'

'Do you mind if Adam doesn't come? I want the girls to meet their cousin without the distraction of what he might say or do.'

'If I am honest, it will be a relief not to have Adam today. I'll make sure he meets his nephew later in the week, when we've adjusted. Can he be left?'

'Charlie Coggins is coming over. He's been great. He stays with him for a few hours every so often so we can go shopping.'

'Who's Charlie?'

'I thought you met him at Adam's leaving do. He's the course facilitator at one of the colleges Adam was involved with. Nice bloke. He distracts Adam with blokey chat and doesn't get much hassle from him.'

'It will be lovely to see you all. Harry's coming over to cook food. Why don't you and the girls join us?'

'Yes please – they'll be over the moon.'

'Okay, see you later.'

She rings off. It suddenly strikes me that this morning Siri and I were a couple. This evening we'll be a family.

'I still can't believe we are talking about our son, Siri. How amazing is that?'

There's no response: Siri's snoring soundly on the sofa. I gently lift up her arm and collect a small warm body. I wonder about switching on the TV. But I decide to watch my son instead.

Chapter 39

'Can you bring over the helium, Tom?' Dawn is in full sergeant major mode.

We've hired the local village hall for Reuben's first ever birthday party.

'Yes, ma'am.'

'Can you believe your little fella is three already?'

'Nope. I always wondered what you were on about when you said the sleepless nights would quickly be a thing of the past. You heard from Liddie?'

'I get the occasional text. She's got a bloke, is back in church. It was good of you to do what she asked about all that.'

'I know. First time I went, I got the time wrong and pitched up half an hour late. Can you imagine? All heads turned and then Reuben started screaming.'

'But you kept going?'

'They were all so nice.'

'So they converted you.'

'Doesn't work like that. Only God has the power to change people's minds.'

'And he changed yours?'

'I realised this wasn't what I'd always regarded as "religion";

it was real. And yes, you could say I've become a Christian. I'm getting baptised at the end of next month.'

'Really? As a grown man, you're going to be sprinkled with water?'

'No, I will be fully immersed into a large pool.'

'I'll look forward to that then, as long as I don't have to hang out with the other God-botherers!'

'Shut up! You'd like them; they've been great. Everyone's praying for Adam, and they've helped us out with childcare when Siri went back to work because her husband is unemployed.'

'I employ you!'

'Not any more.'

'Ah, I keep forgetting that we're partners now.'

'Conveniently,' I laugh.

We are now partners. Siri's mum gave her some of the money she received from the sale of the family home. She said she has enough from a pension, and felt both Adam and Siri needed it now rather than when she dies.

'Did you hear that Siri's having me on the show next month?'

'Well, what you're doing, producing diet plan meals is unique, isn't it?'

'What *we* are doing. Did you get chance to check out that café for sale in Lewes? We definitely need another place.'

'Not yet, but on my to do list when Reuben's at preschool on Thursday. You still don't think we should sell the Tea Cosy?'

'I can't leave the café crowd. What would Philip do? Or Isaac, or Cilla and Peter?'

'I was thinking you could sell to someone who wanted to keep it as a café.'

'Yeah, but the café alone is not sustainable as it is. They'd put up the prices. They'd want our misfits to go. They'd lower the tone.'

'I don't know if you know that you saved my life that first few months. I will always remember that, Dawn.'

'Saved mine too.' Harry gives Dawn a noisy smacker on the lips.

'I still can't get my head around you two being a serious item. Didn't think anyone could tame him.'

Harry takes his partner of eighteen months into a hug too intimate for the public domain. 'Your wife spotted it before we did, though.'

'Women's intuition,' Dawn says, tapping her nose.

'Yuk, don't do that. It reminds me of Leo the slimeball.'

'Talking about me again?' Peter joins the crowd with a plate of Dawn's speciality brownies.

'How's your spots on your tummy?' a small voice says, and the plate is pulled down by its rim.

'Hang on, little fella.' Peter pulls off small fingers from the plate, gives it to Harry and hands Reuben half a slice. Peter gets down on one knee and looks into Reuben's serious eyes. 'Listen, fella, copy me.' He holds up his hand. Spreading out his fingers, he uses his other hand to point to one finger at a time.

'How... is... your... belly... off... for... spots? Now, you say it.' He points to each finger and Reuben is able to repeat his phrase word perfect.

'We'll be back for your teaching when he's doing his GCSEs.'

'Once a teacher, always one.' Peter takes back his plate of cakes with only one left.

Harry keeps two. 'She's getting too skinny.' He pushes one into Dawn's open mouth.

'I can't believe how much weight you've lost,' I say. 'It's taken ten years off you.'

'I need to keep it off, or this won't fit.' She thrusts her manicured hand at me.

'Oh my goodness.' I look at Harry for confirmation that what I'm being shown is an engagement ring.

'I have said I'll marry him on one condition…'

I'm thinking, if he agrees to no more kids, works less, moves to Surrey, keeps feeding her cake…

'If he gets rid of that stupid hot water tap.'

The kids' disco music has been turned up. Harry, Dawn and I join Margaret at the edge of the dance floor.

'I'm losing my hearing. It's a little quieter here, thankfully. But even so it's still a bit much!'

'Go and ask them to turn it down a bit,' I say to Peter, who has his hands over his ears.

Reuben is doing dad dancing with his three cousins. He's having a proper party with twelve tiny preschool friends tomorrow. I keep nagging Siri for over-indulging him, but it's hard not to.

I watch Siri as she talks to Heather. Every celebration is tainted by Adam's absence. He can't cope with big family occasions any more. He's hanging on in there: sometimes I see remnants of who he used to be – the odd quirky joke or kindness. On a Thursday, I spend time with him, to give Heather a day off. His walking is awful and some days we use a wheelchair. Occasionally we have fun, other times we don't. I try not to compare him with the person he was, but just be in the moment with him.

I can't believe how things have turned out for us. Siri could've been Albi's child, and unknowingly passed on the Huntington's gene if I'd not been firing blanks; I could've jumped; Lydia could've changed her mind. I might never even have met Lydia. Instead, I'm as happy as Larry, whoever he is.

I've found my best friend a soulmate, and Siri and I have been given the most precious gift of a perfect son.

Interrupting my thoughts, Reuben bounds over and deliberately crashes hard into Harry's groin.

Margaret winces. 'Be careful with your uncle Harry, young man. He's not as young as he used to be. Say sorry. You've hurt him.' She frequently argues with Siri about discipline. You'll ruin him, she says. All the other kids will hate him if he's spoiled and demanding.

'Do as your gran says.' I try hard not to smile as his features crumple. Margaret says it's manipulation.

Reuben looks up at Harry wearing an exceptionally straight face. He is undeniably gorgeous now: his hair is dark and glossy. If he didn't have such green eyes, he could be mistaken for a child with Asian heritage. 'Sorry, Uncle Harry,' he whispers, standing on tiptoe to give his uncle a kiss.

'No worries, little fella.'

Reuben runs to me. I lift him high, twirl him round, then we slump down together in a chair.

I can see, even from a distance, that Margaret has tears in her eyes.

'Miracle boy. Saved us all, didn't he?'

Harry smiles. 'He really did, Margaret. I don't believe in God, but that child could not look more like your girl if he was artificially designed.'

'Fascinating, isn't it? As Siri says, you couldn't make it up.'

I wander over to Siri; as my arms envelop her, she elbows me away.

'Tom, I'm talking to Heather. Don't be rude! You're as bad as Reuben.' Heather and Siri have matching frowns. I guess they are reminiscing over Adam. 'Carry on, Heather. I apologise for my man.'

'There's nothing more to say, really. It's just – that was the day I knew there was something very wrong. Up until then I'd deluded myself – it was stress, me, work.'

'What day?' I ask.

'Heather was just saying that he'd gone by himself to London, and he'd spent enormous amounts of money on luxuries they couldn't afford when he already had an overdraft.'

'Yes, though he did like to spend, didn't he? Why was that unusual?'

'Because he bought some shoes that wouldn't have looked out of place on a fifteen-year-old. You know how stylish he was. These shoes were ridiculous. That would've been bad enough, but he'd got them in Camden market: he'd commissioned them a few weeks earlier and paid £190 for a pair of Converse I'd have paid £25 for.'

'Oh dear, I bet that caused a row.'

'Then he wore them to a party and came home without them.'

'What do you mean? Was he drunk?'

'Yes, he was still drunk when he arrived home the following day, in his socks. I had to pay the cab as he'd lost his wallet as well.'

'Why were the shoes so expensive?' my mouth asks.

'They were painted with cartoons from *The Lion King*,' Heather replies. 'Ridiculous.'

'Mummy, can we do my cake? Uncle Peter says I can light the candles with him.'

Siri scoops up our boy and carries him over to his audience.

'Tom.'

'Tom, everyone's waiting for the daddy.'

'Come on, Tom... We're doing Reub's cake.'

Happy birthday to you

Happy birthday to you

Happy birthday dear Reuben
Happy birthday to you.

THE END

Acknowledgements

First and foremost, thank you to all the people who over many years have entrusted me with their personal experiences at the most traumatic times in their lives, and to so many marvellous men who've been brave enough to share their 'not good enough' stories with me.

Enormous gratitude goes to my inspiring friend Lucy Funnell for making me finish Tom's story and for being my most consistent cheerleader from first draft to publication.

A huge admiration-filled thank you to Seren Boyd, my unpaid but brilliant editor, for persuading me to get this story out of my filing cabinet, for offering endless kind words to me and unswerving commitment to *Surviving Me*, and for keeping me going when my deepest desire was to give up.

Thank you to my neuropsychology peer supervision group – Dr Richard Maddicks, Dr Jane McNeil and Dr Siobhan Palmer – for being so supportive of my quirky approach to our trade and for not telling anyone that my psychometric tests are covered in dust.

Thank you to my book group friends – Susie, Sandra, Jackie, Lucy, Carole, Mark, Camilla, Judy, Livvy and Gillian – for a decade of interesting discussions about fiction, and for cheering me on as an author.

A huge thank you to my earliest readers who encouraged me when I really doubted myself – especially Viv Cooper, Susan Sale, John Edgington, Margaret White, Elizabeth Hassan, Jane Holbrook, Sue Gatland, Margaret Rice Oxley, Gillian Wieck, Susie Venn, Lauren Densham, Natalie Vellacott, Rachael Thrussell and Judy Crocombe. I'm so grateful to all the people who've kept nodding and smiling throughout all the discussions about how to write and publish a novel.

Thank you to the Vintage Rose Tea Room in Storrington, West Sussex, my own Tea Cosy Café, for caffeine supplies over many hours of writing – my gratitude goes both to the marvellous staff and to the managers, Emma Kennedy and now Sian Church.

Thank you to Jez and Helen Taylor at Kingsley Roofing for their extremely generous pledges.

Thank you to everyone at Unbound for their professional guidance from first draft to publication.

Thank you to Craig Taylor for humbly explaining to me what a good book should look like, and to Mary Chesshyre, my copy editor, for her diligence and professionalism.

Thank you to my parents, Brian and Noreen Frost, who taught me to enjoy reading and writing from an early age. And I've missed the marvellous proofreading skills of Richard Johnson on this project. We all wish you were still around to talk history and politics.

Thank you to my sister Annaliese for listening to endless ideas about Tom's adventures when she doesn't even like fiction, and to Liz Perry for typing the first draft.

Thank you to LuLu for all she's given to our family and for showing me how to be a mother of sons.

Thank you to Oscar and Leah for uncomplainingly doing

their most important exams with no parental support while their mother rewrote her novel and their father provided her with psychological and editing support.

I couldn't have achieved this or anything else in my adult life without the loyalty and wisdom of Lyndon Johnson. Thank you, Professor, for showing (not telling) me what sacrificial, unconditional love looks like.

Unbound is the world's first crowdfunding publisher, established in 2011.

We believe that wonderful things can happen when you clear a path for people who share a passion. That's why we've built a platform that brings together readers and authors to crowdfund books they believe in – and give fresh ideas that don't fit the traditional mould the chance they deserve.

This book is in your hands because readers made it possible. Everyone who pledged their support is listed at the front of the book and below. Join them by visiting unbound.com and supporting a book today.

Nadia Abdo
Julie Abel
Maryann Adsett
Susan Agland
Ben Alcott
Michelle Allan
Nicola Allibone
Ana Amaya
Chloe Andrews
Mark Appleton
Georgina Baker
Katie Banister
Debbie Barber
Leigh Barton
Lucy Blake
Angharad Blossom
Susan Botfield
Seren Boyd
Clair Brown
Liz Burt
Stephanie Byrne
Amanda Cairns
Sian Campbell
Cherril Castle
Victoria Chandler
Sarah Charman
Sian Church
Elise Collis
R Coogan
Elizabeth Cooke
Viv Cooper
Gilly Crossley
Kelly D'Ambrosio
Carla Daley
Ulf Dantanus
Liz Davis
Sally de la Fontaine
Steve Deamer

Tim Dean
Deirdre Dean
Kathryn Denchfield
Emily Denny
Elaine Devenish
Jenny Divall
Deb Dubar
Stuart Duncan
Billybobduncan Duncanw
Ann Edgington
Tracey Euesden
Giles Evans
Debbie Everitt
Steph F
Lorna Felix
Keith Feltham
Jo Ferris
Katy Fischbacher
Joy Foulds
Kim Freeman
Manisha Fritche
Noreen Frost
Brian Frost
Sue & Rob Fuller
Anthony Funnell
Gaby George
Nikki Glover
Vanessa Goss
Sally Gould
Karl Green
Julie Green
Sophie Greengrass
Owen Griffiths
Abbie Haines
Sharon Hammond
Elizabeth Hardy
Tracy Hare
Rachel Hibbs
Andrew Hislop
Mark Holloway
Deborah Holman
Anbesan Hoole
Judith Houghton
Lorna Houston
Sara Hughes
Melanie Hughes
Beverley Iles
Bill James
Karen James
Nicola Jenkins
Josh Johnson
In memory of Beth Jupp
Margaret Jurocko
Emma Kennedy
Mrs Nicky Kirby
Jax Lambert
Shona Lavey-Khan
Cath Leighton
Vicky Lester
Camille Lofters
Sterre Marien
Karen McIvor
Joanna McKnight
Jane McLaren
Jane McNeil
Carolyn McNeilly
Debrs Menear
Helen Moore
Sarah Mumford
Brenda Mumford
Edward Murray
Carlo Navato
Paula Negus
Jane O'Sullivan
Chris O'Leary
Joanna Oliphant-Hope
Katrina Orchard
Cassie Over
Siobhan Palmer
Debbie Parrott
Catharine Pedroza
Zanya Petken
Elizabeth Phillips
Olivia Pinkney
John Pohorely
Matt Pollard
Jacky Powell
Janeen Prinsloo
Susan Quinn
Nikki Read
Sally Roberts
Clare Robinson

Sophie Robinson
Susan Rout
Sally Ruane
Carol Russell
Tom S
Luke Sayers
Sally Scrase
Rachel Searle
Gabrielle Searle
Ben Shanmugam
Nicky Skelton
Jason Skelton
Linda Slater
Katie Smith
Christine Smith
Clare Smith
Susan J Smith
Ruth Spencer
Gail Spring
Linda Stewart
Samantha Storey
Hilary Stovold
Tony Street
Clare Street
Cecilia strong
Fiona Sturrock
Robert Syred
Jess Taylor
Rachael Thrussell
Paula Timmins
Sarah Van Cooten
Mark Vent
Rowena Vincent
Elaine Waight
Kaaren Wallace
Shelley Westgate
Margaret White
David White
Rebecca Whitney
Beth Williams
Tina Williams
Christine Wood
Clare Woods
Sharon Woolnough
Catherine Wright